THEATRE HISTORY STUDIES

Theatre History Studies is an official journal of the Mid-America Theatre Conference, Inc. (MATC). The conference encompasses the states of Illinois, Iowa, Nebraska, Kansas, Missouri, Minnesota, North Dakota, South Dakota, Wisconsin, Michigan, and Indiana. Its purposes are to unite persons and organizations within this region and elsewhere who have an interest in theatre and to promote the growth and development of all forms of theatre.

Theater in the Americas

A New Series from Southern Illinois University Press

ROBERT A. SCHANKE, SERIES EDITOR

QUERIES & SUBMISSIONS

Robert A. Schanke, Editor
Theater in the Americas
Theatre Department
Central College
Pella, IA 50219
E-mail: schanker@aol.com

The goal of the series is to publish a wide range of scholarship on theater and performance in the Americas, defining theater in its broadest terms and including subjects that encompass all of the Americas.

The series focuses on the performance and production of theater and theater artists and practitioners but welcomes studies of dramatic literature as well.

Meant to be inclusive, the series invites studies of traditional, experimental, and ethnic forms of theater; celebrations, festivals, and rituals that perform culture; and acts of civil disobedience that are performative in nature.

We hope to publish studies of theater and performance activities of all cultural groups within the Americas, including biographies of individuals, histories of theater companies, studies of cultural traditions, and collections of plays.

Southern Illinois University Press
P.O. Box 3697, Carbondale, Illinois 62902-3697—www.siu.edu/-siupress

THEATRE HISTORY STUDIES

VOLUME XXIII

CONTENTS

2003

SPECIAL FEATURES

Felicia Londré — The World's Greatest Entertainer: Al Jolson (1886-1950) 1

ARTICLES

Norman Hart — The Selling of *La Cage aux Folles*: How Audiences Were Helped to Read Broadway's First Gay Musical 5

Patty S. Derrick — Julia Marlowe's Ophelia: A Portrait of Resistance and Failure 25

Heidi J. Holder — Outcast London on the Victorian and Edwardian Stage 49

Steven Dedalus Burch — Historical Invisibility: The Vexatious A.P. Wilson and the Abbey Theatre 65

James Wilson — Community, Civility, and Citizenship: Theatre and Indoctrination in the Civilian Conservation Corps of the 1930s 77

Anne Fletcher — The Gestus of Scene Design: Mordecai Gorelik and the Theatre Union's Production of Brecht's *The Mother* 95

BOOK REVIEWS

Kim Marra and Robert A. Schanke, eds., *Staging Desire: Queer Readings of American Theater History*
Reviewed by Bob Vorlicky 109

Patricia McDonnell, *On the Edge of Your Seat: Popular Theater and Film in Early Twentieth-Century American Art*
Reviewed by Felicia Londré 114

Eli Rozik, *The Roots of Theatre: Rethinking Ritual and Other Theories of Origin*
Reviewed by Tice L. Miller 116

Philip C. Kolin, ed., *The Undiscovered Country: The Later Plays of Tennessee Williams*
Reviewed by W. Douglas Powers 117

Freddie Rokem, *Performing History: Theatrical Representations of the Past in Contemporary Theatre*
Reviewed by Don LaPlant 118

Dunbar Ogden, ***The Staging of Drama in the Medieval Church***
Reviewed by Donnalee Dox 121

Michael W. Pharand, *Bernard Shaw and the French*
Reviewed by David J. Eshelman 124

Brooks McNamara, *The New York Concert Saloon: The Devil's Own Nights*
Reviewed by Noreen Barnes-McLain 126

Adam Versenyi, trans., *The Theatre of Sabina Berman:* The Agony of Ecstasy *and Other Plays*
Reviewed by Jean Graham-Jones 128

David Krasner, *A Beautiful Pageant: African American Theatre, Drama and Performance in the Harlem Renaissance, 1910-1927*
Reviewed by James Wilson 130

S.E. Wilmer, *Theatre, Society and the Nation: Staging American Identities*
Reviewed by Rosemarie K. Bank 133

Nathan Stucky and Cynthia Wimmer, eds. , *Teaching Performance Studies*
Reviewed by Lynn C. Miller 135

BOOKS RECEIVED 139

Front Cover: Julia Marlowe as Ophelia. Courtesy of Ford E. and Harriet R. Curtis Theatre Collection, University Library System, University of Pittsburgh.

Theatre History Studies 23 (June 2003)

The World's Greatest Entertainer Al Jolson (1886-1950)

THEATRE HISTORY CROSSWORD PUZZLE VII

FELICIA HARDISON LONDRÉ

Constructed using Crossword Weaver

ACROSS

1. African American bandleader who worked with Al Jolson on *The Singing Kid* and was a guest on Jolson's 1936 radio show.
10. In his 1935 film *Go Into Your Dance*, Jolson sings "Casino - - Paris."
11. Jolson could have seen this 1913 French musical at the Longacre.
12. Jolson treated him and his partner Eubie Blake to dinner in Hartford in 1919; he represented the Negro Actors' Guild at Jolson's funeral in 1950.
13. Top female singer in Jolson's day: - - - a Bayes (1880-1928).

14. Jolson never was a second one of these.
17. "Back in Your Own Back Ya - -" was often sung by Jolson in the 20s.
19. Bi - - more Theatre: where Jolson was playing in L.A. when he signed to film *The Jazz Singer.*
21. Jolson recorded "I'm - - razy for You" in 1929.
22. - - rone Power co-starred with Jolson and Alice Faye in *Rose of Washington Square.*
23. How Jolson would spell French: Parlay - - - Fronsay?
24. Song recorded by Jolson in 1920; title is the name of a river and a state.
26. Eddie - - - nard wrote the song "Ida, Sweet as Apple Cider" for himself, but both Jolson and Cantor popularized it.
27. You can still hear the immortal voice on dozens of compact d - - - s.
28. Blanche - - - - (1876?- 1961) got her audiences to sing along.
29. Jolson sang Berlin's "- - My Mammy" in his 1930 film *Mammy.*
30. Name of Jolson's third wife spelled backwards.
32. Initials of famous band that played for the *Demi-Tasse Revue* (1919) which featured 50 dancers with electric lights in their shoes.
34. Broadway with Jolson.
35. Producing organization for which Jolson was top money-maker.
39 - - - - - - of kings in *Big Boy.*
41. A Jolson show on Broadway always cracked it.
42. Line in song *Ma Blushin' Rosie*: "Your honey boy -- waiting."
43. B.O. condition for most of Jolson's performances.
44. Henry - - nd - was a guest on Jolson's Shell Chateau radio show on 14 September 1935.
45. Garland - - derson, author of *Appearances,* for which Jolson gave initial financial backing.
46. Jolson sings "- - etty Baby" in three different movies.
48. Line in a song: ". . . because my - i - ah might change her mind about me."
49. What Jolson did to all his parts.
50. Familiar name for the great entertainer.
52. "You - - - - Me Love You," song in Jolson's repertoire from 1910s to 1940s
53. Composer whose big break came when Jolson performed "Swanee."
55. Jolson sang "Yes, S - -, That's My Baby" on the Burns & Allen Show in 1950.
56. Crooner on whose radio show Jolson often performed.
57. Song in *Big Boy*: "- -'ry Rose Must Have a Thorn"
58. Jolson goes on them in *The Singing Fool.*
60. - - - - Deslys was the star of *Vera Violetta* (1911), but it was Jolson who led it to 112 performances.
61. Irving Berlin song in *The Jazz Singer*: "- - - - Skies".
62. Jolson and Crosby recorded "- a - ter P - rade" as a duet.

DOWN

1. Banjo-eyed imitator of Jolson.
2. Much - - - : when Jolson followed Caruso on a 1918 benefit program and showed

the audience that they "ain't heard nothin' yet."

3. Composed "Let Me Sing and I'm Happy" especially for Jolson.
4. Line from "April Showers": "And when you see - - ouds upon the hills. . . ."
5. "- I - xander's Ragtime - and"
6. Line in the song "Hallelujah, I'm a Bum": "The m - on'- my ch - ndelier."
7. Theatre where Jolson gave solo Sunday matinees with a runway through the audience.
8. Birth name of Al Jolson.
9. Jolson sang Berlin's "Alwa - -" on several radio shows.
10. Jolson contemporary Peter - - - - - - sang "Wagon Wheels" in 1934 *Ziegfeld Follies.*
15. Jolson's longtime piano accompanist.
16. In Jolson's World War I song "Hello Central," he asks for his daddy in "- o M - n's Land."
18. Minstrels with whom Jolson toured from 1908 to 1910.
20. Jolson would sometimes dismiss the rest of the cast to sing and -- --- with the audience on his own.
23. What Maurice Chevalier had that Jolson didn't.
25. African American architect Paul Williams designed the Jolson monument at - - llside Memorial Park in Los Angeles.
31. Jolson never had a f- - - on Broadway.
33. Jack - - - - - ' - German dialect comedy enlivened Shubert shows like *A Night in Paris* (1926) and *Artists and Models* (1927).
35. A 1912 Jolson song: "- - - - Your Fingers"
36. Demonized in World War I songs by Cohan and others.
37. Initials of the Brooklyn Theatre where Jolson and his brother performed *The Hebrew and the Cadet* in 1904.
38. Jolson recorded "- u - Tum. Tiddle" in 1911.
40. Jolson never minded going on it.
46. Role Jolson would have played if Kern had composed the show instead of Gershwin.
47. Synonym for "my baby's solitaire" in Jolson's song "There's A Rainbow Round My Shoulder."
50. - - rome Ker -'s *Show - oat*.
51. Initials of *Hollywood Reporter* columnist who reconciled feuding Jolson and Walter Winchell.
52. Jolson didn't need one, even after he lost a lung.
53. "Sweet Geor - - - Brown" was sung by Jolson in 1938.
54. Jolson often sang "- Can't Gi - e Yo - Anything But Love" on radio.
56. Initials of all-night radio host who broadcast a legendary impromptu session with Jolson on 6 October 1946.
59. Jolson collaborated with Sigmund Romberg on the melody for "The Rag-Lad of Bag - - d."

C	A	B	C	A	L	L	O	W	A	Y		D	E
A	D	E	L	E			S	I	S	S	L	E	
N	O	R		B	A	N	A	N	A			R	D
T		L	T		K	A		T	Y		V	O	O
O	H	I	O		S		L	E	O		I	S	C
R	I	N	G		T	O		R	E	L	E	E	K
			A	P			A	G	L	O	W		S
S	H	U	B	E	R	T		A	S	P	O	R	T
N	U	T		A	M		S	R	O		F	O	A
A	N		P	R		J		D	N		P	A	D
P		J	O	L	I	E		E		M	A	D	E
	G	E	R	S	H	W	I	N		I	R		R
B	I	N	G			E	V		S	K	I	D	S
G	A	B	Y		B	L	U	E		E	S	A	

Theatre History Studies 23 (June 2003)

The Selling of *La Cage aux Folles*: How Audiences Were Helped to Read Broadway's First Gay Musical

NORMAN HART

After *Hello Dolly!* (1964) and *Mame* (1966) both closed in 1970, Jerry Herman suffered a string of critical and commercial failures that had begun with *Dear World* (1969) and lasted more than a decade, due in large part to the so-called concept musicals of Stephen Sondheim and others that dominated the hearts and minds of critics and Broadway intelligentsia alike during the 1970s. In 1983, Jerry Herman finally scored another success with *La Cage aux Folles.* Although it received mixed reviews, the show was a huge success with audiences and was nominated for a Best Musical Tony Award. Its major competitor was Sondheim's *Sunday in the Park with George*, and as Craig Zadan points out, "the ceremony took on an unusually acrimonious tone when it became a battle for recognition between two different styles of musicals, contrasted by the work of Stephen Sondheim and that of Jerry Herman."[1] Herman confirms that there were indeed "two separate camps in the theater community that year," and asserts that when *La Cage* won Best Musical "it seemed clear to me that a majority of theater people were voting for traditional musical values."[2]

La Cage's dramatic content, however, was nowhere near as traditional as its musical form, given that it centered around the loving relationship of two homosexual men, one of which was a drag queen. Other musicals like *Lady in the Dark* (1941), *Coco* (1969), and *A Chorus Line* (1975) had included gay characters, but they were secondary characters who were either sexless or ashamed of their sexuality, or whose flamboyancy was played strictly for laughs. *La Cage*, on the other hand, was the first Broadway musical not only to feature but to dignify the relationship between two gay men. Moreover, it did so during a time when America was entering a period of neo-conservatism that was determined to reverse what it considered to be a decline in traditional family values brought on by the political and cultural liberalism of the previous decades that had fostered, among other *un*traditional values, a tolerance of homosexuality.

Given the show's dramatic content, *La Cage* no doubt attracted many homosexual theatergoers, especially those who had long waited to be foregrounded in a major Broadway musical. As this essay will show, however, many in the gay community had serious reservations about how they were being represented. It is therefore reasonable to suggest that although audiences for *La Cage* were — like any audience — a complicated group, the show owed its run of 1,761 performances in large part to its ability to negotiate the border between its non-conservative, homosexual content and its mostly neo-conservative, straight audiences. This essay also suggests that *La Cage*'s production and creative teams achieved this negotiation by manipulating (either consciously or unconsciously) what Marvin Carlson has theorized to be the "devices for stimulating and channeling the desires and the interpretive strategies of the spectator."[3] According to Carlson, who based his theory on literary reader response criticism, there are four major devices that "provide audiences with strategies for organizing and interpreting their involvement with the theatre event."[4] He posits that an examination of these devices — which comprise the play's text, publicity and programs, lines of business, and institutionalized critical reaction — can foster a better understanding of a theatrical event and what an audience brings to that event in terms of its "expectations, assumptions, and [reader] strategies."[5] This essay will therefore attempt to achieve a better understanding of the success of *La Cage aux Folles* by examining the way the production and creative teams may have utilized Carlson's devices to ensure that their reader-audience would not feel threatened by a homocentric musical during a time when homosexuality was again being demonized by the New Right.

La Cage aux Folles, written by Jean Poiret, opened at the Théâtre de Palais Royale in 1973. A prime example of French boulevard farce, the play tells the story of a middle-aged homosexual couple, Georges and Albin, who have been living together for twenty years behind their nightclub where Albin performs in drag as Zaza, Queen of the Riviera. The couple has also raised George's son, who announces at the beginning of the play that he wants to marry the daughter of a moralizing, anti-gay public servant. Problems arise when the girl's father insists on meeting the boy's parents before giving his consent. Albin solves the problem by dressing up as the son's "mother," which eventually brings the farce to a happy end.

An immediate hit, *La Cage* ran for seven years in Paris, with many major productions staged around the world. Allan Carr, a former manager for Ann-Margaret, Marvin Hamlisch, and others, had just finished producing the successful film version of *Grease* when he saw *La Cage* in Paris in 1976. He became excited over its audience appeal and eventually obtained the rights to the property by 1978.[6] When Carr announced his plans to turn the play into Broadway's first musical to center around a homosexual love affair, many pundits predicted that his attempt would prove to be a difficult, if not impossible, task. Determined to give birth to a hit rather than the flop that the nay-sayers were predicting, Carr went down the Who's Who of successful Broadway composers, lyricists, librettists, and directors in the hope of finding a winning team. Musical theater talents such as Maury Yeston, Jay Preston Allen, Jack Hofsiss, Tommy Tune, and Mike Nichols were all involved at one point or another, but, for reasons unknown, none of them displayed any desire to remain with the project.

Deciding to begin his search for someone to play Albin, Carr attended a performance of Harvey Fierstein's highly successful Broadway play *Torch Song Trilogy* on the advice of a friend who had described it as a "gay *Nicholas Nickleby*."[7] Intending to concentrate on Fierstein as an actor, the hopeful producer later stated that he was instead "knocked out by the humor and warmth and pathos of the script. When you're talking about Harvey Fierstein, you're talking about the voice of the eighties."[8] Believing that he had finally found the ideal person to write the musical's book — namely, a hot new playwright who had proven that it was possible to create a homocentric theatrical product that could sell on Broadway — Carr asked Fierstein to meet with him to discuss the project that, as the word on the Street had it, was shaky at best. Having heard about the numerous people who had wandered in and out of *La Cage*, Fierstein recounted:

> The idea had been kicking around for years — there was no *way* that it would work. But I wanted to meet Allan because I'd seen him on Tom Snyder and thought he was really camp. [When we met, he talked] like a kid who's got a shopping cart in a toy store and can buy anything he wants. Who wanted to work for a crazy guy like that? I immediately said yes.[9]

But Carr was not yet totally free to say yes to Fierstein. Shortly after meeting with the playwright, Carr asked Jerry Herman if he would be interested in signing on as the show's composer/lyricist. Ironically, Herman had tried (and failed) to obtain the rights to *La Cage* after he had seen the movie version four years earlier. Carr's belated offer convinced Herman that he was indeed "fated" to write *La Cage* and was "floored" that he now had the opportunity to work on "an entertainment that [would make] an important statement about our lives."[10] But before agreeing to take on the project, Herman asked Carr who he had in mind to write the book. Being unfamiliar with both Fierstein and his work, Herman was leery of Carr's latest selection. After attending *Torch Song* with Carr, Herman said simply, "Sign him."[11]

With Fierstein officially on board, Carr was finally able to convince director Arthur Laurents to join the team. Laurents, who had liked the film only mildly and had already turned down Carr's previous overtures to direct the show, was as impressed with Fierstein as Herman had been:[12]

> Harvey Fierstein is not only one of the nicest people I've ever met, he is *the* sensibility of the Eighties. When I went backstage after seeing *Touch Song* and told him it was the best American play I'd seen in a long time, he said he agreed with me. I liked that.[13]

With Laurents, Fierstein, and Herman in place — an eclectic combination that Herman described as "the best of that classy Old Guard generation, . . . a gay man who is more in touch with modern theatrical trends and the political views of the young generation, . . . and me, Mr. Show Business"[14]— Carr was confident that he would be able to produce what he called "the *Ziegfeld Follies* with heart."[15] But by now the Eighties had arrived, and the social-political landscape had changed from when Carr had first obtained the rights to *La Cage*.

Commonly referred to as the "Me Decade," the Seventies fostered a process of self-examination that allowed for a freer public discourse of personal identities, which, in turn, led to an awareness and tentative acceptance of Others. One such group that achieved a foothold in the burgeoning atmosphere of socially acceptable Otherness was the gay and lesbian community, who, by the mid-seventies, had coalesced into a number of activist groups that were "willing to take immediate, direct action against the old array of antihomosexual institutions."[16] The political pressure brought to bear by these groups resulted in a number of significant gains, including the decriminalize of homosexuality in several states; an end to automatic dismissal of gay people from federal employment; and, perhaps most significant, the removal of homosexuality from the American Psychiatric Association's diagnostic manual after a century of pathologizing rhetoric that had fueled a range of antihomosexual practices in the United States.[17]

By the end of the decade, however, the tide of progressive change was stemmed as a new wave of conservatism washed across America. In 1977, the antigay Save Our Children organization convinced the voters of Dade County, Florida, to repeal a newly-established civil rights ordinance that prohibited discrimination on the grounds of sexual orientation. Similar repeals of equal rights laws throughout the United States followed quickly on the heels of the Dade County decision. Soon, an increasingly reactionary climate fostered not only an escalation of police and street violence against gay people but a host of public leaders who could now "shed their veneer of liberalism to attack gay people as immoral sexual predators and threats to the family."[18]

In 1979, the emergence of a New Right political movement helped Ronald Reagan to win a landslide victory that put him in the White House with a clear majority. Two years later, a mysterious disease originally diagnosed as Gay-Related Immune Disorder was identified and labeled Acquired Immune Deficiency Syndrome (AIDS). By the time *La Cage* opened on Broadway, the disease had become "the subject of a widespread panic fueled by the mass media promotion of right-wing demagogues who vilified gay men as a threat to public health [and] 'family values.'"[19]

Given this shift in the social-political climate, the first order of business for *La Cage*'s creative team was to transform a clearly liberal text into one suitable for a reemerging neo-conservative audience. Fortunately, there were a number of given circumstances within Poiret's original script that made this task a bit easier. For one, the action takes place on the French Riviera, which gave audiences a foreign locus in which they could comfortably situate equally foreign behavior such as homosexuality and female drag, thus reassuring themselves that if the location was un-American, so was the behavior.[20] Another comforting given was that both Georges and Albin were middle-aged characters. Because of the stereotypical belief that men at this point in their lives have passed their sexual prime, audiences could set aside any fears they may have had about being made to witness the sexual aspect of the leading couple's relationship. Still, it was crucial that the text strike a universal chord when the lifestyle of its main characters was anything but universal. And Carr firmly believed that it was Fierstein who held the key to this paradox.

As noted, Carr had called Fierstein "the voice of the Eighties." But what was this voice saying, and why did Carr believe that it could speak to the universality that the text required? Perhaps the answer lies in drama critic Ross Wetzsteon's analysis of the backlash *Torch Song Trilogy* was beginning to experience from the gay and lesbian community. According to Wetzsteon, gays and lesbians who had been fighting hard against a heterocentric value system believed that the play was nothing more than a glorification of both middle-class, traditional American family values and Fierstein's openly declared appreciation of "straight" values.[21] This appreciation included the vision of a familial gay lifestyle that was, according to gay cultural critic Simon Watney, a clear example of "[the] bourgeois assimilation rampant among some segments of the gay and lesbian community."[22] Of course, Fierstein's conservative, middle-class vision of homocentric relationships was exactly what the text needed to ensure that it would mirror the audiences' equally conservative, middle-class vision of heterocentric relationships.

According to Fierstein, his first dramaturgical task was to transform Poiret's farcical lead couple into a more traditional, sympathetic one: "The audience has to be absolutely convinced from the minute the curtain goes up that these two men have been a married couple for twenty years. If they don't feel that, we've blown it."[23] The idea that a homosexual couple can sustain a long, loving marriage is central to Fierstein's text, but it is not presented in a confrontational manner. There is no political rhetoric or gnashing of teeth over not being accepted by a heterocentric social order. Instead, Fierstein constructed dramatic moments that allowed Herman to musicalize the naturalness of Georges and Albin's relationship. For example, early in the show, Georges's son, Jean-Michel, sings a song ("With Anne on My Arm") about the love he feels for his fiancée. Georges then sings the same love song to Albin ("With You on My Arm"), thus naturalizing and making concrete both Fierstein's and Herman's view that love, commitment, and family are values that everyone, straight or gay, has the right both to choose and to actuate.[24] That these values were embraced by the text no doubt helped audiences to embrace the text in turn.

In addition to modeling Georges and Albin's relationship on a more acceptable middle-class, hetero-marital paradigm, Fierstein transferred most of the homophobic rhetoric from the original play's prospective father-in-law to Jean-Michel. By making the son the "villain" of the piece, Fierstein was able to craft a text that not only offered audiences traditional scenes of parent-child conflict but again naturalized traditional family values. When, for example, Jean-Michel accuses Albin of not understanding or respecting his wishes, Georges counters angrily that very few sons have received as much understanding and respect from their mothers as Jean-Michel has received from Albin. Thus, as Fierstein summarized his traditional adaptation of a non-traditional text,

> *La Cage* [is] the tale of a marriage of 20 years almost ruined by a son's thoughtlessness. Here, amidst the age-old triangle of mother, father, and child, we found our universality . . . What child has not at some point in its life been ashamed to introduce its parents to friends? What parent has not wondered, "Where did we go wrong?" What marriage has not been tested in these familial flames? [In short,] what *La Cage* comes down to is simple: Honor thy father and mother. [I]f you want a quick phrase, always go to the Bible--it does it so well.[25]

It is possible that Fierstein's conservative view of family was the "voice of the Eighties" to which Carr had referred, given that it was an echo of similar views that were currently being voiced in other forms of popular entertainment. Television, for example, had already shifted away from shows like *All in the Family*, *Maude*, and *Sanford and Son*, in which families were for the most part dysfunctional, their problems were often divisive, and the humor came from coarse insults, to shows like *Happy Days*, *Little House on the Prairie*, and *Eight is Enough*, in which families were loving and supportive, their problems brought them together rather than tore them apart, and the humor was of a kinder and gentler nature. Moreover, although the wives in these families enjoyed an equal status in their marriages, they were assigned nonetheless the traditional, nurturing role of Motherhood[26] — a role similarly assigned to Albin by

Fierstein.

Given the public's desire for more conservative, family affirmative entertainment, it is not surprising that both the pre- and post-opening publicity for *La Cage* attempted to shape the desired audience reader strategies by focusing on Fierstein's almost Victorian application of neo-traditional American family values to the gay lifestyle. *New York* magazine, for example, could assure prospective audiences that *La Cage* would be nothing more threatening than "[a] drag-queen musical with a biblical message . . . a musical celebrating not just monogamy and family but a world in which children want their parents' approval before getting married."[27] Even the *Village Voice*, a liberal, gay-friendly weekly that understandably could have been more critical of Fierstein's conservative reworking of the text, opined that *La Cage* was "a pleasant, professional, shrewdly tactful show . . . with nice old-fashioned songs by Jerry Herman."[28] Still, Fierstein's program credits were carefully crafted in order to ensure that the playwright's apparently safe vision would not become blurred. No overt mention is made of Fierstein's work in gay theatre--including the fact that he had been a performing drag-queen--and Fierstein's only listed work as a playwright was his commercially successful *Torch Song Trilogy*. Other works with easily misread titles like *Freaky Pussy* were omitted.[29]

Another publicity device employed to aid the targeted audience in their reading of *La Cage* was the show's logo, which appeared in newspaper advertisements, on posters, the theater marquis, the Broadway cast album, and the cover of the program (See Figure 1). A seductive, flapper-like "chorine" is decked in feminine signifiers such as furs and jewels, yet at the same time "she" is sporting a tattooed anchor, which is not only a masculine signifier but one that signifies the traditionally masculine occupation of sailor. No doubt these mixed signals alerted audiences to the drag aspect of the show and pointed up what Wetzsteon called "[an] emphasis on disorientation [that would] make the audience more aware of how people traffic in poses."[30] This accurate reading no doubt pleased both Fierstein, who wanted to challenge the exclusive hetero-orientation of love and marriage, and Laurents, who heightened the disorienting authenticity of drag both by casting two female actors to play "male" drag queens and by consciously avoiding camp.[31]

Upon further reflection, however, Carr's publicity team may not have been as pleased that the logo alerted audiences so clearly to the fact that their sensibilities would be disoriented or that they would be made aware of the poses people traffic in--especially poses to which they themselves did not subscribe. After the three million dollar pre-opening ticket rush that sustained the first six months of the show's box office, the *New York Times* display ad featured a new, modified logo (See Figure 2). The chorine was still present, but in a different pose that not only revealed a shapely, clearly feminine leg but an equally feminine arm that was devoid of the masculine tattoo. The chorine appears to be pulling back a curtain (thus foregrounding the theatricality rather than the reality of her pose) to reveal a photograph of Albin and the Cagelles in full drag. Their poses, however, clearly favor the publicity team's desire to present *La Cage* as a harmless campy romp over Laurents's desire to disorient the audience through the authenticity of drag.

The logo used for the display ads was continually modified throughout the run of the show, especially during the family-oriented holiday season when any aspect of the

Figure 1. *La Cage aux Folles*, original program cover. PLAYBILL®. Used by permission.

Figure 2. *New York Times* display ad, (February 26, 1984), Section 2, 10. Marvin A. Krauss Associates. Used by permission.

original logo or other possibly family-*dis*oriented images were completely absent.[32] By 1986, however, the logo underwent a major transformation in which the only thing to survive was the title's typography (See Figure 3). Any unsettling ambiguities that might have been evoked by the original logo were clearly eradicated from the new one. Not only did a photograph of a real, tattoo-less "chorus girl" promise an evening no more disorienting than the Rockette Christmas Show, but it did not take a magnifying glass to confirm that "she" was indeed a she.[33] Moreover, this photograph of a real "she" subtly privileged the two real women in the chorus over the men playing at being women. With the show out on national tours, Carr's publicity team thus provided Middle American towns like Lexington, Kentucky, with a logo that it would have no problem running in its newspaper and that clearly imaged its critical promise that *La Cage* would be "[a] naughty, but nice, sentimental family show."[34]

The numerous changes to the logo did not change the fact, however, that one of the lead characters was a homosexual man who made his living as, and enjoyed being, a drag-queen. Perhaps realizing how easily an actor can become closely identified with his or her role, Laurents, as director, was faced with the difficult task of finding not only an actor willing to risk being labeled a homosexual simply because he would be playing the part of a drag-queen but one whose usual lines of business were masculine enough to reassure audiences that he indeed would only be "playing" the part. Fortunately, George Hearn, who had recently played strong, patriarchal figures in both *I Remember Mama* and *A Doll's Life* and had replaced Len Cariou as the hyper-masculine Sweeny Todd, was willing to take a chance on the role, mainly because he believed that "there are so few musicals these days *about* anything."[35] In fact, Hearn was so willing to take a chance that he appeared at the audition wearing a red dress and wig, size 10 ballet slippers, and belted out "My Heart Belongs to Daddy." He immediately got the part.

Albin's lover, Georges — described in the original play as a "manly fortyish-year-old" (*la quarantaine virile*)[36]— was a less daring character but ironically far more problematic to cast. Whereas Hearn was the first and only actor to audition for Albin, it took months to find someone to assume the role of Georges. Finally, Gene Barry agreed to do the part, but only after much self-deliberation and long talks with his wife and children.[37] His hesitancy was understandable, for he had built his entire career on playing stereotypically macho characters — including the relatively recent role of an investigative lawyer on television's *Burke's Law* — and stood to suffer from what Carlson refers to as "audiences bitterly protesting a popular actor unexpectedly appearing in a role out of harmony with a previously established persona."[38]

Whether or not Laurents was consciously aware of a potential "bitterly protesting" audience-reader backlash, one has to wonder why he wasn't tempted to cast gay actors to portray gay characters; after all, Carr had first scouted Fierstein to play Albin. But perhaps on further reflection and perhaps believing that it would be too dangerous to represent homosexual love so realistically in front of a mostly conservative audience — especially during a time when AIDS was still being referred to as the Gay Plague — Laurents, by capitalizing on both Hearn's and Barry's established hetero-masculine lines of business, was able to comfort potential audiences with the fact that these two men were only pretending to be in love with each other.

The publicity team's next task, therefore, was to ensure that the public would correctly read the actors' own sexual preferences, just as they had helped them to read

Figure 3. *La Cage aux Folles* modified program cover. PLAYBILL®. Used by permission.

the show's message and intent. They concentrated on Hearn first, perhaps because they sensed that audiences would have difficulty reading the female drag aspect of Hearn's character. Shortly after *La Cage* opened on Broadway, a full-length article on Hearn appeared in the September 5, 1983 issue of *People Magazine*. The first page of the article featured a photograph of Hearn that was captioned: "'What identity crisis?' jokes George, as he brings a weensy bit of his drag role to his Connecticut farm" (See Figure 4). It is clear that the female drag aspects of his pose are highly satirized and are far outweighed by the masculine icons of the ax, the pipe, the action of making a muscle, and the woodshed setting. Another photo depicted Hearn row-boating on a country lake with his current girlfriend, with a caption that read, "'I've had lots of ladies,' George boasts, but Betsy Joslyn is the one he takes fishing these days on a golden pond." Again, the masculine images prevail, including that of Hearn manning the oars, and there is a sly reference to the then recent hit film *On Golden Pond*, thus subtly equating Hearn with the All-American actor Henry Fonda, who had starred in the movie. Also, while these photos rate full- and half-page status respectively, the only photo of Hearn in his full drag costume occupied a mere one-column, one-third of a page space situated in the traditionally weak layout position of the upper left hand corner on a page not totally dedicated to the article.

Stating up front that Hearn is a "thrice-married, vigorously assertive heterosexual,"[39] the article goes on to list a number of Hearn's "masculine" activities such as arguing about politics over Irish whisky at a Broadway-area bar and chopping wood on his 20-acre farm in Connecticut where the article's lead photo was taken. The article also gave Hearn the opportunity to verbalize his masculinity with statements such as "Men are enslaved to the hunt. I'm a hunter too. If the skirt is tight and the sweater is tight, I'm gone"; "I love the company of women"; and "After the divorce [from Dixie Carter] I didn't want to get involved with anyone. I put up defenses. I drank a lot."[40]

For reasons unknown, it took Gene Barry three months to get his own article in *People Magazine*. Meanwhile, other publicity channels touted the fact that Barry was the actor who had played Bat Masterson and who did the voice-overs for the Ford and Miller beer commercials that had recently run on television. They also featured Barry's own masculine pronouncements like "the important thing to understand is that I don't play the homosexual part of Georges. I play the love he feels for Albin";[41] and "George and I didn't look at each other as man or woman, but as someone we dearly loved. If I ever had a problem, I'd just think of my own wife."[42] This solution was confirmed by Barry's wife when Barry finally got equal time in the December 5, 1983 issue of *People Magazine*: "When he sang his love songs to Albin, I felt he was really singing them to me."[43] Barry also took the opportunity to emphatically state that he was in no way an advocate for homosexuality in spite of undocumented intimations to the contrary made by Fierstein:

> I don't *care* what Harvey Fierstein is saying on the airwaves. I don't want to be part of his platform. I'm just playing a role. If I have a few genteel gestures I use sparingly, so what?[44]

People reinforced verbal Barry's bravado by running a three-column, three-quarter

Figure 4. *People Magazine*, (September 5, 1983), 47. Photograph by Karin Epstein. Used by permission.

photo-spread of him swaggering down a New York street with his large family dutiful in tow and a caption that read, "Gene Barry, the macho hero of the TV series, *Bat Masterson*, leads the Barry bunch on a stroll in Manhattan" (See Figure 5). As with Hearn, the only photo of Barry in character was conspicuously small and buried at the end of the article.[45]

Hearn's and Barry's well-publicized masculine posturing reflected a similar trend towards such posturing in other forms of popular entertainment. Current, highly-rated television programs like *Magnum, P.I.* and *The A-Team*, for example, featured macho heroes played by equally macho actors, while each week *Monday Night Football* offered up twenty-two gladiators battling it out on the field of masculine sport. In the movies, the hyper-masculine heroes of box-office hits like *Star Wars*, *Superman*, *Raiders of the Lost Ark*, and *Rambo* reflected a growing trend of neo-machoism in American culture, while the films' equally popular sequels confirmed not only that the reflection was accurate but that the trend was ongoing. Indeed, Carr himself had contributed to this trend with his film version of *Grease*, which, like the stage musical, featured a leather-jacketed, masculine young man who eventually ruled supreme over the girl he loved. It is no wonder, then, that *La Cage*'s publicity team focused not so much on the talent that Hearn and Barry would bring to their parts but rather on reassuring audiences that although the actors would be playing homosexuals, they themselves were ax-wielding, hard-drinking, women-loving, family-oriented heterosexuals.

For the most part, the institutionalized critical reaction to *La Cage* echoed the desired readings that Carr and his production teams had constructed with the devices that were within their control, either consciously or unconsciously. All of the major reviews continued to propagate the safe, family fun aspect of the show and encouraged audiences to pick out the two "real" women from among the "real" men in the chorus. Where the show did not fare so well was the "heart" for which it had striven. Amid opinions that "there are times when the show becomes too contrived, even too apologetic for its homosexuality,"[46] that "too often the show simply seems to be showing off instead of building interest,"[47] and that "[while] homosexual theater characteristically rejects ordinary middle-class values, *La Cage* embraces those values,"[48] it is perhaps Frank Rich's review in the *New York Times* that best sums up the critical reaction to Fierstein's stated desire to "make the characters more human, not those ridiculous farce characters in the French play":[49]

> In its eagerness to please all comers, this musical is sometimes as shamelessly calculating as a candidate for public office. . . . Harvey Fierstein has misplaced his craftsmanship and bite, [for] there is a homogenized, sit-com tone to the script which suggests Mr. Fierstein is pandering to what he apparently regards as a squeamish Broadway-musical audience. . . . The parents of the bride are such caricatured villains that even the more zealous homophobes in the audience can feel morally superior to them--and thereby escape the reach of the show's plea for tolerance.[50]

Other critics also opined that *La Cage* presented itself "not as a special pleading but as entertainment,"[51] and that Fierstein's potentially risky onstage representation of gay

Figure 5. *People Magazine*, (December 5, 1983), 71. Photograph by Karin Epstein. Used by permission.

lifestyles "makes 'The King and I' daring by comparison."[52]

Later, Middle-America had the opportunity to voice their own ambivalent critical reaction when, for example, the road company of *La Cage* came through Lexington, Kentucky. The reviewer for the *Lexington Herald-Leader* focused on the comforting fact that the show was nothing more threatening than "[a] big, glitzy song-and-dance musical in the style of those that helped build the New York theater's reputation for lavish entertainment."[53] The editors, however, buried the review on the last page of the entertainment section next to an advertisement for "The Great American Strip-Off," which was being held at a local adult nightclub (See Figure 6).[54] This visual juxtaposition clearly suggested that while the reviewer equated *La Cage* with innocent tease, the editors wanted their reader-audiences to equate it more with blatant sleaze.

As noted, George Hearn claimed that he took the role of Albin because he believed that there were so few musicals *about* anything. But just what did *La Cage aux Folles* ultimately end up being about? Laurents wanted it to be about illusion and disorientation; Herman wanted it to be about "standing up for yourself and fighting bigotry";[55] Fierstein wanted it to be about the universality of love and marriage; and Hearn and Barry wanted it to be about *anything* but the intimation that they themselves might be homosexual.

Utilizing Carlson's reader-strategy devices, this essay has shown that it was perhaps only Hearn and Barry who got their wish, thanks in large part to publicity channels that focused not only on both of the actors' past masculine lines of business but on their current masculine posturing on topics such as women, drinking, and sex. However, these same devices undercut Laurents's desire to disorient his audience through the authenticity of drag by slowly transforming that authenticity into images that privileged real women over men playing at being women. As for the show's text, Herman himself undercut his desire to fight bigotry against homosexual love by creating songs that heterosexualized George's and Albin's love for each other rather than celebrated that love's uniqueness. Even the one quasi-political number in the show, "I Am What I Am," was so generalized that it could have stood safely as an anthem for any minority fighting to be what they are because what Albin is in this song does not include sex.[56] Similarly, Fierstein played it safe in his text by sacrificing homosexual specifity to heterosexual generality, as many members of the critical institutions were quick to point out. Moreover, as one critic later posited, Fierstein generalized George's and Albin's relationship to the point of an unobtainable "Ideal Marriage" that is "so clubby, so cozy, so unswervingly and reassuringly affectionate, it would surely be exceptional anywhere."[57]

But were Carr and his team merely following the current trends of other popular entertainment, or did they consciously manipulate the reader-strategy devices at their disposal in such a way that would have anticipated and dissipated any homophobic backlash that could have threatened the success of their project? Perhaps the answer lies in Herman's response to reviewers who criticized *La Cage* for not living up to its political potential:

> If we *had* written a stronger, tougher political message into the material, the *New York Times* might have loved us more. But that would have given our show too narrow an appeal and it never would have found the huge universal

Figure 6. *Lexington-Herald Leader*, (February 5, 1988), B16.

audience that it did.[58]

Assuming that the "we" to which Herman refers was Carr and the rest of the creative team, it is not merely historical distance that suggests that they did indeed make a conscious decision to privilege commercial success over political content first by building a heterosexual narrative around homosexual characters and then by helping their audiences to read it as such.

Ultimately, what *La Cage aux Folles* was about was a fun-filled, nonthreatening, glitzy, Ziegfeld Follies-like evening at the theatre that was suitable for mass consumption by a conservative, hegemonic audience. That it succeeded as such is evidenced by the show's nine Tony nominations, six awards (including Best Musical), and a run of 1,761 performances.

NOTES

1. Craig Zadan, *Sondheim & Co.*, 2d ed. (New York: Harper & Row, Publishers, 1989), 315.
2. Jerry Herman, *Showtune: A Memoir by Jerry Herman* (New York: Donald I. Fine Books, 1996), 242-43.
3. Marvin Carlson, "Theatre Audiences and the Reading of Performance," in *Interpreting the Theatrical Past*, ed. Thomas Postlewait and Bruce A. McConachie (Iowa City: University of Iowa, 1989), 92.
4. Ibid., 86.
5. Ibid., 86-7, 97.
6. At first, Carr had wanted to make the play into a movie, but by the time he was able to obtain the rights the highly popular French-Italian movie had been released. Rather than competing with the film's success, Carr decided instead to adapt the play into a musical. David Sheward, *It's a Hit!: The Back Stage Book of Longest-Running Broadway Shows, 1884 to the Present* (New York: Watson-Guptil, Back Stage Books, 1994), 285.
7. Originally three separate one-act plays that premiered off-off Broadway at Ellen Stewart's La MaMa in the late Seventies, *Torch Song Trilogy* opened at the Richard Allen Center in 1981, transferred to the off-Broadway Actors Playhouse in early 1982, and then opened on Broadway at the Little Theater on June 10, 1982. Winning the 1983 Tony Award for Best Play, *Torch Song Trilogy* ultimately achieved a run of 1,222 performances. *Cambridge Guide to American Theatre*, s.v. "*Torch Song Trilogy.*"
8. Quoted in Ross Wetzsteon, "La Cage aux Folles Comes to Broadway," *New York Magazine*, 22 August 1983, 33.
9. Ibid.
10. Herman, 244-25.
11. Quoted in Wetzsteon, 33.
12. That Laurents was always less than enthusiastic about *La Cage* is suggested by the fact that he accords the show only two brief mentions in his recently published autobiography, and that he refers to it as "the biggest hit I'd ever been associated with. Not the best." Arthur Laurents, *Original Story By: A Memoir of Broadway and Hollywood* (New York: Alfred A. Knopf, 2000), 412.

13. Quoted in Wetzsteon, 33.
14. Herman, 226.
15. Quoted in Wetzsteon, 33.
16. Barry D. Adam, *The Rise of a Gay and Lesbian Movement*, rev. ed. (New York: Twayne, 1995), 85.
17. Ibid., 87.
18. Ibid., 109.
19. Ibid., 155.
20. In its first incarnation, *The Queen of Basin Street,* director Mike Nichols had planned on placing the action in New Orleans. This idea was totally scrapped when Nichols left the project. Sheward, 285.
21. Quoted in Wetzsteon, 35.
22. Moe Meyer, introduction to *The Politics and Poetics of Camp*, ed. Moe Meyer (New York: Routledge, 1994), 2.
23. Quoted in Wetzsteon, 34.
24. Ibid., 37.
25. Harvey Fierstein, *La Cage aux Folles*, liner notes, RCA RCD14824, 1983, compact disc; quoted in Ibid., 33.
26. S. Robert Lichter, Linda S. Lichter and Stanley Rothman, *Prime Time: How TV Portrays American Culture* (Washington, D.C.: Regnery Publishing, 1994), 153, 61.
27. Quoted in Wetzsteon, 37.
28. Guy Trebay, *Village Voice*, 6 September 1983, 57.
29. *Playbill* 83, No. 8 (August 1983), 37.
30. Quoted in Wetzsteon, 34.
31. Ibid., 37, 4.
32. For example, the display ads for the 1986 Christmas season consisted of only the show's title and other pertinent information under a headline that read "The Perfect Last Minute Christmas Gift!," which was framed by a garland of holly, ribbons, and candy canes.
33. A similar live photograph of a "chorine" in the same high-kicking pose was featured during the month of December, 1985. The telling area of this photograph, however, was overlaid by the show's title, thus interfering with the more than likely correct reading of this Cagelle as a male actor in drag.
34. Dan Smith, "Crowd pleasers: Broadway Live schedule is music to patron's ears," *Lexington-Herald Leader*, 23 August 1987, D1.
35. Quoted in Wetzsteon, 34.
36. Jean Poiret, *La Cage aux Folles* (Paris: Presses Pocket, 1979), 11.
37. Wetzsteon, 34.
38. Carlson, 90.
39. Andrea Chambers, "Gorgeous George Hearn is the Queen of Broadway in a Gilded *La Cage Aux Folles*," *People Magazine*, 5 September 1983, 47-8.
40. Quoted in Ibid., 51.
41. Quoted in Wetzsteon, 34.
42. Gerald Clarke, review of *La Cage aux Folles*, by Harvey Fierstein and Jerry Herman (Palace Theater, New York), *Time*, 29 August 1983, 36.

43. Quoted in Andrea Chambers, "Gene Barry Sings His Love Songs to a Man in Broadway's *La Cage Aux Folles* and His Family Cheers Him On," *People Magazine*, 5 December 1983, 71.
44. Quoted in Chambers, 72. That Barry's uneasiness with the homosexual aspect of his role may have interfered with his ability to develop an acceptable character is suggested by Laurents's revelation that during rehearsals "[o]ne of the two stars would have been fired but a replacement couldn't be found; somehow, I had to get a performance out of him." Although Laurents did not mention the star's name, it is reasonable to assume that he was referring to Barry given the initial difficulty Carr had in finding an actor to play Georges and Hearn's overt enthusiasm about playing Albin. Laurents, 412.
45. Such public heterosexual posturing, both in word and image, was of course not new to Broadway audiences. For example, Julian Eltinge, who specialized in female impersonation during the height of vaudeville, was extremely aware of the need to develop an off-stage image of normative masculinity. Among other tactics, he wore clothes that accentuated the broad shoulders that he artfully disguised while in female drag, developed a masculine swagger, publicized his supposed interest in sports and athletics, and circulated stories about taking on insulting bullies and drunks in barroom brawls. See Robert C. Toll, *On With the Show: The First Century of Show Business in America* (New York: Oxford University Press, 1979), 246-56.
46. Clive Barnes, review of *La Cage Aux Folles*, by Harvey Fierstein and Jerry Herman (Palace Theater, New York), *New York Post*, 22 August 1983, E1.
47. Dennis Cunningham, review of *La Cage aux Folles*, by Harvey Fierstein and Jerry Herman (Palace Theater, New York), *WCBS*, 21 August 1983.
48. Julius Novick, review of *La Cage aux Folles*, by Harvey Fierstein and Jerry Herman (Palace Theater, New York), *The Village Voice*, 6 September 1983, 75-6.
49. Quoted in Wetzsteon, 33.
50. Frank Rich, review of *La Cage aux Folles*, by Harvey Fierstein and Jerry Herman (Palace Theater, New York), *New York Times*, 22 August 1983, B6.
51. Howard Kissel, review of *La Cage aux Folles*, by Harvey Fierstein and Jerry Herman (Palace Theater, New York), *Women's Wear Daily*, 22 August 1983, 46.
52. Douglas Watt, review of *La Cage aux Folles*, by Harvey Fierstein and Jerry Herman (Palace Theater, New York), *Daily News*, 22 August 1983, D3.
53. Tom Carter, review of *La Cage aux Folles*, by Harvey Fierstein and Jerry Herman (Lexington Opera House, Lexington, KY), *Lexington-Herald Leader*, 5 February 1988, B9.
54. It is ironic to note that the stripper pictured on the right could be read as a male performer given the drag aspect of her heavy, overdone makeup.
55. Herman, 226.
56. John M. Clum, *Something for the Boys: Musical Theater and Gay Culture* (New York: St. Martin's Press, 1999), 183.
57. Benedict Nightingale, *Fifth Row Center: A Critic's Year On and Off Broadway* (New York: Random House, Times Books, 1986), 48.
58. Herman, 228.

Norman Hart received his doctorate from the University of Maryland at College Park and currently is Director of Musical Theatre at James Madison University. Recently, he presented a paper entitled "Where Do We Begin the Beguine?: Broadway's Debt to Early English Forms of American Musical Theatre" at Hofstra Cultural Center's conference on the Broadway musical.

Theatre History Studies 23 (June 2003)

Julia Marlowe's Ophelia: A Portrait of Resistance and Failure

PATTY S. DERRICK

In 1904 Julia Marlowe, already an established American star of Shakespearean drama and romantic melodrama, teamed with E. H. Sothern and played Ophelia for the first time, using a text cut by Sothern to highlight his role as Hamlet (See Figure 1).[1] In exchange for Sothern's performing Romeo to her beloved Juliet, Marlowe supported him by portraying Ophelia with what Marvin Rosenberg calls a typically "sweet" Ophelia.[2] A reading of Sothern and Marlowe's 1904 promptbook justifies such a label: unseemly remarks about Ophelia have been excised along with the bawdy song by her.[3] Indeed, Marlowe's desire to depict only good women on the stage, and specifically here a pure Ophelia, can be seen in the textual cuts. However, Marlowe's part book for the role, describing all of her stage business as well as every gesture and facial expression that she used, tells a deeper, more interesting story.[4] Through nonverbal means, Marlowe added more complexity to the role than the simple cutting of lines reveals. Although famous for her rich voice and musical delivery, Marlowe found nonverbal signs that enabled her Ophelia to speak a stronger language, the language of resistance, the language of one whose tragedy, as Marlowe herself stated, lies in her repeated failure. Marlowe's portrayal certainly could not be labeled a "power" Ophelia although elements of strength, intelligence, and rebelliousness can be seen in her gestures and expressions. It was a performance of its time, a transitional time when Shakespearean performance modes were moving away from the grand style of the nineteenth century with its romanticized portrayals of Ophelia but the modern psychological and naturalistic style had not yet fully emerged and developed. Marlowe's Ophelia could likewise be called transitional: progressive and innovative in its nonverbal transmission of protest and resistance, paving the way for the "power" Ophelias to come, but also traditional in its verbal purity and sweetness, linking her portrayal to the romanticized Ophelias of the previous century. Marlowe clearly believed that Ophelia had a compelling story of feminine strength to tell, but it is the story of a nineteenth-century woman habituated to the cult of true womanhood, a woman whose repeated self-sacrifice and failure lead her into the only space allowed her: childlike delirium. Marlowe tells this story partially with the expurgated text but largely with her own face and body.

The American theatre in 1904 was making a hesitant transition from the previous century's grand style, characterized by broad gestures, pictorial realism, and meticulous delivery of blank verse, to a more "realistic" style in movement, delivery, and *mise-en scene*. However, during the first decade of the twentieth century, audiences still applauded and expected the old traditions, a fact lamented by theatre historian Walter Prichard Eaton in 1908:

Figure 1. Julia Marlowe as Ophelia. Courtesy of Ford E. and Harriet R. Curtis Theatre Collection, University Library System, University of Pittsburgh.

> This tight old world is in very little danger from revolutionists, iconoclasts, new ideas in any form. We are compact of an inherited stock of beliefs and ideas, and we adopt as little that is new as possible; we hate change, a readjustment. . . . Old traditions flourish just because they are traditions; old conventions, moldy with time, still prevail and are accepted by audiences long after every one knows they are false and hollow. The stage villain, the stage servant, the stage hero, what are they but conventions we lack the initiative to give up?[5]

One of those conventions that actors and audiences inherited and cherished was the portrayal of Ophelia as an image of true womanhood: pious, pure, submissive, domestic. Barbara Welter describes the cult of "true womanhood" in her book *Dimity Convictions* as a "fearful obligation, a solemn responsibility"; the standards "by which a woman judged herself and was judged by her husband, her neighbors and society, could be divided into four cardinal virtues—piety, purity, submissiveness and domesticity. Put them all together and they spelled mother, daughter, sister, wife—woman."[6] Mrs. Anna Jameson in her 1833 character study of Ophelia found qualities of the true woman: "modesty, grace, tenderness," without which "a woman is no woman." To Mrs. Jameson, Ophelia can be compared to "a strain of sad sweet music which comes floating by us on the wings of night and silence, and which we rather feel than hear. . . ."[7] In 1884 Grace Latham in an essay entitled "O Poor Ophelia" also expressed this traditional notion, "Ophelia lacks the passion which might have lifted her for the moment beyond her fears"; Latham went on to describe the passive virtues that are both noble and necessary for a beautiful female character, virtues that Ophelia possesses: obedience, gentleness, patience, purity, and quiet endurance.[8] In 1897 Jessie Fremont O'Donnell ostensibly rejected the traditional romanticizing of Ophelia and asserted that Ophelia is merely "a simple shallow girl," but she continued by describing the character as "pure and delicate" and "weak and timid," adjectives traditionally used in the nineteenth century to romanticize Ophelia and place her squarely within the mold of the ideal woman.[9]

Also, in 1897, George Bernard Shaw commented on the audience's resentment of Mrs. Patrick Campbell's innovative and realistic portrayal of Ophelia's madness: "The part is one which has hitherto seemed incapable of progress." The audience preferred, Shaw explained, to see maiden lunacy that evokes beauty and pathos rather than a portrait of true madness that made them "horribly uncomfortable."[10] Mrs. Campbell attempted to break with tradition, attempted to play the mad scene as something more than a pretty interlude, and to Shaw, her performance chilled the blood, giving the scene "its right tragic power and dramatic significance."[11] In Mrs. Campbell's hands, a pretty Ophelia became painful, an interpretation used again in 1905 by Lily Brayton (with H. B. Irving's Hamlet), and Max Beerbohm found it misguided: "Lunacy is a painful thing, and Shakespeare did not mean the mad scenes of Ophelia to be painful: he merely meant them to be beautiful. . . . The only right way for an actress to interpret these mad scenes is through her sense of beauty."[12] Beerbohm clearly preferred the portrayal of Ellen Terry, whom Rosenberg calls one of the great "sweet Ophelias"—poetical, dreamy, cool, tender, chaste.[13] Alan Hughes describes Terry's Ophelia as "picturesquely pathetic," or "as Victorians liked to put it, she was 'ideally' pathetic and beautiful." Her madness was played as "a mind shattered but nothing squalid and painful."[14] Anthony Dawson also alludes to Terry's Ophelia as "lovely, pathetic, plaintive," a portrayal admired by audiences because she "fit smoothly into this homey patriarchal atmosphere."[15] Other nineteenth-century actresses established this tradition of beauty and pathos: Mrs. Charles Kean, for instance, whose Ophelia was characterized as charming, harmless, pious, full of timid grace;[16] or Helena Faucit, whose portrayal was both subtle and innovative but struck reviewers as revealing "all the poetry in the madness of Ophelia."[17] One reviewer rhapsodized over Faucit's mad scene: "how pale she [was] already with her future death,"[18] a comment reminiscent of Edgar Allan Poe's declaration that "the death . . . of a beautiful woman is, unquestionably, the most poetical topic in the world. . . ."[19]

The role of Ophelia became a perfect vehicle for exalting the cult of true womanhood; she could be pure and chaste, obedient and submissive, and her madness and death could evoke images of sublime beauty. A. C. Bradley, in his landmark critical study *Shakespearean Tragedy*, published in the same year as Marlowe and Sothern's *Hamlet* (1904), echoes the traditional view of Ophelia. He declares that Ophelia should be "merely one of the subordinate characters" since she lacks the "spirit, power or intelligence" of an Imogen, Portia, or Juliet.[20] He states further, "And in the love and fate of Ophelia herself there was introduced an element, not of deep tragedy but of pathetic beauty, which makes the analysis of her character seem almost a desecration,"[21] a perspective shared by Mrs. Jameson, who insisted that Ophelia's "sorrow asks not words but tears."[22] Bradley, however, does analyze her character briefly and proposes that she is not a weak woman but rather a simple and infinitely unselfish one, whose madness is a blessing, given her situation. Of her madness, Bradley perpetuates the conventional interpretation: "In her wanderings, we hear from time to time an undertone of the deepest sorrow, but never the agonised cry of fear or horror which makes madness dreadful or shocking. And the picture of her death, if our eyes grow dim in watching it, is still purely beautiful."[23] His view of Ophelia resonates with the romanticized portrayals on the stage, the portrayals that audiences preferred. Pathetic beauty and sorrow could reinforce the audience's desire to see Ophelia as a true woman — unselfish, self-sacrificing, and sublimely beautiful as she crumbles and dies.

Even though the role of Ophelia was a small one, generally played by "the second juvenile of the company," Julia Marlowe assumed the role in 1904 as a concession to her new stage partner, E. H. Sothern (See Figure 2).[24] She came to the role at the age of thirty-nine and approached it with her customary scholarly meticulousness, and in many ways her portrayal invigorated the traditional image of Ophelia. After all, Marlowe was the foremost romantic actress of the day, called the "epitome of womanly virtue and feminine loveliness."[25] Nevertheless, she saw more in Ophelia than many of her contemporary actor-managers had and certainly more than contemporary scholar-critic A. C. Bradley, who did not perceive the strength and "deep tragedy" in Ophelia's story. Marlowe clearly disagreed. In 1905 Marlowe gave an interview to the *Washington Post* regarding her portrayal of Ophelia, and she mentions that perhaps her "conception differs somewhat from others" since she sees Ophelia as smart and strong, not the "feeble-minded ingénue" frequently offered to audiences. Marlowe explains that Ophelia is "most assuredly" intellectual: "it is because of the very force of her intellect

Figure 2. Julia Marlowe as Ophelia and E. H. Sothern as Hamlet. Courtesy of the Theater Collection, Museum of the City of New York.

that she goes mad. If she were less great her mental fall would be less." She goes on to assert that Ophelia ought to be viewed as "the pivotal character of the play. . . . Insignificant as she is sometimes made to appear, she really dominates everything."[26] Marlowe's proof of Ophelia's intellect and centrality rests on her relationship with Hamlet: "Hamlet is thirty and a remarkably intellectual man. Ophelia would have to be a strong, well-poised woman to hold such a man, no whining and piping ingénue, no woman of ordinary attainments. I take it she was intellectually the most attractive woman in the Danish court."[27] Her claim that Ophelia's story is tragic and substantial in its own right is repeated again in a 1906 interview with Elizabeth McCracken: "She failed; that was her tragedy that she always failed. She tried to save the persons she loved, and she could not."[28] Marlowe's Ophelia repeatedly tried— tried to assert her own desires, tried to resist being used as a political pawn, tried to comfort and restore the man she loved— and repeatedly she failed. Marlowe's view that Ophelia's tragedy is caused by failure is provocative given a nineteenth-century explanation of failure offered by John Ruskin in his 1864 lecture "Of Queen's Gardens." In a thoroughly romanticized perspective of gender roles, a perspective that fueled the cult of true womanhood, Ruskin describes the "separate spheres" of men and women as being the natural way: "Man's power is active, progressive, defensive. . . . But the woman's power is for rule, not for battle and her intellect is not for invention or recreation, but sweet ordering, arrangement and decision. . . . Her great function is praise. . . . The man, in his rough work in the open world, must encounter all peril and trial—to him therefore must be the failure, the offence, the inevitable error; often he must be wounded or subdued, often misled, and always hardened."[29] Failure, a possible result of doing, acting, creating, lies in the masculine sphere. Marlowe's Ophelia, attempting to bridge the two spheres, experiences the rigidity of their separation, gaining an awareness of the masculine world of doing and failing and of the impossibility of entering and succeeding in that world. Marlowe herself knew much of the failure that comes with trying, risking, doing; she had made her own way in the world since she was a young teenager, deciding for herself the career path she would follow, managing her own Shakespearean productions and tours (prior to her collaboration with Sothern in 1904), and she had not always succeeded. Marlowe, like her Ophelia, was strong yet feminine and delicate, assertive yet virtuous, and ultimately she conformed to the patriarchal order of the day.

The following description of Marlowe's performance, based largely on her own part book, reveals that the actress found an important tragedy to tell, a tragedy of a nineteenth-century woman who attempts to resist and fails.

Act 1, Scene 3

Marlowe's first appearance as Ophelia occurs in 1.3, set in a room in Polonius' house. Seated at a table, Marlowe's Ophelia reads a scroll, presumably a missive from Hamlet because she secretly kisses it before Laertes enters, at which time she hides the scroll behind her. Although her affection for the scroll reveals a young girl in love, attempting to hide the letter from her brother suggests fear or possibly even defiance. Ophelia's first line, "Do you doubt that?" in response to Laertes' request that she write to him (1.3.4), has been described by Charles E. Russell, Marlowe's business manager and biographer, as sounding unsuspected profundities in Ophelia's nature. Marlowe's simple delivery of the line conveyed loneliness and a sense of troubles; inexplicably, Russell contends, Marlowe allowed the audience to understand that Ophelia's mother is dead and that Ophelia seemed wistfully conscious of "tragic boding."[30] Her loneliness alters quickly, however, as Laertes begins to warn her away from Hamlet. Laertes points to the scroll as he mentions "the trifling of his favour" (1.3.5), causing Ophelia to turn resentfully to him (part book). Her resentment shifts quickly to slight fear at his next comment that Hamlet's "favour" is a "toy in blood" (1.3.6), and then fear alters to wonderment as she hears that Hamlet "may not . . . Carve for himself" (1.3.19-20). Sothern and Marlowe cut the intervening thirteen lines in which Laertes refers to "the youth of primy nature" (1.3.7) and to "nature crescent" (1.3.11). As Laertes explains that "the health of this whole state" (1.3.21) depends on Hamlet's choice of a bride, Marlowe's Ophelia shows a thoughtful realization of Hamlet's inability to choose freely. Her apparent understanding shifts immediately to pain as Laertes warns her to "weigh what loss your honour may sustain" (1.3.29), the pain appearing at the mention of "honour." As he cautions her to ignore Hamlet's love songs, Ophelia takes a couple steps away from her brother. The next passage from Laertes, with its references to Ophelia's "chaste treasure" (1.3.31) and to "contagious blastments" (1.3.42), has been cut by Sothern and Marlowe, but Laertes' repeated admonition, "Fear it" (1.3.33), remains along with his comment about the "chariest maid" unmasking "her beauty to the moon" (1.3.36-37). Although the unseemly references to Ophelia have been cut, Marlowe still has sufficient opportunity to unveil a range of thought and emotion in Ophelia. Already moving away from her brother, she then sinks into thought, staring forward as he refers to unmasking "her beauty"; she begins her clear response still looking forward, "I shall the effect of this good lesson keep/ As watchman to my heart. But good my brother . . ." (1.3.45-46), at which point she turns to him and places her hand on his shoulder, an unexpected gesture of authority, confidence, perhaps equality or even dominance, as she then instructs him, "Do not . . . Show me the steep and thorny way to heaven . . . " (1.3.47-51). Laertes immediately softens with "O, fear me not" (1.3.51) as their father enters. Marlowe's Ophelia steps away, stealing a glance at the scroll she still holds in her hand, her mounting confidence fading in her father's presence.

Such is our first view of Ophelia. The cutting of the text allows Marlowe to highlight the purity and sweetness that surround Ophelia, but the revelation of many distinct emotions— girlish love, loneliness, fear, wonderment, pain, independence, pensiveness, confidence, all in a twenty-five-line span (the same exchange in Shakespeare's text is fifty-two lines) — suggests the latent power and intelligence within Ophelia, noted by the *New York Herald* reviewer, "Marlowe invested [Ophelia] with more mentality than usual."[31] In this brief opening scene with Laertes, the audience could catch a glimpse of Ophelia's inwardness, her mystery. Marlowe found silent ways to unveil qualities of a "power" Ophelia, qualities that Marlowe's contemporaries found new and interesting. Oscar Firkins in 1913 commented that Marlowe's Ophelia was "less drooping and spiritless than the majority of the lacklustre sisterhood"; he saw in this Ophelia a woman who "submits rather than succumbs; she obeys with decision; she keeps her heart, if not her will, in her own custody."[32] Charles Russell perceived the complexity of Marlowe's portrayal, ". . . she suggested dignity, worth, a self-respect, without loss of sweetness and innocence."[33] Furthermore, Russell believed that in Ophelia's scene with Laertes, Marlowe conveyed "a wistfulness in the voice and an undertone of tragic foreboding that clutched at the sympathies and held them afterward."[34]

The scene continues with Polonius' admonitions to Ophelia, his advice to Laertes having been cut. Polonius gestures for Leartes to leave, and Ophelia quickly crosses to her brother, bowing to her father as she moves; she lays her hand on Laertes' arm, and he responds by grasping both of her arms with ". . . remember well/What I have said to you" (1.3.84-85), causing Polonius to shoot a quick glance of inquiry in their direction. Laertes kisses her forehead as he bids her farewell, and she stands motionless watching him depart. Polonius then asks, "What is't, Ophelia, he hath said to you?" (1.3.88), prompting her to turn, to respond with ". . . something touching the Lord Hamlet" (1.3.89), and timidly to hold out the scroll. Her inner turmoil grows as Polonius chastises her for being too "free and bounteous" (1.3.93) with her time with Hamlet and for not understanding herself and her "honour" (1.3.97), a word that elicits a cry of exclamation from her. She certainly does understand herself, her honour, and the dilemma that her father is introducing. Marlowe's part book directs that she "extend hand holding scroll, in gesture of expostulation," an earnest but unspoken protest to her father's taking and reading the letter. She attempts an explanation as he reads, "He hath, my lord, of late made many tenders/ Of his affection to me" (1.3.99-100), and then extends her hand appealingly for the letter. When he questions her, "Do you believe his tenders, as you call them?" (1.3.103), her protest shifts to bewilderment as she responds, "I do not know, my lord, what I should think" (1.3.104). As he berates these "tenders," all confusion fades, and she again attempts to protest, reaching out for the scroll with the insistent declaration, ". . . he hath importun'd me with love/ In honourable fashion" (1.3.110-111), causing Polonius to turn away from her, which in turn causes her to move a couple steps toward him. All that remains in Sothern and Marlowe's production of Polonius' subsequent explanation of Hamlet's deceptive ardor and vows is, "Ay, springes to catch woodcocks, I do know/ When the blood burns, how prodigal the soul/ Lends the tongue vows" (1.3.134), a suggestion that shocks Ophelia, prompting her to cover her face with horror. She removes her hands from her eyes only when he forbids her to "give words or talk with the Lord Hamlet" (1.3.134). Still holding the scroll, he demands, "Look to 't" and "Come your ways" (1.3.135). Marlowe's Ophelia glances at the scroll and crosses expectantly to him, but then realizing the hopelessness of retrieving her love letter, she submits tearfully, "I shall obey, my lord" (1.3.136), and exits in front of him.

Although she ultimately submits to her father's command, Marlowe's Ophelia clearly exhibits signs of protest and independent thought; in repeatedly reaching for her love letter and in covering her face, blocking out her father's unpleasant pronouncements, this Ophelia shows that she has chosen to believe Hamlet's vows over her father's warnings. However, she must obey. Polonius is not only her father but also a high-ranking official at court, a fact that Marlowe considered in her interpretation of Ophelia. According to Charles Russell, Marlowe's Ophelia "felt a sense of place in the court as a daughter of the lord chamberlain of the kingdom of Denmark, the man next to the king himself."[35] Whereas the reality of her father's position lends her the dignity and strength to protest her father's assessment of Hamlet, it also dooms that protest to failure. By the end of this short scene, then, Marlowe has laid her character's foundation: sad but not pathetic; pure and chaste but certainly not ethereal; independent in her thought and desires but incapable of little more than nonverbal protest because of her keen awareness of her family's court position; deeply emotional and deeply in love but not confused or puzzled by her emotions as many "sweet" Ophelias have been. While Marlowe's Ophelia could satisfy a 1904 audience's entrenched expectation of feminine loveliness and virtue through an expurgated text, the actress could quietly subvert those expectations and offer a fresh insight into Ophelia's mysterious interiority by enhancing and illuminating her few lines with gestures, facial expressions, and movements, many of which suggest resistance, protest, independent thought, qualities that certainly stretch, even challenge, the notion of ideal womanhood.

Act 2, Scene 1

The consequence of Ophelia's obedience soon becomes clear to her as she reports to her father her encounter with an apparently crazy Hamlet in 2.1 (Act 2 is one continuous scene in the Sothern-Marlowe version). Ophelia runs into the castle's throne room where Polonius has been giving spying instructions to Reynaldo (very abbreviated in this production), and she glances back over her shoulder as she approaches, "betraying alarm" (part book). She again looks back over her shoulder as she begins, ". . . as I was sewing in my closet" (2.1.77); Marlowe's Ophelia describes Hamlet's unbraced, hatless, pale, knee-knocking demeanor, eliminating the unpleasant reference to his fouled, ungartered stockings. Polonius hypothesizes that Hamlet is "Mad for thy love?" (2.1.85), to which Ophelia agrees and begins to imitate Hamlet's gestures, with observable force and precision in Marlowe's portrayal. During her speech, she seizes Polonius' wrist at 2.1.87 ("He took me by the wrist"); backs away arm's length from him; raises her hand to her brow and slowly nods her head up and down; releases her hold on Polonius, throwing his hand from her at 2.1.96 ("he lets me go"); turns from him, glancing back over her shoulder at him; and on "to the last, bended their light on me" (2.1.100), she crosses toward Polonius with her eyes fixed on him. Marlowe's gestures reveal an Ophelia who is deliberate, even forceful; she is not weeping, and she does not seem to be struggling to understand what happened. Some Ophelias, as reported by Rosenberg, run through the speech smoothly; others cannot look at Polonius during the speech; many have wept and sobbed.[36] Marlowe's Ophelia defiantly re-enacts Hamlet's gestures, suggesting instead a nonverbal accusation of her father (i.e., "See what you've made me do?"). At the end of the speech, she sinks down on a stool and covers her face with her hands, a gesture that speaks loudly after the preceding defiance. Clearly, there is much she does not want to face, much that she would rather not see: Hamlet's growing madness, her unwilling rejection of Hamlet's attention, and her necessary but resistant obedience to her father.

The realization that she has contributed to Hamlet's madness, that she has probably driven away their love and hope for marriage, could commence a softening or weakening of Ophelia, but not in Marlowe's hands. As the scene continues with Polonius' plan to reveal her encounter to the King, Marlowe's Ophelia continues to resist. On his first command, "Come, go with me; I will go seek the king" (2.1.101), she removes her hands from her face, recoils, then moves away, sitting in Hamlet's chair, an action that intimates her desire to disobey, to follow her own heart. However, when

Polonius accusingly asks if she has given "any hard words of late" (2.1.107) to Hamlet, she begins to weep, "No, my good lord" (2.1.108); his question suggests that she is to blame entirely for Hamlet's instability, but they are tears of frustration, perhaps even anger, because almost immediately she wipes them from her eyes on ". . . denied/ His access to me" (2.1.109-10). Polonius repeats his command, "Come, go we to the king" (2.1.117), and starts to move off but hesitates, waiting for her. Marlowe's Ophelia rises and starts to follow but thinks again and stops, prompting her father to insist, "This must be known . . . " (2.1.118). Her choice has been made clear, but she dare not resist further. She crosses to Polonius and exits in front of him. Once more, her father's position at court takes precedence, so her resistance can end only in failure. A London *Sunday Times* reviewer of Marlowe's 1907 performance of the role believed that in Ophelia's resistance to Polonius, Marlowe showed "almost too much forcefulness for Ophelia,"[37] an indication that Marlowe's portrayal in some ways undermined the audience's traditional expectations despite the sanitizing of the play text.

Act 3, Scene 1

As the third act begins, Gertrude is sitting in Hamlet's chair (again in the throne room) with Ophelia sitting on steps beneath her, holding her hand. A small silver book hangs from Ophelia's belt, and Polonius holds a small jewel casket. After Claudius dismisses Rosencrantz and Guildenstern, he turns to Gertrude, "Sweet Gertrude, leave us too" (3.1.28), at which Gertrude rises and Ophelia, too, stands with her father's assistance. But the assurance and protection she feels with Gertrude quickly fade as Claudius reveals his plan: Hamlet has been sent for in order that he "may here/Affront Ophelia" (3.1.30-31). At this suggestion, Marlowe indicates with her expression "the shock which your sensibilities suffer by such a plan" (part book). According to *The Times* reviewer in 1907, Marlowe's Ophelia demonstrates her unwillingness "to play decoy. She ran to tell her father that she would not, came back crestfallen and disgusted at the task."[38] She must listen as Claudius explains that he and Polonius will spy on the two to determine "If 't be th' affliction of his love or no/ That thus he suffers from" (3.1.35-37), a statement that clearly reminds Ophelia of her complicity in the "affliction" and that causes her to "show pain" in Marlowe's portrayal. Gertrude crosses to her, takes her hands as she wishes "That your good beauties be the happy cause/Of Hamlet's wildness" (3.1.39-40), and finally kisses Ophelia's brow before departing, leaving Ophelia utterly abandoned with two masculine authority figures. Her isolation and vulnerability are intensified by her prior closeness with Gertrude, her only ally and source of hope. Polonius approaches his daughter and thrusts the jewel casket toward her, but Marlowe's Ophelia refuses to take it, a weak attempt (but an attempt nevertheless) to resist any further interference in her love for Hamlet. However, Polonius taps the box commandingly, and "seeing the futility of further refusal, Ophelia reluctantly takes it" (part book), as he instructs her, "walk you here" (3.1.43). The nonverbal exchange between Ophelia and Polonius is intended to show that Ophelia does not initiate the return of Hamlet's gifts, contrary to A. C. Bradley's assertion in 1904 that she originates the idea.[39] Clearly, Marlowe draws attention to the jewel box as further evidence of Ophelia's unwilling participation in what is entirely her father's plan. As Polonius and Claudius hide themselves, Ophelia paces, "showing great distress" as she hears Hamlet's approach; she extends her hand "indicating great tenderness toward Hamlet" and then, according to the part book, "with an expression of regret at the scene you know is to follow, you hurriedly exit R.3.E. still glancing back in the direction from which Hamlet approaches." The extending of her hand towards Hamlet suggests a desire to reach out to him, to help him, a gesture of great sympathy and anguish that she will repeat later in the scene.

At the end of the "To be" soliloquy, Polonius shows himself in an archway because he must force Ophelia back into the room: "Ophelia looks at Hamlet and recoils from her task, turning appealingly to Polonius who points to Hamlet, and directs her to enter" (promptbook). Realizing again the futility of her protest, she lifts the book hanging from her belt and pretends to read as she moves toward Hamlet. When he notices her and asks to be remembered in her prayers, she responds "with an assumed indifference" (part book), even walking away as she asks, "How does your honour for this many a day?" (3.1.91). Sothern's Hamlet is surprised by Ophelia's tone and immediately "adopts a formal attitude" with her (promptbook), which, in turn, causes Ophelia to indicate "grief at Hamlet's sudden coolness" (part book). Quickly, however, she recalls her task and glances up toward the balcony where Polonius and Claudius hide. Resuming her indifferent demeanor, Ophelia attempts to return the casket, but first she opens it, takes out a few pearls, fondles then replaces them: "Take these again" (3.1.100). She extends the jewel box tenderly, and Hamlet takes it, walking away from her, an action that elicits a small sob from her. The conflict between duty to her father, who watches from above, and love and pity for Hamlet becomes excruciating; a sob escapes, but it quickly turns to embarrassment as Hamlet turns and attacks, ". . . are you honest?" (3.1.103), and the embarrassment increases as Hamlet refers to beauty transforming honesty "to a bawd" (3.1.112), causing Ophelia "to shrink" at one of the few blatantly unseemly words used in her presence in this production. (At some point during the "honest/fair" exchange, Sothern's Hamlet must have thrown the jewel casket down although the 1904 promptbook doesn't indicate the action. Later gestures, however, depend on his having cast the box away.) Ophelia then turns toward him as he turns away to admit, "I did love you once" (3.1.115), and having lost her facade of indifference, she responds, "Indeed, my lord, you made me believe so" (3.1.116), accompanied by a "hardly heard cry" (part book). Charles Russell describes this moment in the production, "The whole history of her love, her hope and its irretrievable ruin seemed to be told in the single line, so simple and so moving, 'Indeed, my lord, you made me believe so' and 'I was the more deceived.' It seems impossible to make five words convey more than these five words conveyed as Miss Marlowe spoke them. A new drama opened in them; for the time we lost all thought of the problem laid upon Hamlet, and saw, in a flash, the whole course of his wooing and the sombre tragedy of its end."[40] In a handwritten note in her part book, Marlowe instructs herself to "cry" and to turn her back to Hamlet at this point, allowing him a moment of hidden and unspoken tenderness. As he says, ". . . for virtue cannot so innoculate our old stock but we shall relish it" (3.1.117-18), he takes a lock of Ophelia's hair, presses it to his lips tenderly then puts it down and resumes his formal attitude: "I loved you not" (3.1.118-19).

Still with her back to Hamlet, Marlowe's Ophelia moves away a few steps until he says, ". . . it were better my mother had not borne me" (3.1.123-24), at which she turns with an "exclamation of protest" by placing her hands on Hamlet's shoulders (part book). Earlier she had asserted control and confidence with Laertes with this same gesture — her hand on his shoulder — and despite her own conflicted emotions now, she is attempting to steady what she thinks is an increasingly mad, self-destructive lover. She is trying to solve a problem, one to which she contributed, by offering sympathy, compassion, and strength. Marlowe explained in her 1905 *Washington Post* interview that at this moment Ophelia's "one idea is to help him, to restore him and save him . . . she believes him to be mad, and that is the controlling note of her attitude toward him — an attitude of deep pity and concern."[41] Sothern's Hamlet takes her hands and continues railing, "What should such fellows as I do crawling between earth and heaven?" (3.1.128-29), at which Marlowe instructs herself, "You remonstrate with same business" (part book). Again she protests nonverbally; again she offers to balance or anchor him with her hands on his shoulders, and again, her efforts fail. On "believe none of us" (3.1.130), Hamlet takes Ophelia's hands and "throws them away from him" (part book), and in a handwritten note Marlowe directs herself, "Try to put arm up higher" at which he again throws her arms down, causing her to turn slowly from Hamlet (part book) as he commands, "Go thy ways to a nunnery" (3.1.130). At this point, Marlowe's Ophelia catches a glimpse of Polonius, eliciting a slight cry and a sudden movement of her upraised hand; Hamlet, noticing the gesture, takes her hands, turns her toward him, and looking directly into her eyes, asks, "Where's your father?" (3.1.130-31). "Avoiding Hamlet's glance guiltily and speaking falteringly" (part book), she lies ("At home"), prompting Hamlet's outrage at her deception. Russell describes the effect Marlowe's Ophelia created when she lies: "the lie seemed wrung out of her by an invisible racking; she hated to say it and still that knowledge was heliographed to us and not to Hamlet."[42] Marlowe believed that Ophelia was trying to save Hamlet by lying to him because she "understood that if Hamlet were to know that Polonius was at hand he would be projected into one of his violent attacks. Hence it is for his own good, as she conceives it that . . . she replies untruthfully . . . and the sacrifice of truth in a woman as pure and good as Ophelia is itself a tragedy. Her one idea is to help him, to restore him, and save him from despair."[43] At several points during Hamlet's angry speech— "Let the doors be shut upon him" (3.1.133) — she "turns appealingly to him" with outstretched hands (part book), but her attempts to reach out and help with him only enrage him further. To C.E. Russell, her plea "O help him, you sweet heavens" (3.1.135) seemed "torn out of a stricken soul and from that time her disaster was foreshadowed upon us not as the weakness of a commonplace intellect overthrown, but as the inevitable and only possible ending of a great and shattered life."[44] Hamlet takes her outstretched left wrist on "no more marriages" (3.1.149) then throws it down and paces away on "the rest shall keep . . ." (3.1.151), leaving her behind him, still with extended arms. Before his exit, Sothern's Hamlet stops in front of Ophelia and covers his face with his hands, "as if to vanish her from his thoughts" (promptbook), a gesture she earlier exhibited with her father, a gesture suggesting a desire to protest present reality by denying it. Marlowe's Ophelia watches Hamlet's exit, and Russell chronicles this moment as Ophelia realizes the loss of Hamlet's love: "she made a tragic passage of an astonishing compulsion. For the first time one felt how much of an exalted passion lay latent in this neglected character."[45] She opens her speech, "O, what a noble mind . . ." (3.1.152), crossing to the throne area and sinking on the upper throne step midway through the lament, back to the spot where she received some small support from Gertrude; as she recalls that she "suck'd the honey of his music vows" (3.1.158), she picks up the casket, which Hamlet had previously dashed to the floor, and rises on "O, woe is me . . ." (3.1.162), exiting alone, leaving the jewel box behind. Polonius and Claudius do not re-enter until she is gone, so she receives no consolation from her father. Clearly, this Ophelia expects none.[46]

Marlowe's part book never indicates that her Ophelia breaks down sobbing, and the *Daily Telegraph* reviewer of a 1907 performance even refers to the fact that "her eyes swimming with unshed tears, touched us to the heart."[47] Marlowe non-verbally enunciated Ophelia's inner struggle, which as Rosenberg notes, was considered "something new" to observers[48]: her desire to reach out and reform her bond with Hamlet, her awareness of her guilt, her attempt to bolster his mind and spirit with shows of strength, her fear of betraying her father. According to the *New York Herald* reviewer in 1904, "Here was not a gentle lady going daft to slow music, but a woman of strong passions and fine intelligence who succumbs to a terrible catastrophe."[49] However, Marlowe did not sacrifice Ophelia's womanly tenderness and beauty despite her visible efforts to take control and shore up Hamlet's frantic mind; a *Chicago Tribune* reviewer noted in her 1910 performance of the role, "There was sounded a note of sorrow at the loss of Hamlet's love which has not before been found in any other impersonation of the part."[50] The outstretched arms created an image of sad and lyrical beauty but not of fragile instability. Julia Marlowe herself commented on this scene, "Polonius was annoying to Hamlet, under any circumstance. Ophelia couldn't have lived all her life at the court of Denmark without having discovered that. How unendurably it would have nettled Hamlet to hear that Polonius has been listening behind the arras to his so personal, so private words to Ophelia! She knew that; and she tried both to protect her father and to spare Hamlet. She failed; that was her tragedy that she always failed. She tried to save the persons she loved, and she could not."[51] Marlowe's Ophelia is not a passive victim; repeatedly, she tries to repair the wrongs surrounding her by sacrificing her own desires and well-being, and repeatedly, her actions fail to make any difference.

Act 3, Scene 2

Ophelia's presence in the Mousetrap scene (3.2) is greatly diminished in Sothern and Marlowe's version since the indelicate banter between Hamlet and Ophelia has been excised. However, her presence is felt. Prior to Ophelia's entrance, Hamlet is on stage with a Jester, who picks up the jewel casket Ophelia left behind. He offers it to Hamlet, as Ophelia had previously done; Hamlet takes it then throws it back to the Jester and walks to his chair. According to the Sothern-Marlowe promptbook, "the Jester shows disappointment at Hamlet's treatment, stands looking at Hamlet. Hamlet turns and beckons the Jester to him . . . and puts his arm around his shoulder." The dumbshow provides a visual echo of Hamlet's unforgiving treatment of Ophelia earlier; the audience knows that she had attempted the impossible— returning his gifts while extending a sympathetic hand—and that her gesture found bitter anger. Repeating her gesture now, with the opposite response from Hamlet, certainly draws attention to Ophelia and the sorrow she feels, sorrow that leads to her tragic breakdown in the next act. The connection between her madness and her earlier actions becomes clear; Ophelia's breakdown occurs not because she has a fragile, passive spirit that cannot survive in a corrupt world but rather because her repeated and active struggles to love and be loved are thwarted—all misunderstood, all failing. Marlowe's Ophelia enters for "The Mousetrap" escorted by Horatio. Marlowe directs herself, "You notice Hamlet and give a slight indication of pain" (part book), before proceeding to sit next to the throne. When Hamlet makes his way to her and asks, "Lady shall I lie in your lap?" (3.2.110-11), her response is only "You are merry, my Lord" (3.2.120), the intervening eight lines regarding "country matters" having been cut. As Hamlet rants about his father's death only two months before, Marlowe's Ophelia glances at Horatio, "conveying your pity for Hamlet's condition" (part book). Later in the scene, when Hamlet comments on the Player who is "one Lucianus, nephew to the King" (3.2.239), Ophelia responds to him, "You are as good as a chorus, my lord" (3.2.240), and while the entire court watches the player, Ophelia keeps her gaze fixed on Hamlet, a small attempt to reconnect with him that he quickly brushes off. He responds, "I could interpret between you and your love if I could see the puppets dallying" (3.2.241-42), but their subsequent exchange at 3.2.243-45 ("You are keen, my lord" . . . "It would cost you a groaning to take off mine edge") is decorously cut. When the King ends the play by shouting for lights, in the chaos of everyone's running off stage, Ophelia hurries off with the Queen. Again, the audience sees Ophelia associated with Gertrude, her only source of feminine guidance and sympathy in the play. Marlowe's Ophelia is not entirely isolated; however, her alliance with the Queen, visually established in two scenes, represents yet another attempt by Ophelia to save herself, mend Hamlet, and rescue their love, but the attempt is doomed to fail because of Gertrude's own powerlessness.

Act 4, Scene 5

Her repeated attempts to save her lover's soul and mind while protecting her father's position at court leave Marlowe's Ophelia lost, unconsoled, and nearly unnoticed by either man. Marlowe chose to portray Ophelia's resulting madness in Act 4 as many of her nineteenth-century predecessors had done — with pathos and beauty as audiences preferred; however, her particular interpretation of the insanity grows logically out of Ophelia's previous self-sacrificing struggles (See Figure 3). Phyllis Chesler in her book *Women and Madness* describes the role that self-sacrifice plays in the cult of true womanhood:

> Women are impaled on the cross of self-sacrifice. Unlike men, they are categorically denied the experience of cultural supremacy, humanity, and renewal based on their sexual identity. . . . In different ways, some women are driven mad by the fact. Their madness is treated in such a way as turn it into another form of self-sacrifice. Such madness is essentially an intense experience of female biological, sexual, and cultural castration, and a doomed search for potency.[52]

In the first three acts, Marlowe portrays Ophelia as caught between the masculine and feminine spheres, searching for, often attempting, potency through resistance, protest, and support, and each attempt leads to self-sacrifice and then failure. This inevitably doomed chain of events leads to her final sacrifice: her adult will and intellect. Carroll

Figure 3. Julia Marlow as Ophelia in the "mad scene." Courtesy of the Theatre Collection, Museum of the City of New York.

Smith-Rosenberg explains that among nineteenth-century women, the hysterical fit "must have been the only acceptable outburst—of rage, of despair, or simply of energy—possible. But as a form of revolt it was very limited. . . hysterics don't unite and fight."[53] Having failed at all efforts, albeit non-verbal ones, either to fight back or to nurture, Marlowe's Ophelia sublimates her anger, her despair, her energy and reverts to childhood, a place outside the masculine and feminine spheres. Her entrance early in Act 4 (the first four scenes of Act 4 having been cut in this production) is described in her part book, "The entrance of Ophelia should strike, at once, the key-note of the scenes to follow: her hurried entrance and inquiring glance from side to side, her childlike simplicity should all suggest the shattered mind." While Marlowe's interpretation has a psychological reality and coherence based on her previous scenes, it never approaches the startlingly painful and naturalistic portrayals of some of her contemporary actresses (Mrs. Patrick Campbell, for instance).

She enters with a delicate white scarf draped over her left arm and a lute in her right hand, searching for the only ally she has had, the Queen, who agrees immediately to speak with her. (In Shakespeare's text, Gertrude initially refuses to speak with her.) Many of the Gentleman's lines (transferred here to Horatio) regarding Ophelia's madness are cut; the audience hears nothing of her hemming and beating her heart or of her "winks and nods and gestures" (4.5.11) so that Marlowe can create her own image of the true woman-turned-child. As she sings, "How should I true love know" (Shakespeare's text is "<u>your</u> true love know"), her face is bright, and she strikes a chord on the lute at the end of each line. Marlowe then describes in her part book how she intends to portray this childlike insanity: "One of the most effective means of suggesting insanity, in this scene, is by rapid transition of mood; from brightness to sadness and vice versa." Her idea for this image of feminine insanity certainly is derived from Ellen Terry's portrayal, which itself was based on Terry's visit to a madhouse where she observed a young woman whose vacant stare suddenly shifted to excitability as "she sped across the room like a swallow."[54] An instance of Marlowe's use of this effect is in the transition from her bright inquiring glance and almost bird-like utterance of the words "Say you" followed immediately by a despairing look and low wail of "Nay, pray you mark" (4.5.28), at which point she resumes her singing and strumming of the lute. In the middle of the song's line, "At his head a grass-green turf" (4.5.31), Marlowe glances down, suggesting a grave at her feet, and a small sob escapes here and again in the middle of the next line, "At his heel a stone" (4.5.32). At the conclusion of this line, Marlowe instructs herself, "As you moan, pass your hand over your brow. Add 'oh, oh'" (part book). The Queen moves toward her, showing great sympathy, but Marlowe's Ophelia "pays no attention to the Queen," shifting back to brightness on "Pray you, mark" (4.5.35) then immediately back to a plaintive mood as she continues her song, "White his shroud as the mountain snow" (4.5.36). Claudius enters, and he and Gertrude watch as Ophelia sings and strums her lute, but his presence adds a new emotion to her poignant vacillation between brightness and sadness. When he speaks to her, "How do you, pretty lady?" (4.5.41), Marlowe's Ophelia turns toward him about to respond; then "instinctively shrinking from him" (part book), she pushes her lute at him. This "shrinking from him" and the proffering of her lute suggest a childlike fear, certainly, but also intimate a deeper revulsion or horror, an emotion that she displays again later in the scene. In her next short speech, her mood shifts several times. She begins by addressing Claudius in a bright but confidential tone, "They say the owl was a baker's daughter," but then her tone changes to sadness on "Lord, we know what we are," at which point she shudders before continuing, "but know not what we may be" (4.5.42-44). She glances down at the imaginary grave at her feet, turns and brightly curtsies to the Queen with "God be at your table" (4.5.44). Claudius mentions the dead Polonius at 4.5.45 ("Conceit upon her father"), causing her to snap back harshly at him, "Pray, you, let's have no words of this" (4.5.46). At this moment, according to Marlowe's part book, "occurs a marked contrast of manner; your mood changes to one of excessive gaiety, which expresses itself a moment later in song." However, Marlowe's Ophelia sings only the first stanza:

> Tomorrow is St. Valentine's day,
>   All in the morning betime,
> And I a maid at your window,
>   To be your Valentine. (4.5.48-51)

Marlowe eliminates the bawdy stanzas to preserve the purity of her Ophelia and to sustain this image of delirium as a reversion to simple juvenile emotions.[55]

After her brief Valentine song, Claudius tries to move toward her as he asks Gertrude, "How long hath she been thus?" (4.5.67), but Ophelia again recoils from him then shoves him away from her. Her fear and anger shift quickly to sadness with "I hope all will be well" (4.5.68), the sadness further deepening on "I cannot choose but weep" (4.5.68-69), at which she kneels and spreads her white scarf before her, suggesting a grave, a piece of stage business used by several actresses in the nineteenth century. To this imaginary but now explicitly depicted grave, she speaks her next line, "To think they should lay him i' the cold ground" (4.5.69-70), causing her to break down crying. But this touching picture of beauty is brief because Marlowe's Ophelia rises suddenly and while both glaring at and recoiling from Claudius, she angrily addresses him, "My brother shall know of it" (4.5.70), her emphasis on "brother." Just as quickly, her manner changes again to "one of extreme courtesy as you address the Queen" (part book): "and so I thank you for your good counsel" (4.5.71). Marlowe's Ophelia curtsies several times and beckons imaginary attendants as she makes her way toward an archway for her exit. Just as she crosses through the archway, the audience hears "a burst of half delirious laughter" (part book).

In describing Marlowe's Act 4 Ophelia in 1913, Oscar Firkins makes particular mention of her "aspen-like mobility and variability" and categorizes this depiction of madness as "drifting," a sort of "helmlessness of the uncontrolled mind."[56] He chronicles Marlowe's Ophelia not as heartbreakingly sad but rather as heartbreakingly cheerful: "She nestles into her grief, she makes bereavement a playfellow, she comforts herself with laments; we are touched with the immeasurable sadness of her not being immeasurably sad."[57] Arthur Symons reports similar impressions of this mad Ophelia: "she suffers and is pitifully unaware of it. . . ." revealing "the very soul naked and shameless with an innocence beyond innocence."[58] Her reversion to childlike innocence is the greatest self-sacrifice this Ophelia could make because while evoking sympathy in her observers, she does not cause discomfort, pain, or suffering in them.

Preceding Ophelia's re-entrance later in 4.5, shouts and screams are heard offstage.

She enters through an archway, humming a tune she later sings, carrying an armful of flowers, and trailing a garland in her right hand; Russell specifies that Marlowe chose to use all white rose petals.[59] She shows no sign of recognition towards a stunned Laertes because, as her part book directs, "your attention [is] being given entirely to the flowers in your arms, with which you toy." Laertes attempts to draw her attention to him by calling out, "O rose of May!/ Dear maid — kind sister — sweet Ophelia" (4.5.157-58), and for the first time Marlowe's Ophelia glances up from the flowers and stares "abstractedly" at Laertes. Her part book further instructs, "Your glance leaves no doubt in Laertes' mind of your madness." After Laertes laments the mortality of both their old father and her young wits, she returns to the imaginary grave — her scarf spread out on the floor earlier — and begins to sing sadly, "They bore him barefac'd on the bier,/ And on his grave rains many a tear" (4.5.164-65). In the middle of the second line, she drops flower petals onto the grave, and Russell describes this moment, "The manner of it was beyond all words pathetic; nothing could have brought home to us so intimately the sense of Ophelia's infinite disaster and wrecked mind."[60] She breaks off her singing, and as she speaks "Fare you well, my dove" (4.5.166), her glance wanders from the grave; she extends her hand as if following "the flight of an imaginary dove" (part book). Still lost in her imaginary funeral rites, she enlists the participation of her onstage listeners. To Laertes, she brightly instructs, "You must sing 'A-down, a-down-a'"; then turning to Claudius but in a higher register of voice, she directs, "You call him a-down-a" (4.5.169-70). Marlowe's part book spells out that the last note ("down-a") should fade away to a faint echo at which Ophelia should cup her ear as though listening to the refrain. Suddenly, however, she seems to recognize the man before her — the King— and she shrinks in fear, directing her allusion ("It is the false steward, that stole his master's daughter" at 4.5.170-71) to him. The word "daughter" seems to soothe her, and she returns to toying placidly with the rose petals she still carries in her arms.

With Laertes' commentary "This nothing's more than matter" (4.5.172), Marlowe's Ophelia turns to him and offers a rose petal, "There's rosemary, that's for remembrance, — pray you, love, remember" (4.5.173-74), looking into his face and caressing his brow. She selects another petal and handing it also to Laertes, says, "and there is pansies, that's for thoughts" (4.5.174-75). In this production, the thoughts and memories that Ophelia seeks to share with her brother are not altogether bad because they seemed to have a sort of equality in their earlier scene. However, as she gently caresses his brow, she offers him sympathy, probably for their father's death, offers to share his pain, but his response is not a return of pity and love but simple astonishment: "A document in madness, thought and remembrance fitted" (4.5.176-77). Marlowe's Ophelia then turns her attention to the King, crossing toward him, holding out some rose petals, but as she speaks ("There's fennel for you, and columbines" at 4.5.178) and as he reaches out to take the flowers, she quickly pulls them back "with repulsion, dropping them" (part book). She shifts immediately to Gertrude, to whom she offers a petal, "There's rue for you" (4.5.178-79); her manner and tone are "entirely sympathetic," and she takes a petal for herself "with evidence of pleasure" (part book) as she says, "and here's some for me; we must call it herb of grace o' Sundays" (4.5.179-80). Her gesture makes Gertrude uncomfortable, so Marlowe instructs herself, "assume a sympathetic tone to make amends" (part book) as she continues to address Gertrude, "O, you must wear your rue with a difference" (4.5.180-81). Sinking back into herself for a moment, she holds a rose petal before her, "There's a daisy" (4.5.181), and her private thoughts precipitate hysterical laughter followed by a tossing of the flower in the air.[61] As the rose petal falls, her laughter turns into "tears and passionate sobbing" (part book), and her grief reminds her again of Laertes, to whom she crosses on "I would give you some violets, but they withered all when my father died" (4.5.181-83). She turns then to the imaginary grave, made visible with her scarf, and begins to toss petals over it and sing brightly, "For bonny sweet Robin is all my joy" (4.5.184). Marlowe's part book instructs her to "sink down above imaginary grave and begin to croon first few lines, body swaying to the rhythm of the music. As you sing, form outline of cross with flowers which she has let fall." The song "becomes crescendo" (part book) at the beginning of the second verse, and no doubt Marlowe's well-trained contralto voice enthralled both the onstage and offstage audiences. At the song's end, her Ophelia starts to rise, and Gertrude crosses to help her; the part book directs that the Queen "places her arms sympathetically about you, to assist you: you shrink from the touch but glance at her, and recognizing the Queen you are reassured and accept her assistance." Before exiting, Marlowe's Ophelia bends over the grave and addresses it, "God be wi' ye" (4.5.197), and Gertrude must begin to move her away. With one last act of resistance and protest, this Ophelia turns back to the grave, with extended arms, and repeats "God be wi' ye" a couple times; however, realizing for the last time the futility of resistance, she turns away and with a low wail buries her face in her hands, "moaning piteously" as she exits.

In many ways, Marlowe's mad scene summarizes the progress of her Ophelia: her attempts to reach out and support others at the cost of her own needs and desires; her attempts to be seen and heard and understood, all failing; and her realization of her failures in her final gesture of covering her face — the clearest non-verbal expression of protest to the realities around her that she could make, even in lunacy. Charles Russell describes the effect of Marlowe's performance in this scene, ". . . when she went out a sound arose in the theatre like the long-drawn sigh of many persons, an echo of a pent-up feeling too deep for applause."[62] Although Marlowe certainly saw Ophelia's story as more than a lovely and lyrical interlude in Hamlet's tragic tale, she never "played for points," a nineteenth-century practice that Marlowe deplored. Instead, she played the mad scene, according to John Corbin, with "admirable restraint," and with "full recognition of the scene's essential connection with the entire play, disregarding the temptation to stress her own moments at the expense of the unity of the whole."[63]

Conclusion

Marlowe's Ophelia struggles but ultimately fails to break the mold of true womanhood. She had only two spaces in which to reside: silent, submissive womanhood or childlike delirium. While she desired the purity and gentleness of the feminine sphere, she tried to incorporate the energy and problem-solving action of the masculine sphere. Failure was inevitable. Julia Marlowe places her Ophelia squarely within a tradition, both critical and theatrical, while simultaneously and subtly subverting that tradition. According to Anthony Dawson, "The theatre is shaped by, and helps to shape, the cultural needs and meanings of a particular historical moment.

Hence, though tradition generally plays a conservative role, participating in the reproduction of cultural orders, there is always some kind of negotiation between tradition and innovation, ways that what is known is re-shaped into new forms that speak to new imperatives."[64] Marlowe's Ophelia is precisely such a "negotiation." Just as Marlowe herself was an actress caught between traditions in the early years of the twentieth century, her Ophelia is equally transitional.[65] Despite Marlowe's friendship with Susan B. Anthony, whose battle cry for women was "failure is impossible," Marlowe's Ophelia struggles to assert herself yet indeed fails, caught between old and new cultural ideals and expectations.

Julia Marlowe continued to play Ophelia until her retirement at the end of the 1924-25 season, when she was sixty years old. To her the age of Ophelia was irrelevant; she never tried to look as Ophelia might have looked but rather tried "to be as she was, do as she did."[66] Also irrelevant to her was this production's diminution of an already small role. The number of lines did not matter because as Marlowe herself wrote, "Great acting . . . does not depend upon the voice solely. . . . A look often speaks volumes and reveals what the tongue could not."[67] In Marlowe's hands, Ophelia's story was deep and tragic, a tale of protest and failure, and she told much of that brief tale with her eyes, her gestures, her movements. Charles Russell likened her Ophelia to a great Italian portrait: "masterful, compact, intense . . . still looking out of the canvas when the canvas is gone."[68]

NOTES

All references to the text correspond to the Arden *Hamlet*, ed. Harold Jenkins. London: Routledge, 1990.

[1]Marlowe debuted as Ophelia 4 October 1904 in Chicago. Marlowe and Sothern then took this production, along with *Romeo and Juliet* and *Much Ado About Nothing*, to the Knickerbocker Theatre in New York, stopping to perform in Pittsburgh along the way.

[2]Marvin Rosenberg, *The Masks of Hamlet* (Newark: Univ. of Delaware, 1992), 244.

[3]The promptbook for this production is Folger: Hamlet 34, dated 1904 by Charles Shattuck.

[4]Julia Marlowe's part book for Ophelia is held at the Museum of the City of New York: 43.430.683.

[5]Walter Prichard Eaton, *The American Stage of To-Day* (Boston: Small, Maynard and Co., 1908), 59.

[6] Barbara Welter, *Dimity Convictions: The American Woman in the Nineteenth Century* (Athens: Ohio University Press, 1976), 21.

[7]Anna Jameson, *Shakespeare's Heroines: Their Moral, Poetical and Historical Characteristics* (Philadelphia: John E. Potter, n.d. [1833]), 62.

[8]Grace Latham, "O Poor Ophelia." Read at 94th Meeting of the New Shakspere Society, 8 February 1884. Rpt. in *Women Reading Shakespeare 1660-1900*, ed. Ann Thompson and Sasha Roberts (Manchester: Manchester Univ. Press, 1997), 166-67.

[9]Jessie Fremont O'Donnell, "Ophelia." *The American Shakespeare Magazine*, March 1897. Rpt. in *Women Reading Shakespeare 1660-1900*, ed. Ann Thompson and Sasha

Roberts (Manchester: Manchester Univ. Press, 1997), 241-42.
[10]George Bernard Shaw, Review of *Hamlet* in *The Saturday Review*, 8 April 1905. Rpt. in *Shakespeare in the Theatre: An Anthology of Criticism*, ed. Stanley Wells (Oxford: Oxford Univ. Press, 2000), 149.
[11]Shaw, 149.
[12]Max Beerbohm, Review of *Hamlet* in *The Saturday Review*, 8 April 1905. Rpt. in *Shakespeare in the Theatre: An Anthology of Criticism*, ed. Stanley Wells. (Oxford: Oxford Univ. Press, 2000), 180.
[13]Rosenberg, 246.
[14]Alan Hughes, *Henry Irving, Shakespearean* (Cambridge: Cambridge Univ. Press, 1981), 68.
[15]Anthony B. Dawson, *Hamlet*, Shakespeare in Performance Series (Manchester: Manchester Univ. Press, 1995), 64.
[16]Rosenberg, 241.
[17]Carol J. Carlisle, *Fire and Ice: Helen Faucit on the Victorian Stage* (London: Society for Theatre Research, 2000), 135.
[18]Carlisle, 135.
[19]Edgar Allan Poe, "The Philosophy of Composition," *Graham's Magazine* 28 (April 1846). Rpt. in *Edgar Allan Poe: Selected Prose, Poetry, and Eureka*, ed. W.H. Auden (New York: Holt, Rinehart, and Winston, 1950), 425.
[20]A. C. Bradley, *Shakespearean Tragedy*, 2nd edn, 1905. (Rpt. New York: St. Martin's, 1978), 160.
[21]Bradley, 160.
[22]Jameson, 62.
[23]Bradley, 164-65.
[24]E. H. Sothern, *Julia Marlowe's Story*, ed. Fairfax Downey (New York: Rinehart, 1954), 169.
[25]Garff Wilson, *History of American Acting* (Bloomington: Indiana Univ. Press, 1966), 148.
[26]*Washington Post* (5 February 1905).
[27]*Washington Post* (5 February 1905).
[28]Elizabeth McCracken, "Julia Marlowe, Including Comment By Her on Characters She Has Played," *The Century* 51 (November 1906): 52.
[29]Kate Millett, "The Debate Over Women: Ruskin vs. Mill," *Suffer and Be Still: Women in the Victorian Age*, ed. Martha Vicinus (Bloomington: Indiana Univ. Press, 1972): 126.
[30]Charles E. Russell, *Julia Marlowe: Her Life and Art* (New York: Appleton, 1926), 324.
[31]Rosenberg, 244.
[32]Oscar Firkins, "Sothern and Marlowe—An Estimate," *Theatre* 18 (October 1913): 32.
[33]Russell, *Julia Marlowe*, 322.
[34]Russell, *Julia Marlowe*, 324.
[35]Russell, *Julia Marlowe*, 322.
[36]Rosenberg, 365-66.
[37]Rosenberg, 244.
[38]Rosenberg, 462.
[39]Bradley, 165.
[40]Charles E. Russell, "A Notable Achievement: Miss Marlowe and Mr. Sothern in

Shakespeare," *Critic* 45 (December 1904): 531.
[41]5 February 1905.
[42]Russell, *Julia Marlowe*, 323.
[43]*Washington Post*, 5 February 1905.
[44]Russell, *Julia Marlowe*, 323.
[45]Russell, *Julia Marlowe*, 323.
[46]Rosenberg reports that Marlowe's promptbook reveals that Ophelia returns after Claudius and Polonius exit in order to gather up her trinkets and weep over them, an added bit of business giving Marlowe the scene-end (543). Neither the 1904 promptbook nor Marlowe's part book shows this addition, which must have been used in a later production.
[47]Rosenberg, 244.
[48]Rosenberg, 244.
[49]Rosenberg, 244.
[50]Rosenberg, 244.
[51]McCracken, 52.
[52]Phyllis Chesler, *Women and Madness* (New York: Four Walls Eight Windows, 1972), 71.
[53]Barbara Ehrenreich and Deirdre English, *Complaints and Disorders: The Sexual Politics of Sickness* (New York: Feminist Press, 1973), 41.
[54]Ellen Terry, *The Story of My Life: Recollections and Reflections* (New York: McClure, 1908), 169.
[55]Rosenberg reports that the bawdy stanzas were usually censored "to preserve the 'decency' of Ophelia and the ears of the spectators." He describes Helena Modjeska's treatment of the song in her production with Edwin Booth: "At the end of the first stanza she breaks into a wordless song, to the music of which she dances up the stage and down again to the King" (785).
[56]Firkins, 121.
[57]Firkins, 121.
[58]Sothern, 190.
[59]Russell, "Notable," 531.
[60]Russell, *Julia Marlowe*, 323.
[61]In later productions, Marlowe must have altered the presentation of the flowers. In an interview as early as 1905, she commented on the scene: "It does not seem to me natural that an insane person could discriminate between different kinds of flowers. . . . To her all flowers must seem alike. Then how much stronger and better to have her give the flowers to imaginary instead of real persons! How much more in keeping with the state of her mind" (*Washington Post* 5 February 1905).
[62]Russell, "Notable," 531.
[63]John Corbin, *New York Times* (30 October 1923).
[64]Dawson, 24.
[65]See Patty S. Derrick, "Julia Marlowe: An Actress Caught Between Traditions," *Theatre Survey* 32.1 (May 1991): 85-105.
[66]McCracken, 52.
[67]Julia Marlowe, "The Eloquence of Silence," *Green Book Magazine* 9 (March 1913): 398.

[68]Russell, *Julia Marlowe*, 325.

Patty S. Derrick is Professor of English at University of Pittsburgh-Johnstown, where she teaches Shakespeare, Shakespeare and Film, and Renaissance Literature. She is currently editor of the New Variorum edition of *Two Gentleman of Verona* and is writing a book on Julia Marlowe's Shakespearean interpretations and portrayals. She has published other articles in *Theatre Survey*, *Theatre History Studies*, *Shakespeare's Sweet Thunder* (ed. Michael Collins), *Two Gentlemen of Verona: Critical Essays* (ed. June Schlueter), and *Analytical and Enumerative Bibliography*.

Theatre History Studies 23 (June 2003)

Outcast London on the Victorian and Edwardian Stage

HEIDI J. HOLDER

In the nineteenth-century English theater, dramas that promised audiences authentic scenes of London life enjoyed an enormous and enduring popularity. From W.T. Moncrieff's adaptation of Pierce Egan's *Tom and Jerry* (Adelphi 1821) to such late Victorian and Edwardian plays as G.R. Sims's *The Lights O'London* (Royal Princess's 1881), Arthur Shirley's *How London Lives* (Princess's 1897), Elizabeth Robins's *Votes for Women!* (Court 1907), and G.B. Shaw's *Pygmalion* (Haymarket 1912), audiences were entertained by the city's color and variety.

These London dramas offered not only striking images of urban life, but also dramatic representations of the prevailing "urban theories" of their time. Plays from the 1820s-40s borrowed from and enacted the kind of "London" sketches created by Egan and Dickens; in the latter half of the century, the drama was more likely to be influenced by (and in turn to influence) the writings of the so-called "social explorers" such as Henry Mayhew, James Greenwood, Andrew Mearns, and George Sims. There is a noticeable movement in the theater, shadowing a change in the popular press, from a tone of revelry to one of social concern. Later in the century the poor would fade into the background, as the society drama exemplified by Arthur Wing Pinero and Oscar Wilde became the dominant theatrical form. Ultimately, such reformers as G.B. Shaw, John Galsworthy, and Cicely Hamilton would revisit the all-encompassing mid-Victorian melodrama in which the classes mingled and social problems were at the forefront.

Spectacular recreations of London settings were ubiquitous on the Victorian stage, and include such scenes as Covent Garden market, the Burlington Arcade, Rotten Row in Hyde Park, the Elephant and Castle, Trafalgar Square, the Old Bailey, Charing Cross, Paddington Station, the Borough Market, the Royal Academy, Vauxhall Gardens, and St. Katherine's Wharf. Audiences clearly took great pleasure in these effects, which were much vaunted for their realism. Playbills proudly listed the latest "sensations," which are often attributed to whole teams of scene painters — men who rivaled the authors and actors in credit for a play's success. But this realism, this mania for authenticity, provided the settings for genres of a fantastic and formulaic kind, such as melodrama and farce. Hyper-realism in the *mise en scène* was thus balanced—or contradicted — by mechanical plots that sometimes seem drawn from fairy tales. Nowhere is this theatrical paradox more evident than in the dramas depicting the plight of London's poor.

London's impoverished districts and citizens were objects of fascination as early as Egan's whirlwind London tour in *Tom and Jerry*; this immensely popular novel, promptly adapted for the stage, followed the escapades of young bohemian gentlemen in London's high life and low life (See Figure 1). This type of London experience,

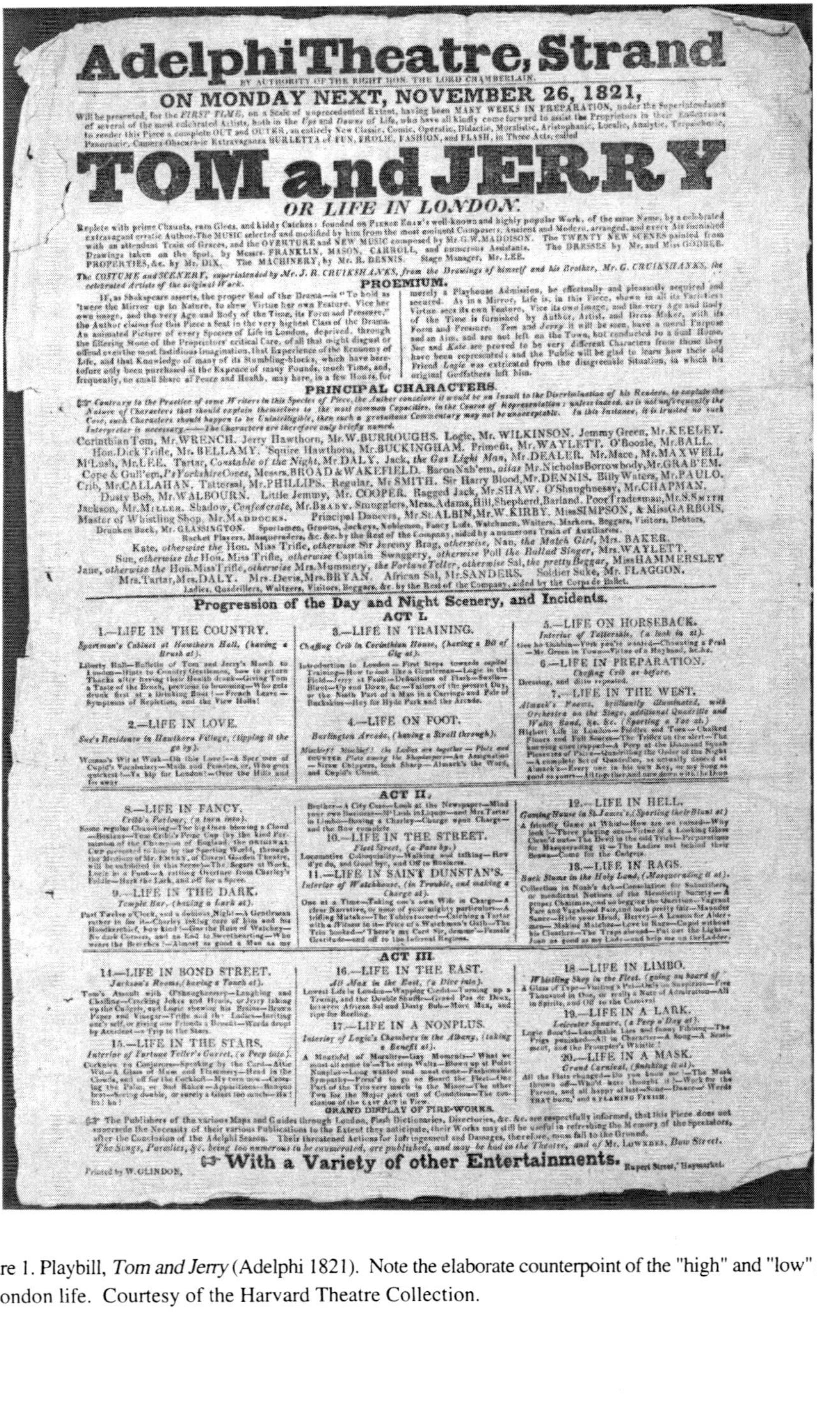

Adelphi Theatre, Strand

ON MONDAY NEXT, NOVEMBER 26, 1821,

TOM and JERRY

OR LIFE IN LONDON.

PROEMIUM.

PRINCIPAL CHARACTERS.

Progression of the Day and Night Scenery, and Incidents.

ACT I.

1.—LIFE IN THE COUNTRY.

2.—LIFE IN LOVE.

3.—LIFE IN TRAINING.

4.—LIFE ON FOOT.

5.—LIFE ON HORSEBACK.

6.—LIFE IN PREPARATION.

7.—LIFE IN THE WEST.

ACT II.

8.—LIFE IN FANCY.

9.—LIFE IN THE DARK.

10.—LIFE IN THE STREET.

11.—LIFE IN SAINT DUNSTAN'S.

12.—LIFE IN HELL.

13.—LIFE IN RAGS.

ACT III.

14.—LIFE IN BOND STREET.

15.—LIFE IN THE STARS.

16.—LIFE IN THE EAST.

17.—LIFE IN A NONPLUS.

18.—LIFE IN LIMBO.

19.—LIFE IN A LARK.

20.—LIFE IN A MASK.

GRAND DISPLAY OF FIRE-WORKS.

With a Variety of other Entertainments.

Printed by W. GLINDON,

Figure 1. Playbill, *Tom and Jerry* (Adelphi 1821). Note the elaborate counterpoint of the "high" and "low" scenes of London life. Courtesy of the Harvard Theatre Collection.

thoroughly jolly in tone and received via an upper-class sensibility, held sway through the 1840s; but around mid-century there is a notable shift. As the work of such journalists and reformers as Henry Mayhew, John Hollingshead, and James Greenwood described the "crisis" of "outcast London," audiences in the theater developed a taste for plays that offered both realistic scenes of London poverty and fantastic resolutions of the problems it presented.

Plays exhibiting the details of London's "dark side" had always been a risky business. Theater managers were perennially being accused of staging corrupting scenes of vice; in turn, the managers — and sometimes authors — would declare a pedagogical interest in the material of the drama, claiming that their plays were intended to warn audiences, especially the young, away from the pursuit of vice.[1] Thus, audience members who were attracted to the theaters by the promise of scenes of vice were supposedly intended to be repulsed and chastened by the very images they desired to see. Moncrieff's wildly popular *Tom and Jerry*, for instance, was lambasted in the press, and in letters to the Lord Chamberlain, as a "poisonous and disgusting item."[2] Its playbills and its preface to the published text are masterworks of moral justification. The preface declares that

> the obnoxious scenes of life are only shown that they might be avoided; the danger of mixing in them is strikingly exemplified, and every incident tends to prove that happiness is only to be found in the domestic circle.[3]

The playbills insist that the "moral purpose" of the play is intricately tied to its "truthful" images: its "twenty new scenes," we are told, were "painted from drawings on the spot."[4] Douglas Jerrold felt similarly compelled to defend his successful play *Martha Willis, The Servant Maid* (Pavilion 1831) in a rather long-winded, pious statement at the front of the published text:

> It is the object of the present drama to display, in the most forcible and striking point of view, the temptations which in the metropolis assail the young and inexperienced on their first outset in life — temptations which, if yielded to, inevitably conduct their victim to wretchedness and shame. It being the peculiar province of the stage to 'hold the mirror up to nature,' to deter by example, and warn by precept, — it is trusted that the present Drama, which abounds in strong and highly wrought pictures of real life, — which contains characters whose originals are to be met with in almost any street in London, will be found not only worthy of the attention of those whose situations in the world it more immediately applies [sic], but also interesting to those Patrons of the Theatre who are desirous of finding in a drama skillful combinations of powerful, yet naturally wrought incidents, and vivid portraitures of men and manners as they really are. One of the great geniuses of modern times has said 'truth is strange — stranger than fiction.' This great metropolis teems with persons and events, which, considered with reference to their dramatic capabilities, beggar invention: — every knave has his mystery, every dupe his sorrow, every street its romance of real life. It is these scenes of everyday experience — it is these characters, which are met in our

> hourly paths — that will be found in the present Drama, but so displayed and grouped, that, whilst they gain an animations and a strength from contrast, they sacrifice no jot of their identity or nature; they lose nothing, save their original grossness. In the Drama, Vice is anatomized, in order to be shunned and hated — and not robed in specious finery, to lure and destroy.[5]

Clearly, "truthful" plays of London life were highly popular yet morally suspect; if London's "dark side" was to be put on display, it must come with a lesson appended.

The controlling viewpoint in plays such as *Tom and Jerry* was that of the roving gentleman, the vaguely disreputable "man of the world" who is familiar with the customs and language not only of his own class and neighborhood but also of the larger world — in this case the world of London. In *Tom and Jerry*, the urban specialist "Corinthian Tom" provides lessons in London life to his unschooled country cousin, Jerry (presumably a stand-in for those members of the audience who might be similarly unschooled). The argument <u>for</u> such plays as *Tom and Jerry* was that by being a man of the world, you could protect yourself from the city's darker elements. Forerunners of the dandies, these bohemian seekers of knowledge and culture could blur class and cultural boundaries and be the safer for it. An opposition was set up <u>between</u> this kind of urban bohemianism and crime; armed with knowledge of the ways of criminals, you could move among them unscathed. The country Squire in *Tom and Jerry* wonders at the changed nature of a "cultural tour" of London:

> Well now, I always thought living in London was going to see the lions in the Tower, making a call at the Whispering Gallery, leaving one's card atop of the monument and taking a peep in Westminster Abbey — 'twas so in my day — how things are altered.[6]

To which Tom replies, "London teaches valuable lessons"; later Jerry will learn to "talk to a rogue in his own language and fight him with his own weapons."[7]

In melodramas of London life the central characters are typically seen <u>among</u> the poor, but are not <u>of</u> the poor. In the "bohemian" plays of the first half of the century, we have as our "tour guides" to London such upper-class characters as Tom and Jerry. In mid-century plays, however, rather than tracking the path of Egan's dandies, or of their lower-class counterparts, we typically follow the travail of characters who have experienced a "fall" from wealth and status — or at least from the middle class. In W.T. Moncrieff's *The Crossroads of Life; or, The Scamps of London* (Sadler's Wells 1843), young Herbert, who has ruined himself by attempting to live the London high life, presents his case thus:

> For upwards of a week I have been a wanderer through the streets by day, an outcast here by night, pursued by hunger and remorse. Vainly have I sought employment, unused to work I have been unable to command it. Ah, the most destitute among these miserable wretches is far less to be pitied than I am. They can sleep soundly. . . .[8]

Robert Wild and his family, who appear in James Elphinstone's *London Labour,*

London Poor; or, Want and Vice (Pavilion 1854), are living in paupers' lodgings in Clerkenwell (he was disowned by his wealthy father for marrying a milliner); as the family suffers insult and degradation, Robert's wealthy brother Charles is following closely behind, determined to restore his brother to his rightful place. In C.H. Hazlewood's *The Casual Ward* (Marylebone 1866), one of a number of plays capitalizing on the interest provoked by James Greenwood's *A Night in a Workhouse*, (serialized in the *Pall Mall Gazette* in 1866), the scene opens on one Richard Glover fleeing the authorities. He pauses to lament that he is "brought to poverty by too great a confidence in those I thought my friends."[9]

This focus on the upper (or at least middle) classes reduced to poverty was no less popular in theaters of the West End than in those in the working-class East End and South Side — and similar plots are seen in George Sims's *The Lights O'London* (Princess's 1881), Dion Boucicault's *The Poor of London* (Grecian 1864), and *How We Live in the World of London; or, London Labour and London Poor* (Surrey 1856).[10]

This plot line allows the mingling of classes, the crossing of the city's geographical and psychological boundaries, without making the poor themselves the object of direct attention. Even in those plays that seem to make a character born to poverty the central interest, we observe a determination to rewrite the character's story. In *The Street Arab; or, Adrift on the World* (Garrick 1871), we may think that Clement, the "king of the Street Arabs," is a native of the East End, but he turns out to be a titled lord. Just when the audiences have had the thrill of watching the lower-class Clement marry the upper-class Roberta, the villain says in an aside, "He little thinks he's heir to 5,000 a year . . . besides a mine down in Cornwall."[11] This effect of simultaneous closeness and distance is reflected in the contemporary debates — especially in the grim period of the 1860s — over charity and the "poor laws." Gareth Stedman Jones has examined the anxieties provoked by "the immense geographical gulf which had grown up between the rich and poor of London": "it was increasingly suggested," he notes, "that this severance of rich from poor was at the root of the dangerous social situation that momentarily had seemed to threaten upper-class London in the 1860s."[12] The appearance of so many characters whose class status is unsettled until the play's conclusion shows that the theater was offering a dramatic embodiment of and resolution to a widely-perceived problem of interclass contact.

This determination to solve the problem of poverty via the predictable mechanisms of melodrama is most evident in plays more closely connected to journalistic exposés. In Henry Mayhew's series of articles for the *Morning Chronicle* (1849-50), later published as *London Labour and the London Poor*, one of the most distressing images was that of the unnamed eight-year-old "Watercress Girl": "There was something cruelly pathetic," Mayhew writes, "in hearing this infant, so young that her features scarcely formed themselves, talking of the bitterest struggles of life, with the calm earnestness of one who had endured them all." Mayhew reports that at first he did not know how to speak with her, since "her knowledge begins and ends with water-cresses." She has no dolls, expresses amazement that London has parks, is too tired to play games, knows nothing of religion, and indeed shows an astonishing ignorance of everything unconnected with the purchasing and sale of watercress — "I'm a capital hand at bargaining," she asserts.[13] Mayhew's interviews with children such as this revealed a world of poverty and degradation that was deeply alarming and embarrassing to Londoners. But this disturbing material was soon transported into the world of the melodramatic stage. Along with the rise of reformist journalism there came an upsurge in the number of plays focusing on the problem of London's poor.

Mayhew's Watercress Girl herself was to appear, in rather a new light, in a highly popular East End play, William Travers's *The Watercress Girl* (City of London Theatre 1865). The play opens with a spectacular scene in Covent Garden market in which the costermongers and stall keepers are all anxiously awaiting the appearance of their "pet," little Alice Green, who, upon her arrival, passes out her unsold bunches of greens to her many friends. In contrast with the grim ignorance displayed by her counterpart in Mayhew, little Alice teaches the other children how to read, and even leads Sunday school lessons. True to the usual pattern for plays of outcast London, little Alice turns out to be an heiress; her reprobate father restores her to her rightful status as he dies, and she is happily reunited with her mother (who had been imprisoned, naturally, in an insane asylum). Significantly, Alice is initially happy in her lot as a street-seller, as in this scene when she is "tempted" by the villain:

> Graft: How should you like to be a lady and live in a fine house and have servants to wait upon you, eh?
> Alice: I — I don't know sir. I'm very happy here sir.
> Graft: Ah, you think so — wait till you've tried the other.
> Alice: I don't care about being a lady, Sir, thank you all the same, they're all very kind to me in the market.[14]

The Watercress Girl, "Betty Clearbrook," in *How We Live; or, London Labour and London Poor* (Surrey 1856), is treated to like kindness and good fortune. A solicitous gentleman buys six bunches, telling her to "keep them until I call for them"; such a time will be "when you keep a four-wheeler and ask me to dine with you in Belgrave Square."[15]

Typically, the plays of "outcast London" exhibit a wide range of scenery. Andrew Halliday's *The Great City* (Drury Lane 1867) includes representations of the gates of an East End workhouse, Paddington station, Charing Cross Hotel, A Street near St. Paul's, and a panoramic view of London by night; Travers's *The Watercress Girl* moves from Covent Garden market and a house in the Seven Dials, to a fine house in the suburbs and a sensational view of London bridge. The story of the central characters acquires an authority and representative quality when merged with an overview of London. Rather than being grounded in one place, one scene, the story is literally all over the place. Part of the enjoyment for an audience is precisely this unfixed quality of characters, the way in which their relation to their surroundings is uncertain yet central.

A paradigmatic example of the problem of "placing" the individual can be observed in the heroine's famous leap into the Thames in Dion Boucicault's *After Dark* (Princess's Theatre 1868); Louisa, apparently a poor, fallen woman, jumps from Waterloo Bridge and is rescued at the last possible moment. After various revelations of identity Louisa will be restored to her father and husband. Crucial to the scene is the unmistakable, ubiquitous presence of London: this is not simply a moment of peril, but one that relies for much of its effect on its context, its background. Such "leaps," or "falls", (or near leaps and falls) are also seen in *The Scamps of London; or, The Crossroads of Life* (Sadler's Wells 1843), *London by Night, St. James's and St. Giles's* (City of London 1853), *The Poor Girl's Temptations; or, A Voice from the Street* (City of London 1858), *London Highways and Byeways* (Pavilion 1864), *The Lights O'London, The Great City* (Drury Lane 1867), and *In Darker London* (West London 1894). Advertising woodcuts would typically show the individual — usually a woman — in mid-fall, suspended against the backdrop of the city. These scenes were usually nightscapes, and their effect is ambiguous: the city can be seen as threatening, as a marker of boundaries, or as an image of limitless possibilities.

The use of spectacular London scenes reinforces the fascination with mingling of classes. Very many of these scenes are places of meeting and/or transit: railway stations, street corners and squares, bridges, markets, and pleasure gardens. These are places, in fact, where all types of Londoners (as well as out-of-towners and foreigners) might cross paths. In the reiteration of such images, one senses a keen interest in the possibilities inherent in such locations; these are spaces of and for coincidence, fortuitous or ill-fated meetings, and missed assignations. The villain in Halliday's *The Great City*, standing in the middle of the hubbub of the terminus at Charing Cross, imagines London as "the big net."[16] A scene from Selby's *London by Night* offers an early and instructive example, depicting a chaotic yet carefully choreographed nighttime crowd at the Elephant and Castle. An elderly man, Mr. Bloomfield, has arrived from the country to find his nephew (he will also find his niece here), and when he appears he is besieged by cadgers vying to assist him and literally fighting over him. He is rescued by Bawling Jack, a street Arab with some half-dozen professions, who happens to know Bloomfield's nephew:

> Bawling Jack: Chronicle — Times? or the latest of news overland mail!
> Duffy: Taters all smoking hot.
> Nibble: Coppers for jack keeps the mud from your shoes.
> Omnibuses: Brighton or Worthing, New Cross or Dover, Greenwich or Deptford . . . Strand, Waterloo — Go by the river. Lots o' prime buses for ladies who will.
> . . .
> Bawling Jack: Now here you have it my customers—Globe! Globe! latest intelligence from —
> Omnibus conductor: Strand, Waterloo!
> Bawling Jack: Her Majesty's return from —
> Conductor: Fleet Street! Islington!
> Bawling Jack: Arrival of the King of the French from
> Conductor: King's Cross, King's Cross — Oh
> Bawling Jack: News from Ireland, second edition — arrival of great and glorious and free first flower of the earth and gem of the sea in the —
> Conductor: Hold Bailey — Hold Bailey! Newgate St.
> Duffy: Baked Taters all hot![17]

Bloomfield, guided by Jack, must hunt through London (including a *Bal Masque* at Vauxhall Gardens) before finding his nephew and rescuing him from impoverishment at the hands of a usurer. Despite Bloomfield's condemnations of London's dangers, the audience, of course, has thoroughly enjoyed the depiction of urban revelry offered by the play. Jack himself is a highly typical and eminently useful figure: the benevolent street lad, who helps the central characters put their affairs in order.

To give a sense of how intensely visual these local scenes would be, listen to this description of a scene (The steamboat pier at Hungerford Bridge) from Dion Boucicault's *Lost at Sea: A London Story* (Adelphi 1869):

> The pay office R & L; the river Thames is seen under the space of the trestle railway. Westminster Bridge crosses the river in the distance. The opposite bank, with St. Thomas's Hospital and Lambeth Palace in the distance, is seen over Westminster Bridge, while the line of the South Embankment with its lights twinkle amid the gloom. The coloured lights over the arches of Westminster Bridge indicate the water-road. The lamps on Westminster Bridge, and the railway lamps and semaphores on the railway bridge, are seen. A red lamp projects from the pay-office, R.H. The clock tower of the Houses of Parliament in the distance, extreme L.H. (During the following scene the traffick of cabs, omnibuses, waggons, &c., is maintained across Westminster Bridge. The Dark form of a barge, with sails set, floats slowly up the river, it lowers the mast to pass under the bridge. A locomotive and train passes across the railway bridge above. These incidents occur at intervals. Woman and child at pay-office, R.H., in which at an open window facing the audience discover the Money-Taker, reading paper by lamp. Two Boys asleep against the pay office, L.H. Man walking up and down at back.)[18]

This scene features remarkably little dialogue. A young lower-class woman is considering suicide in consequence of a tragic misunderstanding. The woman doesn't jump after all, having been diverted from her purpose by several characters, including the ever-present helpful and knowing street-lad. What at first seems a play about the poor shifts focus to become a play about an upper-class character resuming his rightful status — this piece features the usual class and identity confusion, including a Dickensian "drowned man who's really alive and masquerading as someone from a lower social class."

The enlightenment of the young woman in *Lost at Sea* could have taken place anywhere; instead, it was set within an elaborate vision of the city. Since the stories told are often about the problem of fixing or locating a character in his or her proper place, the effect of such elaborately familiar productions was to give the audience the enjoyment of seeing order established in their own world as well as on the stage. Contemporary London life is not only displayed, it is rendered neat and comprehensible.

The unmooring of identity often found in melodrama — and part of its paranoid appeal — is very intense in these play, in which the connections between the rich and poor, the criminals and the virtuous, are often literalized in blood ties. In a dramatic version of Douglas Jerrold's *St. James and St. Giles*, staged at the City of London Theatre in 1853, the districts of London usually named as representing London's poles of wealth and poverty have been embodied in characters bearing their names. These characters turn out, in the end, to bear close ties: "St. Giles" turns out to be "St. James's" older brother from an early "hidden" marriage, and St. James's love, Clarissa, is prevented from going astray by her own mother, who "abandoned" her family years earlier (one gets here, by the way, a marvelous sense of the tradition from which Wilde pulled his plot lines). St. Giles, accused of crimes perpetrated by "Master Willis," an upper-class fellow supporting himself as a highwayman, later stops him from murdering his uncle. St. James, initially a pleasant enough fellow, turns to perjury and kidnapping once he knows that his status as heir is threatened. In the play's "sensation scene" at Westminster bridge, St. Giles, seeking for St. James in order to kill him, hears a cry of help from the water: "Help! It is a sacred cry!"[19] It is, of course, St. James in the water; St. Giles, of course, rescues his brother.

St. Giles is a liminal figure: he is not only half brother to St. James, but also half brother to Jingo, a degraded East End youth. St. Giles will in the end assume St. James's role in the family, and also responsibility for Jingo, whose criminal father dies, begging St. Giles to "make an honest man out of him." The point seems fairly clear; in a pointed reversal of roles, Eastenders ultimately make better Westenders. What in the West End could be a paranoid fantasy of experiencing poverty, a scary ride safely experienced in the theatre, could in the East be a thrilling fantasy of the collapse of the distinctions made by geography, class, and money. Quite simply, the issue is <u>who</u> gets to go <u>where</u>.

The critique of the West End dramas of London life by the East End theaters extended also to their mania for "authenticity." If *The Scamps of London* could tout its recreation of a rookery in St. Giles, and *The Lights O'London* could create a sensation with its depiction of the Borough on a Saturday night ("almost too real, too painful, too smeared with the dirt and degradation of London life," according to one critic), then perhaps the East End theaters could claim the same privilege.[20]

A fine example of such an attempt is *Glad Tidings*, a huge hit for the Standard Theatre in 1883 (by this time several East End theaters had established themselves as powerful venues with "respectable" reputations). *Glad Tidings* owed much of its renown to its recreation of the sinking of the steamer "Princess Alice" (here renamed the "Glad Tidings"); the production showed not only the disaster, but also the makeshift morgue on the docks, a scene that led to much debate in the press over the proper limits of realism and good taste.

A good deal of the press coverage for *Glad Tidings* (which was more extensive than for most East End plays) focused on the question of whether or not the play could conceivably be compared favorably to a West End production, and — more importantly — whether an East End theater could present, accurately and with authority, the more fashionable districts to the West. A crucial scene in Hyde Park's Rotten Row, with fashionable loungers plotting while riders capered by on real horses, was a sticking point for many West End critics. Some critics called it a "singularly clever recreation," "worthy of any theatre in London . . . all details being perfect" *(Daily Chronicle* 10 Sep. 1883); "this scene is worth seeing by the most fastidious West-ender" (*Funny Folks* 15 Sep. 1883). Others balked at acknowledging that an East End theater could pull off such a feat; one critic insisted that "the illusion is sustained by the introduction of horses, though the riders are not good imitations of the class seen near Knightsbridge on an afternoon in May" (*Echo* 31 Aug. 1883); another comp lains that the Standard couldn't get its details quite right in the end, pointing out that "from Rotten Row we ride off to the home of rank and fashion, where the ladies and gentlemen disport themselves in full dress early in the morning" *(Evening News* 30 Aug. 1883).[21]

The mingling of anxiety and curiosity seen in the reviews reveals the theater's power to define. In the West End tradition of staging the "world" of London, the power to sample and to know all of London's variety belongs not only to the Toms, Jerrys, and other gentlemen on the town, but to a particular audience at a particular venue. By staking a claim, through manipulation of plot, character, and *mise en scène*, to the prerogatives of such gentlemen, the East End theaters attempted to appropriate this power to define, if only, at times, to blur the carefully drawn distinctions in the West End theatre between the different worlds of London. Like Tom's country cousin Jerry, they have learned the language and adopted the weapons of their exotic urban counterparts.

By the end of the nineteenth century, the inclusive *mise en scène* of the Victorian melodrama, the careful patterning of "high" and "low" settings designed to emphasize the need for characters to find their proper position in the world, was being challenged by the rise of newer hybrid genres. While the use of mixed settings would continue, in plays such as Henry Arthur Jones's *The Middleman* (Shaftesbury 1889) and George Moore's *The Strike at Arlingford* (Independent Theatre Society at the Opera Comique 1893), the movement in the West End theater was toward a unified social scene, often representing the homes and haunts of the upper-middle class and the aristocracy. Elaborate recreations of London settings were still popular, but they were often limited to the haunts of the rich; even when public places were recreated, the poor were often invisible. As the apex of the theater of London's rich, one can cite the production at Drury Lane of Cecil Ralegh's *Hearts are Trumps* (1899), which features dazzling depictions of such scenes as the exterior of the Burlington House, the Royal Academy, the Botanical Gardens in Regent's Park, the interior of a fashionable music hall, and a Bond Street dress shop.

In the East End theaters, the juxtaposition of high and low settings remained popular throughout the late Victorian period. However, the influence of the society drama was felt here as well — in the growing proportion of wealthy or fashionable settings. The Standard Theatre, one of the largest and most "respectable" of the East End houses, adopted many of the qualities of the society plays, but nonetheless maintained a stronger connection with the ethos of the earlier drama. In many of the Standard's offerings, particularly the rather lurid dramas written by the Melville brothers, London's poor remain very much in evidence, but they are likely to pop up amid fashionable surroundings. In *The Worst Woman in London* (1902), a tramp surfaces in Rotten Row and ultimately helps to foil the villainess; a similarly helpful sweep appears outside the hero's villa in Regent's Park. And, true to form, the play offers theatergoers a sensational "panorama" scene, in which the downtrodden heroine escapes from a burning building by sliding along a telephone wire against a backdrop of London's rooftops.

In the West End, the reformer-dramatists of the Edwardian period revived the practice of mingling high and low settings. When G. B. Shaw and, later, Harley Granville-Barker, John Galsworthy and Cicely Hamilton used working-class settings or characters, they were very pointedly playing against the vogue for fashionable scenes. Rather than using lower-class settings within a formulaic structure that contained them and neutralized distinctions, Shaw and his Edwardian successors employed these settings — in such plays as *Candida* (Strand 1900 / Court 1904), *Major Barbara* (Court 1905), *The Silver Box* (Court 1906), *Diana of Dobson's* (Kingsway 1908), and *Pygmalion* (Haymarket 1914) — to make sharp contrasts that are pointedly not resolved. When G.B. Shaw opens *Pygmalion* at the porticoes of Covent Garden, showing rich and poor thrown together while seeking shelter from the rain, he is invoking an earlier Victorian stage tradition of depicting the classes of London. What follows, of course, is almost a parody of the fairytale melodramas of outcast London that were popular fifty years before. On one level the ending is entirely traditional: Eliza marries an upper-class man. But on another the picture goes askew: Eliza is no misplaced heiress but an authentic cockney flower-seller, and rather than embarking on a life of ease the couple go into business (ironically enough, as owners of a florist's shop).[22]

Cicely Hamilton's *Diana of Dobson's* likewise effects a novel twist on the role of class in the "London scene." Her play, a great success in its staging at the Kingsway in 1908, tells the story of a downtrodden London shop-girl living in a dormitory attached to a department store (part of the "living-in" system for employees). When she comes into a small inheritance, rather than being prudent she decides to go to the continent and live like a lady for a month. There she is courted by the Hon. Victor Bretherton, who grows cold when she tells him of her true social and economic position. Confidently, she makes a bet with him: that he could not support himself for six months by his own labour. In the final scene, on the Thames Embankment, Diana and Bretherton, both impoverished, meet up at 3:00 in the morning (the light rises during the scene). He admits his failure, and tells her that he has decided that he can indeed live on his own income (a mere six hundred a year) and marry her, though they cannot be "fashionable." United and content, they borrow money for their breakfast from a bobbie who was once in Bretherton's army unit (See Figure 2).

Reviewers picked up on Hamilton's political edge here. The *Pall Mall Gazette* saw a "suffragist sensibility" at work: "the ladies . . . enjoyed seeing one of the tyrants (audi Mrs. Pankhurst!) put in his proper place."[23] The *Ladies Pictorial* reassured its readers that "with the economics of the piece we need not trouble ourselves. . . . much of it savours of that spirit of revolt which represents capital as the inevitable enemy, instead of the indispensable aid of, labour."[24] As with Shaw's plays, the reviewers were often in dispute over the nature of the play's relation to "real life." While the reviewer for the *Evening News* called *Diana of Dobson's* "a 'real' play," with "genuine people, not stage puppets," the *Pall Mall Gazette* sniffed at Hamilton's pretensions to authenticity:

> . . . this is not real life. In the world of fact Victor would have obtained a berth somewhere, or his friends would have done it for him. . . . while Diana with her gifts of speech, presence, and general capability, would surely have found a situation as a companion, or, at the worst, as a general servant. But it makes an amusing comment.[25]

Hamilton, like the other Edwardian reformer-dramatists, was using long-standing, even old-fashioned, notions of "stage realism" precisely to provoke debate on the subject

Figure 2. The "Embankment" scene, *Diana of Dobson's* (Kingsway 1908). Victor and Diana share a breakfast purchased with borrowed change. Courtesy of the Mander and Mitchenson Theatre Collection, London.

of "authenticity." By invoking a theatrical genre usually considered highly realistic and then manipulating it, Hamilton was drawing attention to the ways in which the drama reflects social problems. While the earlier plays of Boucicault, Sims, and Travers ultimately offered solace and reassurance, Hamilton's aim was to unsettle. As one reviewer pointed out, "the audience, at the back of its mind, must have a vague uneasiness about the suitableness of the match and the likelihood of happiness."[26] In the earlier melodramas of poverty in London, one wasn't supposed to wonder about such things.

Whereas London had conventionally been used as a backdrop for revelations of identity, for shifts in class from lower to upper, Hamilton works against expectation to adjust the characters' — and the audience's — notions of place. Both Diana and Bretherton "play" at being rich or poor (at the opening of the final scene the characters are posed so that we do not know, at first, that it is Bretherton sleeping on the park bench (See Figure 3); in the end, however, Hamilton refuses to come through with the fantasy ending that would place these characters at one extreme or the other of the class continuum. It is a mild, prosaic ending, but it goes against a long theatrical tradition in its determination to let the characters' untransformed social and economic standing determine their future. The formula for dealing with anxieties about life in London, in which the poor would be on display in all their misery but would then turn out to be rich, is as it were, quoted, parodied, and finally discarded.

NOTES

1. For a useful overview of dramatic representations of London's dangerous side, see Michael Booth, "The Metropolis on Stage." In *The Victorian City: Images and Realities.* Eds. H.J. Dyos and Michael Booth. London: Routledge, 1973. pp. 211-24.
2. See letters to the Lord Chamberlain, collected with the licensing copy of the text of *Tom and Jerry* (Larpent Plays, L.A. 2262), at the Huntington Library, San Marino, CA.
3. W.T. Moncrieff. *Tom and Jerry; or, Life in London: An Operatic Extravaganza in Three Acts.* London: W.T. Moncrieff, 1826. The play, it should be noted, came with a helpful "Key" to the "flash"—slang—used by the play's bohemians and low-lifes.
4. Playbills, Theatre Museum, London.
5. Douglas Jerrold, *Martha Willis, The Servant Maid: An Original Domestic Drama.* London: Thomas Hailes [1831]. p. 2.
6. Moncrieff, *Tom and Jerry*, p. 3.
7. Moncrieff, *Tom and Jerry*, pp. 12-13.
8. W.T. Moncrieff, *The Crossroads of Life*, L.C.P. 42785, British Library. p. 330.
9. C.H. Hazlewood, *The Casual Ward*, L.C.P. 53048I, British Library, p. 3.
10. The West End theaters mentioned in this essay include Theatre Royal, Drury Lane; Theatre Royal, Haymarket; the Princess's Theatre; the Adelphi; and the Shaftesbury. East End theaters include the City of London Theatre, the Britannia Theatre, the Standard Theatre, the Effingham (later East London) Theatre, the Royal Pavilion Theatre, the Grecian Theatre, and the Garrick Theatre. South-Side (or "Surrey-Side") houses are the Victoria, the Surrey, and Astley's Amphitheatre. The geographical

Figure 3. "Embankment" scene, *Diana of Dobson's* (Kingsway 1908). The vagrant at the left turns out to be the Hon. Victor Bretherton, who is losing his bet. Courtesy of the Mander and Mitchenson Theatre Collection, London.

boundaries did not necessarily limit audiences according to class and/or neighborhood. Astley's was a popular destination for West-enders, and the Marylebone, near Regent's Park, was a solidly working-class house despite its West-End location. Sadler's Wells, with its slightly out-of-the-way location in Islington, was often grouped together with West End theaters.

11. *The Street Arab; or, Adrift on the World.* L.C.P. 55032, British Library. p. 14v.

12. Gareth Stedman Jones. *Outcast London: A Study in the Relationship Between Classes in Victorian Society.* Oxford: Clarendon Press, 1974. p. 247. Jones's chapter "The Deformation of the Gift: The Problem of the 1860s" gives a lucid description of the tortured debates over charity and "alms-giving."

13. Henry Mayhew. *London Labour and the London Poor.* Ed. John Rosenberg. New York: Dover, 1968. Vol. 1, pp. 151-52.

14. William Travers. *The Watercress Girl.* L.C.P. 53045T, British Library. p. 11.

15. *How We Live,* L.C.P. 52958CC, British Library. p. 15. The scene's origin in newspaper accounts of the poor such as those of Mayhew is clearly seen in several of the play's didactic speeches, such as this one made by the kindly gentleman who refuses to take the watercresses: "Hers is a hard lot, she might walk a long distance before she'd clear as much as the trifle I have given her. Cold—heat—wet or dry, her little feet must walk her weary round. . . . The press has recently become a powerful advocate for the poor and some of its noblest spirits have laid their hands upon the plow and guided by such hands there's little fear but the harvest will be a bright one" (16).

16. Andrew Halliday, *The Great City,* L.C.P. 53058, p. 6.

17. Charles Selby, *London by Night.* L.C.P. 42985, British Library. pp. 18-19.

18. Dion Boucicault, *Lost at Sea,* L.C.P. 53079P, British Library. p. 35.

19. *St. James's and St. Giles's.* L.C.P. 52942J, British Library. p. 45v.

20. Review in *The Theatre,* 8 Oct. 1881: 239.

21. Reviews cited are from collections of clippings in the Mander and Mitchenson Theatre Collection, London. For further discussion of *Glad Tidings,* see Heidi J. Holder, "Other Londoners: Race and Class in Plays of Nineteenth-Century London Life" in *Imagined Londons,* ed. Pamela Gilbert. Albany: SUNY Press, 2002. Pp. 31-44.

22. The details of Eliza and Freddy's married life are included in a long note at the end of the playtext. Shaw was a master at reworking Victorian plots and conventions to his own ends. Martin Meisel has analyzed *Pygmalion*'s roots in the "Cinderella" plots common in the Victorian theater (see *Shaw and the Nineteenth-Century Theater,* Princeton: Princeton UP 1963, pp. 169-77). Such plays were certainly the primary models for *Pygmalion*; I think, however, that the dramas of London's poor provide another source for Shaw's play.

23. *Pall Mall Gazette* 13 Feb. 1908. Clipping, Mander and Mitchenson Theatre Collection.

24. *Ladies Pictorial* 13 Feb. 1908. Clipping from the Mander and Mitchenson Theatre Collection.

25. Clippings, Mander and Mitchenson Theatre Collection.
26. Unidentified clipping, Mander and Mitchenson Theatre Collection.

Heidi J. Holder is an Associate Professor of English at Central Michigan University. She has published on British, Irish, and Canadian drama and theater in such journals as *Essays in Theatre* and the *Journal of Modern Literature*, and such collections as *Playwriting and Women in Nineteenth-Century Britain* (Cambridge UP 1999) and *Imagined Londons* (SUNY Press 2002). Her current project is a full-length study of working-class theater in Victorian London.

Theatre History Studies 23 (June 2003)

Historical Invisibility: The Vexatious A. P. Wilson and the Abbey Theatre

STEVEN DEDALUS BURCH

From 1914-15 Andrew Patrick Wilson, a journalist/columnist for the *Irish Worker*, the Socialist organ of the Irish Transport and General Workers' Union, was also the manager of the Abbey Theatre, as well as a director, actor and the company's resident dramatist. His term at the theatre was brief and contentious, and it ended in a controversy that has been rewritten and subsequently removed from most of the official histories of the Abbey. Some of his plays have survived, though not in revival, and, if remembered at all, Wilson would be rated a competent if minor playwright.[1] But it is Wilson's position of invisibility in the Abbey Theatre's history, the controversy over his leaving the company, as well as his prescient achievement of an urban, politically-charged drama that would come to fruition in the works of O'Casey a decade later, which I will attempt to explore in this essay.

The early history of the Abbey Theatre and the Irish Literary Theatre has been written and commented about on many occasions in numerous books and articles and is fairly familiar ground to even the most casual of theatre historians. Its first decade, from the meeting between Lady Gregory and W.B. Yeats in September 1897 in Galway to the historic riots accompanying the Abbey's premier production of Synge's *The Playboy of the Western World*, has been heralded frequently as a great period of theatrical fecundity. Such playwrights as Synge, Yeats, Gregory, Douglas Hyde, Edward Martyn, Fred Ryan, T.C. Murray, George Moore, Seumas O'Kelly, and Padraic Colum brought an almost frenzied level of literary creativity to the Irish theatre while William and Frank Fay revitalized the level of production and acting with their trained professionalism and their devotion to the tenets of realism.

The second decade of the Abbey's existence, however, is less generally well known. Overshadowed in part by the country's political events — from the 1913 Lock-out to the 1916 Easter Rising and the subsequent War of Independence and Civil War that followed when violence tore at the social fabric of Ireland, and more specifically Dublin — and in part by the emergence of Sean O'Casey in 1923, the theatrical history of the Abbey during their second decade is less made up of artistic triumphs than with the more mundane matters of the company's economic survival struggling with and against its artistic ambitions.[2]

Though this period would begin with Irish police batoning Irish citizens and end with Irish armies shooting Irish soldiers and civilians, the Abbey Theatre contrived to present mostly apolitical peasant dramas and folk tales of ancient Celtic glories. Terence Brown identifies the typical Abbey season at this time as containing "realistic plays in

English about Irish rural and small town life that [were] the staple of Abbey Theatre productions" while D. George Bryce characterizes their plays as "ignoring divisive political questions,"[3] even though the Abbey's earlier production of Yeats's nationalistic call to arms, *The Countess Cathleen*, was not without creating public controversy. Yet during this decade the Abbey did venture to produce three social dramas that for the first time specifically addressed Irish urban poverty and, more importantly, brought the working class struggle to the Abbey's largely middle-class audiences: *The Slough* (1914) by A. P. Wilson, *Blight* (1917) by Alpha and Omega (a pseudonym for Oliver St. John Gogarty), and *The Labour Leader* (1919) by Daniel Corkery.[4]

Wilson's *The Slough*, a long-forgotten and unpublished drama, was the Abbey's first attempt to bring the highly politicized world of the urban underclass to its predominantly middle-class audience. Written in the immediate aftermath of the Lock-out during 1914 and produced in November of that year, barely nine months after the Lock-out's ignominious finale, Wilson's play attempted to indict the political and economic structure of the city for its urban conditions and to arouse his Dublin audience's sympathy by exposing the plight of Dublin's starving poor. His strategy lay in reawakening his audience's memory of the excitement stirred by the dynamic labor leader Jim Larkin, here presented as the narrative's formal antagonist, and by utilizing a form of playwriting developed in Paris at Antoine's *Theatre Libre* in the 1890s called *comedie rosse*. This French drama, according to Jean Chothia, was an "offshoot of plays of psychological realism and social enquiry [that were] noted for [their] *rosserie* or gratuitous nastiness [and demonstrating] how the fittest survive in the contemporary world, indicting society with scenes in which characters used violence for self-gratification or self-protection."[5]

Wilson's three-act drama is structured along these very lines and presents a grim and, to its initial reviewers, unsavory and pessimistic portrait of tenement life in the notorious north Dublin slums. *The Slough* focuses on a single family torn apart by the lack of social and economic agency that was as absolute as it was chronic at that time. Its characters are indelibly marked by their unrepentant activities as strikebreakers and prostitutes, conditions so forced upon them that another character describes them as "products of a rotten social state."[6]

Wilson's use of the Dublin vernacular further connects this play to the *comedie rosses*. Writing about the French theatre, Chothia notes that the dialogue often included "colloquial expressions, criminal jargon and phrases which defied verbal taboos, particularly with reference to sexual activity."[7] With swiftly moving action and often containing a savage, bitter cynicism these plays were seen as dramatic photographs which, as Daniel Gerould writes, "tore away the veils of piety, discretion and decency that had always shielded audiences from contact with certain shocking facts of life." Gerould adds that this *tranchȩ de vie* or "slice of life" drama:

> takes sardonic pleasure in undermining the high ideals of traditional religious morality by showing how harsh economic facts and biological drives render those ideals hollow and inoperative. Without comment or condemnation — and only the trace of an ironic sneer — the playwright allows the bare truth to expose the falsity of society's hypocritical pretensions.[8]

Bettina Knapp adds that this theatrical form purposely attempted to expose the underbelly of society, to present unsentimentally the "drunken and besotted rejects of humanity crying out their despair — their disgust with the world"[9] in an attempt to shock a complacent, middle-class audience into clamoring for social change.

This stress on realism becomes integral to the study of Wilson's *The Slough* as his play can be easily traced in both style and substance to this group of mostly one-act *comedie rosses* initially produced at Antoine's *Theatre Libre*. Following their example Wilson, formerly a columnist for Larkin's Socialist newspaper, *The Irish Worker*, strove to expose both the conditions of Dublin slum life and its profound effects on the spirits and the bodies of its inhabitants.[10] In *The Slough* Wilson stages alcoholism, prostitution, disease, chronic unemployment, bitter marriages, violence, and despair as his characters and their vices jostle against the backdrop of an unidentified failed and protracted labor strike for dominance in the lives of the characters. Indeed, reviewing *The Slough*, the critic of the *Freeman's Journal* complained of the Abbey's taste for realism, echoing the very complaints made about the *comedie rosses* at Antoine's theatre:

> [It] is dismal realism. The Abbey, fortunately or unfortunately, according to one's point of view, has no philosophic doubts as to whether it is well that people should see themselves as bad or even worse than they are. Then, too, the absence of squeamishness in the matter of life's squalid realities, which is characteristic of the Abbey, makes for photographic accuracy. The author of *The Slough* has not failed to take advantage of these facts in the working up of his play.[11]

The Slough was first performed November 30, 1914 at the Abbey Theatre under the direction of Wilson, who also played the Jim Larkin-surrogated role of Jake Allen. The three-act play's action is set just before and just after a major syndicalist strike which collapses in failure after several months. The first and third acts present a melodramatic portrait of the Hanlon family headed by Peter Hanlon, an arrogant, lazy, drunken paterfamilias who has earned his children's wrath for his drinking, and his fellow workers' wrath for having once scabbed during an earlier strike. As the new strike is about to commence — the union's leaders are only waiting to count the votes by the members — Hanlon faces expulsion from the union for not having paid up his dues, and his contentious attitude toward the union and its leadership is questioned by some union firebrands who are convinced that he will betray their cause again.

Further tearing at the Hanlon family are the fortunes of its three grown children. The play begins with an angry exchange between the two older children at their worthless father, starting with the spoiled, peacockish son Jack who resides most rancorously with the family. The other, a daughter Peg, is planning a move to Liverpool to look for shop work only to return in the final act as a marginally successful prostitute. The third child, the younger daughter Annie, is a physically frail factory worker beloved of the stalwart union worker Tom Robinson. She has contracted tuberculosis, a condition that is treated by both her and the family as if it were only a bad cold. At the play's end Annie dies from a combination of her illness and the severe shock on learning that Tom has been viciously beaten on the street by baton-wielding policemen and dragged off to jail.

Wilson deftly establishes the family's unhappiness and sordid physical living conditions and he underscores the harshness of their lives in two ways. First, the imminence of the syndicalist strike in the first act elevates some of the play's characters from their previously numbing acceptance of their lives and living conditions into a state of temporary hope and exhilaration. Secondly, this harshness is further underscored in the unfulfilled love of Tom for Annie, who only agrees to marry him once the strike has ended. Occasionally, Wilson skillfully subverts some of the more melodramatic conventions to concentrate more on character in place of a plot. Peter is a defiantly unsympathetic head of this dysfunctional family, as much a victim of the economics of the slums and the mentality that is bred within them, as from his own selfishness and chronic substance abuse. To be sure, many of the other principals are well within the clichéd mold of the melodramatic structure: Peter's wife Mary is stoically long-suffering, the virginal Annie is pure of heart, and Tom is a fine-spoken and heroically manly figure. Yet all their fates are predetermined neither by the plot's narrative strategy nor the characters' stereotypical goodness or badness, but by their class, and, in the end, all are crushed by their seemingly inescapable poverty.

It is in the play's center, its second act, that Wilson breaks most with the formal, narrative melodramatic clichés, and concentrates the play less on the family's and the working-class community's crisis and more on the union's pre-strike decision-making process. At the same time, the play progresses from its melodramatic genre and shifts into a mode of historical drama as it offers its Dublin audience a thinly fictionalized surrogation of the leader of the recent Lock-out, Jim Larkin. What this surrogation will mean to the community of the play becomes a primary focus of Wilson's study of slum dwellers in crisis.

The second act of the play takes place in the Committee Room of the union where the union's leaders are awaiting the results of the strike vote by the membership. Working from broader issues to more specific ones, the officials argue both over the strength of the sympathetic strikes that other unions have pledged to the status of various individuals in the union, most particularly that of Peter, who remains in arrears in his union dues and who had openly scabbed during an earlier strike. A tenement neighbor of the Hanlons, Edward Kelly, introduced in the first act while attempting to get from Peter a commitment to show up at this meeting, provides a spirited defense of the father. It is here that Wilson complicates our impression of Hanlon by Kelly's revelation of what Peter was like in his younger days, and of how this once-solidly union man was reduced to scabbing in that earlier strike because his wife was seriously ill and in need of expensive medical attention.

Wilson places, in narrowing concentric circles, the issues affecting the union, from a solidarity of support from outside to the question of solidarity from within. We watch and listen to the arguments and counter-arguments, absorbing the reasoning behind each of the decisions that will effect profound consequences on the principals in the play. Central to this act, and to a 1914 audience's reception barely nine months following the massively disruptive and emotionally traumatic Lock-out, is the success or failure of Wilson's Larkin surrogate, Jake Allen.

Jake is the union's general secretary (Larkin's own position within the Irish Transport and General Workers' Union), and even though the union has a nominal president, Jake is its obvious leader. It is Jake who determines the fates and disciplines of problematic members, such as Peter. As the act opens, Jake demands from the committee that another delegate be asked to resign for failing to render assistance to a worker in need. Without waiting for a vote Jake then scribbles his decision on the matter in a written order to be acted upon by the downstairs officials. One of the committeemen, Crocker, objects to Jake's high-handed action and questions whether this is in order, only to be rebuked by Jake:

> This man has been practically victimized through the callous action of one of the Union's officials, and when I right a wrong a member of this Committee asks if it's in order. What sort of man are you?[12]

Within the first two minutes of this act Wilson presents a recognizable composite of the general public's perception of "Larkin": bellicose, highhanded, megalomaniac, as headstrong a leader and protector of his men as he is recklessly confrontational against certain union delegates whom he perceives as more concerned with the formalities of meetings than with principles of right and wrong. Jake dismisses cavalierly Crocker's concerns and effectively, if only temporarily, squelches further debate. He then moves with equal alacrity against Peter, characterizing him as a "dangerous man to our movement" and demanding condemnation from the Committee:

> He'd sell his brothers, not for the thirty pieces of silver that even a Judas could obtain, but he'd sell them for as little as the price of a pint of porter. By a man's works shall he be known. Hanlon scabbed before, and he'll scab again. Very well, then, we may as well have our enemies out in the open at once. If he is allowed to prowl around this hall information will go to the enemy. Out with him now then before he can harm us. I move that Peter Hanlon's name be struck off our books, and that he be expelled from the membership of the Union at once.[13]

Jake rides roughshod over another delegate's question, leaving the delegate to object and demand his right to free speech. But Jake permits Peter's neighbor Kelly to set out his defense of Hanlon, a defense that paints a far more sympathetic portrait of a man struggling against overwhelming odds than we have heretofore seen. Jake acknowledges both Kelly's eloquence and, to a certain degree, the justification for Peter's past actions, contextualizing them as the "product of a rotten social state," before articulating the reasons for his harsh judgment:

> If you have your finger blood-poisoned, and there's a danger of it spreading up your arm, then you cut the finger off. That finger was once useful. It has become a danger – it threatens your life. So you destroy it remorselessly. The same thing applies to scabs. You can't destroy them — then banish them — away with them![14]

Jake's persuasiveness sways the other delegates and Peter is expelled without opposition. In barely five pages of dialogue, Wilson has swiftly presented his Larkinite figure as a moral whirlwind that sweeps away everything in its single-minded path with a damn-the-torpedoes-full-speed-ahead vigor. In this scene Wilson drew from both Larkin's public personae and his own personal experiences. At the time of the Lock-out Larkin was already well-known as a labor gadfly and agitator. Even though the Irish labor movement was decades old, Larkin personified it to such a large degree that for many they were indistinguishable from each other. One effect of this personification was to shift emphasis in the local press from the issues that drove the strikers to the inflammatory actions of Larkin himself. This in turn fueled resentment among labor's other leaders, both within Larkin's union and outside it.

F.S.L. Lyons provides an eloquent assessment of Larkin's intense hold on the imaginations of both supporters and enemies, the sense of danger that he carried with him, and it agrees in large measure with most other biographies and, more particularly, to what Wilson effectively manages to put on stage. Lyons writes that though Larkin was not an intellectual and did not possess the ability to effectively analyze the economic structure within the principles of socialism, he did possess

> a natural gift, or rather genius, for flamboyant oratory. Larkin's speeches were larger than life because Larkin himself was larger than life. Physically a very powerful man, he had a big presence and an even bigger voice, which allowed him to dominate vast meetings even in the open air. . . . But his emotions, too, seemed more intense than those of ordinary men. He was driven by a deep compassion and tenderness for the poor to preach 'the divine gospel of discontent.' The other side of that gospel was a *saeva indignatio* against employers who exploited their workers or against trade union officials who failed to protect their members. Larkin, once enraged, respected neither laws nor conventions nor individuals, and his creative years were passed in a frenzy of passionate involvement and controversy. He was the archetypal bull in a china-shop and it was a moot point whether irate industrialists or staid trade unionists were more alarmed by his irruption onto the Irish scene.[15]

Syndicalist historian Emmet O'Connor concurs and writes of the historical Larkin that he was "difficult to work under. Egotism skewed his judgment. His recklessness and arrogance contributed to defeat in the 1913 lock-out," though O'Connor readily balances this with his overall assessment that Larkin "had a coherent, radical vision of trade unionism that is of relevance both historically and politically."[16] ITGWU leader and Larkin's principal rival and successor William O'Brien noted Wilson's *The Slough* in his memoir and called it "very true to life," adding that "it showed Jim up rather badly."[17] This is an opinion frankly not borne out by a reading of the scene as quoted above, which appears to buttress O'Connor's more recent reassessment. Overbearing, high-handed, and even a bit ruthless, Wilson's textual surrogate is nonetheless morally unambiguous and very principled in his leadership. But in Wilson's performed surrogation, Larkin/Allen became a contested site for the opening night audience's memory.

The initial reviews would seem to bear out this contestation. In newspapers that were unfriendly to Larkin during the Lock-out there remained nevertheless a sense of acknowledgment of Larkin's extraordinary forcefulness, even a whiff of nostalgia for his turbulent presence, though not one single review at that time specifically recalled Larkin by name.[18] Interestingly two of the reviewers faulted not Wilson's script but his performance of Jake/Larkin. The *Irish Times* commented that the character is "important enough in such a play to be granted more forceful delineation," a complaint which was echoed by the *Freeman's Journal* critic who stressed that Wilson the actor had "failed to throw into his role the masterful passion and dominating influence which his lines intended, and that failure robbed the scene at the committee meeting of a great deal of its effectiveness."[19]

Yet while the critics may not have been inclined to name Larkin specifically, Wilson's surrogated portrait was, in fact, fairly apparent to most audiences. Joseph Holloway kept a journal about many of the opening night productions he attended at the Abbey, an invaluable resource for any theatre historian, and on November 3, 1914 he wrote enthusiastically about *The Slough* and its Larkin representation:

> Wilson's three-act slum play . . . was a complete success . . . it is chockfull of human nature. All three acts are excellent in their way, and the whole play gripped. . . . A reverend gentleman seated near me remarked at the end of Act I, "It seems like a skit on Larkinism." And he wasn't far wrong, for the "Jake Allen" of the play, forcibly enacted by the author, is in very truth drawn from Jim Larkin, and the realistic committee room scene in Act Two I have little doubt is very like the real thing too. On the stage it appeared so at all events.[20]

In spite of these initially strong reviews the play was not a success, though its opening during wartime in a city still devastated by the effects of the Lock-out provides some highly probable clues as to why audiences spurned it: likely they had had enough of Larkin. Only two years earlier, Larkin and his cause had earned enough support in Dublin to win seats for him and several other Labor candidates in a general election, but in January 1914, Larkin's candidates for the Dublin Corporation were resoundingly repudiated at the polls. This was the final, crushing blow to Larkin and the union and it forced an end to the Lock-out. As a former columnist for Larkin's newspaper, *The Irish Worker*, Wilson undoubtedly felt it necessary to attempt to rehabilitate his audience's memory of a man who had only recently united many of them in protest against the living conditions of Dublin's poor. But crisis fatigue had apparently set in, if only temporarily, and it was too soon, except among some of the reviewers, to begin sounding notes of nostalgia.

Curiously, the play is not mentioned in any of the Abbey's official histories, by Lennox Robinson (a former general manager of the Abbey), Peter Kavanaugh, and Hugh Hunt, except in appendices offering dates and cast lists of all productions.[21] While evidence and anecdote offer meager means in piecing together the story of Wilson's tenure at the Abbey, nevertheless as its manager during 1914-1915, he engaged in several rancorous disputes with the Abbey's board generally and with Yeats specifically over the season, resulting, in these official histories, in either a whitewash of Yeats's position by his supporters or a complete silence about Wilson's Abbey existence.

As a former columnist for Larkin's union newspaper *The Irish Worker*, under the pen name of "Euchan," Wilson's sympathies were strongly prolabor. In one account, from Holloway's journal, the argument that led to Wilson's severing his ties with the Abbey was over Yeats's insistence on adding Synge's *Deirdre of the Sorrows* to the season. Wilson argued in March 1915 that Synge's plays did not return a profit and that to put one on would require the expense of an additional rehearsal. Holloway reports that Yeats insisted, proclaiming that "Synge has left us a glorious heritage, and I have worked to make the theatre a Synge theatre."[22] Exhausted from mounting a string of productions to commit himself to a play requiring yet further rehearsal, Wilson balked, disputing Yeats's judgment and arguing fruitlessly that there were already several plays that could be quickly mounted without the expenditure of time and money on further rehearsals. Finally, Wilson fumed that the directors' personal finances made them oblivious to the concerns of the working actors, suggesting some failure on the part of both Yeats and Lady Gregory to acknowledge realistically the commercial nature of their theatre and the economic needs of their actors. Wilson complained to Holloway that by producing "non-drawing plays [Yeats and Lady Gregory were] robbing [the actors] of their livelihood; Yeats and Lady Gregory had their homes and didn't mind, but it was different with the players."[23] Wilson resigned his position that very night. The Abbey's directors mulled the problem for three days before accepting the resignation. They accused Wilson of breach of orders for refusing to do "legitimate work in not rehearsing Synge's play."[24]

Furthermore, Yeats later accused Wilson of raiding the Abbey's acting company to produce his own plays with the newly formed rival company, the Irish Theatre, created in 1915 by the Abbey's cofounder, Edward Martyn, and Yeats characterized his dismissal of Wilson as caused by Wilson's "turning to his own purposes, offers that were intended for us."[25] Later histories have continued to circulate this story, occasionally with some embroidery. In his recent study D.E.S. Maxwell writes that between 1914 and 1919 four managers were successively in charge of the Abbey, and "three of them [only] intent on advancing their own careers,"[26] further suggesting without naming Wilson that Yeats' characterization of his tenure remains current. Peter Kavanaugh's history reports Wilson's termination as resulting from financial mismanagement, and Robert Hogan and Richard Burnham, in discussing the Abbey's 1925 production of Frank Hugh O'Donnell's *Anti-Christ*, comment that the play's size "probably strained the resources of the theatre more than any other play since A. Patrick Wilson's *The Slough*."[27]

In 1919 Ernest Boyd published his history of contemporary Irish drama and he had both praise for Wilson's efforts and scorn for the current theatrical fare in Dublin: "The newcomers whose work has not yet been published show few signs of wishing to contribute something really personal to the repertory of the Irish Theatre, with the exception of A.P. Wilson's study of industrial life, *The Slough*."[28] But fifteen years after Wilson's termination Andrew E. Malone reassessed this period of Irish theatre and, whether or not he was influenced by the "official" history of the Abbey's productions, he dismissed *The Slough* as "little more than a picture of the terrible conditions of the slum districts of Dublin," adding that it has had a life since then exclusively as political propaganda, though I have failed to locate a single reference to any but its original Abbey production.[29] More recently, Robert Hogan and Richard Burnham mention Wilson's play again but only in passing as the second play ever produced at the Abbey about social conditions.[30]

What remains for the historian, beyond the few sides of an incomplete restoration of the text, is a lamentable portrait of invisibility. Wilson's single season at the Abbey has been dismissed as relatively inconsequential, caught between the more acclaimed managements of Lennox Robinson and St. John Ervine, Wilson's successor. Even Boyd, after praising Wilson's play, fails to mention Wilson by name in either of his discussions on the Abbey or the Irish Theatre companies. Caught in the giant shadows of Yeats, Robinson, Martyn, and Ervine, Wilson and his play appear to have been forgotten.[31]

In their study of the Irish theatre from 1916 to 1920, Hogan and Burnham, after giving a single mention to *The Slough* as a play about social urban conditions, spend time on the Abbey's next production of an urban social drama about a slum family, Oliver St. John Gogarty's 1917 *Blight*. Here the authors find many thematic and narrative elements that correspond to O'Casey's celebrated Dublin trilogy from the 1920s, most specifically *Juno and the Paycock*, as Gogarty's play uses a slum family as "a macrocosm of what is wrong with the slums" and they point to the "poverty, drunkenness, prostitution, disease and early death [that] are the topics to be embodied in the unavoidable members of a slum family: father, mother, son and daughter."[32] But I contend that this description holds very strongly for Wilson's earlier play as well. Admittedly lacking any specific evidence, I would like to posit the possibility of O'Casey's having seen or at least been aware of *The Slough* and the possibility of his having used it as a partial model for his 1924 masterpiece. The very qualities that Hogan and Burnham connect *Juno* to *Blight*, both in their respective themes and characterizations, would also seem to hold for *The Slough*.

Its position as the first Abbey play to deal with urban poverty from the perspective of the poor themselves and the play's obvious leftist politics lead the observer to question its absence in the critical commentary regarding O'Casey's literary and political development, especially in his published letters and the third volume of his autobiography, *Drums Under the Window*. Yet given O'Casey's passionate love of theatre, his attendance at Abbey productions, his membership in Larkin's union and his personal involvement in the Lock-out, it does not seem overly fanciful to suggest that O'Casey might have seen and been influenced by Wilson's innovative tenement drama of working class lives self-destructing from within. That O'Casey makes no mention of *The Slough* is lamentable, especially when he praises the later *Blight*.

But a possible answer may be found in the great and intense acrimony that passed between Wilson and O'Casey in the pages of the *Irish Worker* in February and March 1913. The then fervently nationalistic O'Casey took great wailing exception to Wilson's overtly socialist column attacking the naïve romanticism of the Irish nationalists and proclaiming that the "coming of Home Rule will [only] bring Ireland into commercial line with its neighbors" and asserting that the "battle of the future in Ireland will be between Capital and Labour."[33] In the pages of Larkin's weekly O'Casey repeatedly challenged "Euchan" to a verbal duel to settle the matter,[34] a challenge that Wilson scoffed at as ridiculous: "it strikes me as the funniest thing I have read for a long time."[35] Wilson also got in the last word when he later wrote in answer to yet another challenge from O'Casey, "You've a big, swelled head (the result of consorting with a crowd of boys, possibly) but you have a very small mind. Take care the mind doesn't sweep you off your feet someday."[36] As O'Casey's subsequent career and autobiographies make abundantly clear, it was his experiences in the Lock-out and with Larkin that radicalized O'Casey, and he remained a devoted socialist for the rest of his life. Given O'Casey's nearly legendary penchant for nursing decades-old grudges throughout his life, and his own political turnaround toward Wilson's socialism, one can sadly contemplate a possible revenge of silence, of the greater writer's deliberately consigning his minor antagonist to oblivion.

After writing the earliest urban play in Ireland to address the urban poor from their own vantage point and after attempting to run unsuccessfully two companies Wilson left Ireland by the end of the decade. He settled in Scotland where he continued to write and produce with some minor success for both the theatre, co-founding the Scottish National Players in 1921, which he consciously and openly modeled after the Abbey, and for the radio up to the mid 1950s. By the 1930s his writing concentrated less on class-consciousness and other leftist themes and more on a folksy conservative Scottish nationalism, as in such scripts as his 1940s comedy radio series *Sandy and Andy.*[37] In his rancorous relationships, especially with Yeats and O'Casey, Wilson appears to have imprudently burned some bridges, resulting in his virtual invisibility in the history of Irish drama.

This invisibility succeeds primarily in ignoring the Abbey's somewhat tentative development between the ages of Synge and O'Casey during the country's period of intense social and political upheaval, and contributes to an incomplete history of this remarkable institution. Yet the Abbey, to its credit, continued to broaden its dramaturgical identity through the socially diverse and contentious voices of its members, even though the process was neither smooth nor completely successful. *The Slough*, along with *Blight* and *The Labour Leader*, deserves to be exhumed from the archives and reexamined as more than merely a historical record of its time and place, as it attempted to connect its audiences with their own recent history and to effect a change in their attitudes toward the weaker members of their community. When this is done we may find that *The Slough* is not only Wilson's most fully achieved political and Irish play, but that it is also a drama that, especially the second act, can still surprise and engage us with its form, its substance and its passion.

NOTES

[1] I have been unable to verify any dates for Wilson's life; his earliest writing, a one-act play *Victims*, dates from 1912 and his last, *Gypsy's Warning*, is from 1956. By 1913 he was writing a regular column for the *Irish Worker* under the pen name of "Euchan" and from January to March of that year he engaged in a rancorous debate with Sean O'Casey, then writing as S. O'Cathasaigh. O'Casey biographer David Krause notes that in Ireland Wilson called himself A. Patrick Wilson and that in Scotland he signed his works Andrew P. Wilson. See Sean O'Casey, *Letters, Volume One* (New York: Macmillan Publishing, 1975), 13.

[2] There were controversies during this period, however. The Abbey's 1909 production of Bernard Shaw's *The Shewing Up of Blanco Posnet* and its 1911-12 American tour of *The Playboy of the Western World* met with hostilities, as well as the Abbey's attempt to produce Shaw's *O'Flaherty V.C.* in 1915. See Lucy McDiarmid's illuminating essay,

"The Abbey and the Theatrics of Controversy, 1909-1915," *A Century of Irish Drama: Widening the Stage*, eds. Stephen Watt, Eileen Morgan, and Shakir Mustafa (Bloomington: Indiana University Press, 2000), 57-71.

[3] Terence Brown, *Ireland: A Social and Cultural History, 1922 to the Present* (Ithaca: Cornell University Press, 1985), 104; D. George Boyce, *Nationalism in Ireland* (London: Routledge, 1995), 243.

[4] Frederick Ryan's 1902 satire on municipal politics, *The Laying of the Foundation*, is the earliest Irish "urban" play, but its point of view is distinctly that of its middle-class characters. The two later plays share *The Slough*'s perspective. See Oliver St. John Gogarty, "Blight: The Tragedy of Dublin," *Plays* (Newark: Proscenium Press, 1971); Daniel Corkery, *The Labour Leader* (Dublin: The Talbot Press Ltd., 1920).

[5] Jean Chothis, *Andre Antoine* (Cambridge: Cambridge University Press, 1991), 92.

[6] A.P. Wilson, *The Slough* (Dublin: Abbey Theatre Archives, National Library of Ireland, 1914). Pagination in referencing this play would be frankly arbitrary as it was never published and exists only in an incomplete form through several actors' sides in the Abbey's archives. Some of the sides are missing and I have reconstructed approximately 80-85% of the text from these remaining sides.

[7] Chothia, *Andre Antoine*, 92.

[8] Daniel Gerould, "Oscar Metenier and Comedie Rosse: From the Theatre Libre to the Grand Guignol," *The Drama Review* 28:1 (Spring 1984): 16.

[9] Bettina L. Knapp, "The Reign of the Theatrical Director: Antoine and Lugne-Poe," *The French Review* 61 (May 1968): 869.

[10] In 1912, Wilson wrote *Victims*, a one-act *comedie rosse* about a tenement couple in the grip of economic catastrophe that was produced by the Irish Workers' Dramatic Company on Boxing Day 1912 at Liberty Hall as part of the Irish Transport and General Workers Union; it was revived several times by that company in an attempt to raise funds in support of the 1913 strike. See Steve Wilmer, "Travesties: Ideolgies and the Irish Renaissance," *Theatre Journal* 28 (Summer 1992): 36.

[11] "Review of *The Slough*," *Freeman's Journal* (5 Nov 1914): 6.

[12] Wilson, *The Slough*.

[13] Ibid.

[14] Ibid.

[15] F.S.L. Lyons, *Ireland Since the Famine* (London: Weidenfeld and Nicholson), 274.

[16] Emmet O'Connor, "Essay in Review: An Age of Agitation," *Saothar* 9 (1983): 68.

[17] William O'Brien, *Forth the Banners Go* (Dublin: Three Candles Limited, 1969), 260.

[18] At the time of the Abbey's production of *The Slough* Larkin was in the United States, attempting to raise funds to replenish the union's treasury after the strike's collapse in February. The outbreak of the war detained him from returning and he spent the war years vociferously protesting it. At the war's end, he was arrested for seditious activities and imprisoned in Sing-Sing prison until Governor Al Smith pardoned him in 1923. When he returned to Ireland, his old enemies had taken over both the union and

the country.
[19] "Review of 'The Slough,'" *Irish Times* (4 Nov 1914): 6; "Review of *The Slough*," *Freeman's Journal*: 6.
[20] Joseph Holloway, *Abbey Theatre: A Selection from his Unpublished Journal,Impressions of a Dublin Playgoer.'*eds. Robert Hogan and Michael J. O'Neill (Carbondale: Southern Illinois University Press, 1967), 167.
[21] See Lennox Robinson, *Ireland's Abbey Theatre: A History, 1899-1951* (London: Sidgwick and Jackson Ltd., 1951); Peter Kavanaugh, *The Story of the Abbey Theatre: From Its Origins in 1899 to the Present* (New York: The Devin-Adair Company, 1950); Hugh Hunt, *The Abbey: Ireland's National Theatre, 1904-1979* (Dublin: Gill and Macmillan, 1979).
[22] Holloway, *Abbey Theatre*, 170.
[23] Ibid., 171-173.
[24] Ibid., 172.
[25] Reported in Hunt, *The Abbey*, 110-111.
[26] D.E.S. Maxwell, *A Critical History of Modern Irish Drama, 1891-1980* (Cambridge: Cambridge University Press, 1984), 80.
[27] Kavanaugh, *Story of the Abbey Theatre*, 101-103; Robert Hogan and Richard Burnham, *The Years of O'Casey, 1921-1926* (Gerrards Cross: Colin Smythe, 1992), 266.
[28] Ernest Boyd, *The Contemporary Drama of Ireland* (Boston: Little Brown, 1919), 169.
[29] Andrew E. Malone, *The Irish Drama* (New York: Charles Scribner's Sons, 1929), 275.
[30] Robert Hogan and Richard Burnham, *The Art of the Amateur, 1916-1920* (Mountrath: The Dolmen Press, 1984), 109.
[31] In Donal Nevin's recent celebration *James Larkin, Lion of the Fold* (Dublin: Gill & Macmillan, 1998), there is no mention of Wilson's play even though Nevin discourses on other dramatic representations of the leader.
[32] Hogan and Burnham, *Art of the Amateur*, 111.
[33] See O'Casey, *Letters*, 14.
[34] Ibid., 17.
[35] Ibid., 20.
[36] Ibid., 26-27.
[37] Adrienne Scullion, "Scottish theatre and the impact of radio," *Theatre Research International* 17:2 (Summer 1992): 117-131.

Steven Dedalus Burch is a playwright and theatre historian at the University of Alabama. He has published articles and reviews for the *Journal of Dramatic Theory and Criticism* and *Theatre Journal*. Most recently, he has three essays included in *Holocaust Literature: An Encyclopedia of Writers and Their Works*, edited by S. Lillian Kremer (Routledge).

Theatre History Studies 23 (June 2003)

Community, Civility, and Citizenship: Theatre and Indoctrination in the Civilian Conservation Corps of the 1930s

JAMES WILSON

In July 1933, President Franklin D. Roosevelt welcomed the first group of young men into the Civilian Conservation Corps (CCC), a relief organization established as part of the New Deal. In a greeting published in the CCC camp newspaper, *Happy Days*, Roosevelt gestured to the personal and national import of this employment effort. He wrote to the new recruits:

> You young men who are enrolled in this work are to be congratulated. . . . Physically fit, as demonstrated by the examinations you took before entering the camps, the clean life and hard work, in which you are engaged, cannot fail to help your physical condition. You should emerge from this experience, strong and rugged and ready for entrance into the ranks of industry, better equipped than before.[1]

The CCC, which lasted for only nine years, 1933-1944, was a bold economic and social experiment, and it was one of Roosevelt's most highly-regarded and controversial relief measures. Yet while the governmental organization offered the young men of the camps a number of benefits, including the chance to earn an education and learn new job skills, the CCC treated the men as bodies to be molded, shaped, and transformed into ideal American citizens.

The theatre in the camps, which was supplied by the Federal Theatre Project, was one of the tools used in this indoctrination. This is especially evident in *CCC Minstrel Revue*, which was written for the young men to perform in their mess hall, and *The CCC Murder Mystery*, the most famous Federal Theatre Project show to tour the camps. These two dramatic productions merged the boundaries of fiction and "real life" and made the enrollees themselves the focus, as well as actors in the presentation. Purposely an experiment in audience participation and community building, *The CCC Murder Mystery* in particular both modeled and inscribed democratic and industrial values and reflects the attempts to modernize, moralize, and normalize the boys of the CCC.

Roosevelt himself is credited with devising the plan for the agency, which he envisioned would not only provide employment for a large number of young men, but would also be beneficial in forest protection and renewal. Special camps were organized for blacks, veterans, and Indians, but the targeted population consisted of young, unemployed white males. Selection was limited to unmarried men, eighteen to twenty-five years old (which was later expanded to seventeen to twenty-six years old), who served a minimum of one six-month term, but they had the option to re-enroll for one additional term. As the primary aim of the CCC Act was to provide relief, the enrollees of the camp received a salary of thirty dollars a month (or roughly a dollar a day), twenty-five of which was automatically sent to their families.

The "boys" as they were generally called, spent their days, five days a week, fighting fires, building dams, logging, planting trees, and completing other projects related to environmental conservation; in the evenings, the camps offered a variety of educational and recreational programs (See Figure 1). Because of this, theatre was integrated naturally into the organization's regular operation, and in the summer of 1935, the Federal Theatre Project assumed control of the theatre programs in the camps by providing scripts for the boys to perform and by sending touring productions from camp to camp. The CCC division of the Federal Theatre Project, however, determined that the camp dramatic productions, in keeping with the CCC's goal to improve the moral and spiritual fiber of the boys, should not consist simply of escapist mass entertainment, but should contain evidence of cultural and educational merit.

Prior to the Federal Theatre's intervention, however, theatre in the camps was encouraged primarily for its recreational usefulness. As of 1935, a few camps had designated drama teachers, assigned by such organizations as TERA (Temporary Emergency Relief Administration), but many camps that had their own drama programs were organized by advisers from other academic disciplines. The local community, as in the case of a 1934 production by Camp 1615 near Pontiac, Michigan, often played an important role in putting a play on its feet. For their production of R. C. Sherriff's *Journey's End*, a British play set during World War I, the enrollees were provided with sound and lighting equipment from the local power company, while the town's high school allowed them to use the school's auditorium, and the school's band furnished the musical accompaniment.[2] But because scripts, materials for scenery construction, costumes, props, and lighting were nearly impossible to requisition, maintaining a drama program was exceedingly difficult.

Standard fare on the makeshift stages or open areas in the mess halls, where the performances were generally staged, was mostly emulative of the popular entertainment of the early 1930s. Vaudeville shows, minstrels, and one-act plays (often written by the enrollees) were most common. The "CCC Footlights" column in the December 14, 1935, edition of the national CCC weekly newspaper, *Happy Days* (three months before the FTP's radical revision of the theatre in the camp's program), reflects the diversity of offerings. Five examples of amateur theatrical productions are noted. One mentions that a class of sixteen enrollees at Camp 1268 in High Bridge, New Jersey is "rehearsing a play 'based on aeronautics and filled with action' as its fist production."[3] The column also states that the dramatic class of Co. 1701 presented a public performance of their minstrel show, *Chasing the Blues Away* in the Mound City, Montana high school auditorium and charged "one old book for admission"; thus, "the camp library benefitted to the tune of 150 volumes."[4] Finally, the column captures the intended spirit of the drama programs in its tribute to amateur productions:

Figure 1. CCC Enrollee Planting a Tree. Governmental publicity generally depicted the physical benefits the Civilian Conservation Corps had on the young men as well as the natural, wholesome setting of the camps. Reproduced from the Collections of the Library of Congress.

> Men who sit in vast stadia to witness the dramatic clash of traditional rivals on the football field do no begin to experience thrills comparable with that received by members of Co. 2664, Mt. Carroll, Ill., when they sit in their mess hall and watch the members of their camp dramatic club perform on Saturday nights. . . . True there is not the finesse of professionalism, but there is the joyful realization of uncovering unknown talent. There is a great deal of honest fun which fills an aching void in the lives of men busied usually with field work and camp area improvements.[5]

Camp officials gradually recognized that theatre could indeed "fill an aching void" caused by homesickness and hard work, as well as boost morale among the company. With that as its goal, more and more dramatic clubs began to appear, and they were nearly always greeted with enthusiasm.

Also extremely popular and genuine morale-boosters were the professional productions which toured the camps. Before the Federal Theatre had assumed leadership, the Works Progress Administration (WPA) and state-run theatre operations sent entertainments from camp to camp in a given state. The forms of these also varied, but they were uniformly light as to appeal to the men, the majority of whom had never seen a live production upon arriving at the camps.[6] In the "Footlights" column of the same *Happy Days* edition, one also gets a clear sense of the professional productions offered in the various camps, which included, *Turn to the Right* and *The Fall Guy*, both three-act comedies, and several vaudevilles, which featured comedy sketches, harmonica players, blackface comedians, and a "realistic naval battle" scene as part of a shadowgraph show.

The presentation of shows incorporating a variety of acts had a practical foundation as well. These shows required little scenery, no set script, and could be performed nearly anywhere. The productions did, however, require an unusual amount of adaptability from the performers and technicians. The traveling units went from camp to camp in army trucks, often over bumpy, treacherous roads, and furthermore, each venue meant a different kind of auditorium to which the performers and crew had to adjust.[7] Lighting technicians in particular also had the added difficulty of having to convert a company mess hall into a "theatre." Mess halls were not electrically equipped for this function and finding the electrical lines and making the necessary connections was always a chore.[8] The shows, nevertheless, were nearly always greeted with enthusiasm by the boys, and in many ways, these entertainments may be considered the equivalent of the USO shows presented to soldiers during times of war.

Because of the boys' isolation, arduous work duties, and uncomfortable living conditions in the camps, it is no wonder that theatre was welcomed with such delight. With the launching of the Federal Theatre Project in 1935 and its association with the CCC shortly afterward, theatre took on a new role. Shortly after its creation in the summer of 1935, the Federal Theatre Project assumed control of the by-then flourishing theatre programs in the camps, demonstrating its commitment to producing entertainment geared toward audiences who would not normally attend and who could not afford the cost of admission. No longer would their sole purpose be to provide an evening of pure escapism, but dramatic presentations would be used for their social and educational ends. Hence, the types of theatre presented in the camps began to embody the philosophy behind the CCC.

At a conference focusing on CCC Camp Play Needs in August 1936, the dramatic division developed a list of playwriting ideas and subjects for productions to tour the camps. These included: "A CCC Wedding," "Plays on Camp life — burlesque, comedy, farce," "Scenes from theatrical milestones and styles in acting," "A Peace Play," and a "History of the Women's Movement." Antiwar plays and those dealing with controversial themes were strictly forbidden.[9] Supplementing the conference notes is "Callen's Report," in which the writer provides a rationale for bringing theatre to the camps: "The camps afford these youths their first chance at wholesome living and takes from them the strain of family burdens. They become freer, more mentally relaxed and in a better position to enjoy the arts and develop culturally."[10] And reiterating the CCC's intention to prepare the boys for "the ranks of industry," Callen wrote: "Considering the hypothesis that the drama should be a mirror of real life, it naturally follows that plays, shown at the camps, should deal with the problems created by factory life and modern industrial conditions."[11] Not only would the productions offer a model of moral behavior, but in their simulation of recognizable situations with the boys taking part in them, they may be viewed as a rehearsal for "real life."

This preparation of the boys for a democratic, capitalist society was an underlying goal of the CCC in general and the theatre reinforced it. Publicity for the agency, for instance, quotes one enrollee proclaiming, "As an Americanizing influence, the CCC is perhaps without an equal."[12] But in one of the few studies of the relief agency, Eric Gorham questions the practices and methodology of the organization.[13] Using the Foucauldian model of "Discipline and Punish," Gorham maintains that "the CCC treated its enrollees as 'docile bodies' to be worked upon and improved."[14] The isolation of the camps, uniform lay out of the buildings, and the functionalized space, which was coded by "distinguishing each building carefully from another," contributed to the "sense of being in a regulated environment."[15] The work day schedule also reflects the rigidity of the camp structure, and the boys' leisure time was as carefully controlled.[16] As Kenneth Holland and Frank Ernest Hill point out in their report to the American Council on Education in 1942, the typical day was rigorously scheduled with specific tasks, work assignments, and educational activities, which extended from the reveille at 6:30 A.M. to bunk check at 11:00 P.M.[17] The inflexible structure of time and space, in addition to an emphasis on developing a solid work ethic, aimed to prepare the boys for a modern, industrial society. As even its name suggests, the Civilian Conservation Corps strove to meet this goal by imitating a military model, although this aspect was deliberately downplayed by the government.[18]

As indicated in Roosevelt's greeting to the CCC enrollees, the physical condition of the boys was an indicator of the agency's success, and the boys were constantly monitored and examined by the agency. The improved healthy body of the enrollee, for example, became the symbol for the organization's accomplishments. In fact, reports on the average amount of weight gained by the enrollees were promoted and publicized to show the benefits of the CCC on young men coming from poor families. These were used to encourage other youths to join and to maintain public favor for the program.[19] To accomplish these ends, the boys were subjected to frequent physical and medical examinations. An African-American enrollee, for example, explains that on a Monday he went to Pier 1 in New York City to register for the CCC, received a complete physical examination (his record stamped "C" for "colored), and the following day after being separated into the "colored" camp, he received yet another complete examination.[20] In Foucauldian terms, the CCC enrollee's body was "entering a machinery of power that explores it, breaks it down and rearranges it"[21] so that it may prove useful in a democratic nation.

A major element of CCC indoctrination had to do with instilling morals in the boys. The most crucial societal standards to be upheld were social manners, respect for one's community, and most important, masculine conduct. Venereal disease was a constant threat as a cause for dismissal and the boys were checked monthly, so the focus of sexual relations was on courting women rather than on intercourse. To ensure healthy, heterosexual practices and habits, the camps sponsored dances to which young women in the local towns were invited; also, classes and discussions were presented on acquainting themselves with girls and behaving appropriately.[22] Presumed deviant and unmanly behavior, including masturbation and homosexuality (which was grounds for dismissal), was discouraged and controlled. Holland and Hill report:

> It should be added that masturbation seemed to be fairly common among CCC youth, but that those admitting the habit usually asserted that camp had a tendency to break or lessen its hold upon them. In general, the enrollees despised homosexuality, and only a few cases were reported.[23]

The unstated, underlying philosophy of the CCC was that through discipline, hard work, and moral indoctrination, the enrollees would enter as boys but exit as men.

This philosophy is particularly evident in the theatre offerings that developed out of the union of the CCC and FTP. One such script, the *CCC Minstrel Revue*, "An Original Compilation of Music, Fun, Laughter" by Will Glickman and Ned Snyderman[24] was written as a result of the August conference. This and similar plays, including *CCC Vaudeville*, *Old-Time Minstrel*, and *Jail-Bird Minstrels* were available through the FTP CCC Division's Script Service and could easily be staged by most camp drama clubs.[25] A playwriting contest was also intended to serve as an edifying experience for the boys in the camps.[26] The *CCC Minstrel Revue* does not attempt to "mirror real life" through a presentation of social and political issues on stage, but it involved the boys and camp life directly. The interesting feature of this entertainment is the way in which it is written to incorporate in-jokes, names of the enrollees, and particularities of the camp and area. The character names in the script are listed as "Adviser," "Black," "Brown," "White," and "Green," but instructions are given to substitute the "real names of the enrollees" and the educational adviser throughout. The script itself is a series of fill-in-the-blanks to make the rather standard vaudeville and minstrel jokes more topical and amusing. For instance, the final skit concerning a football game concludes with the following gag:

BLACK

And the guy who blocked for you . . . he's a marvel! Who is he?

ADVISER

Didn't you know? It was Jimmy Smith! . . . (USE REAL NAME OF ANY ENROLLEE WHO IS KNOWN TO BE MISCHIEVOUS OR WHO IS

ALWAYS INVOLVED IN MINOR DIFFICULTIES IN CAMP)

BLACK

Jimmy Smith? How did you know *he* could run interference?

ADVISER

How did I know?

(laughs)

When the educational adviser of a CCC camp wants interference . . .

BLACK

Yes?

ADVISER

HE KNOWS HE CAN DEPEND ON JIMMY SMITH! (USE REAL NAME)

(BLACK OUT)[27]

The adaptability of the show is also demonstrated in its use of ten specialty numbers, thereby allowing for greater participation from the men in camp.

The chief intention of the play is clearly to build community and instill camaraderie among the boys. The use of local names and places further obscures the distinctions between reality and script, and the in-jokes add to the sense that performers and spectators are all participants in the show. Even though the spectators were not precisely "actors" within the entertainment, they were incorporated into the proceedings by becoming the butts of the humor and references in the skits. But clearly the sense of community that the play seeks to foster is based on the boys' sameness. This is not surprising for it was fairly well publicized that the camps were strictly segregated by race, and only a small percentage of the men who were accepted into the program were black.

Luther Wandall, an African-American enrollee, claimed that the organization typified, "to some extent, all the practices and prejudices of the U. S. Army."[28] Another black enrollee, Eddie Simons of Harlem, New York and serving at a camp in New Jersey, experienced the indignities of this prejudice firsthand. Simons, according to a Norfolk newspaper, received a dishonorable discharge when he "refused to stand and fan flies from a white officer," telling the officer that "he did not think fanning flies was part of his duty." The NAACP intervened, and the youth was given an honorable discharge and paid all allowances he had lost as a result.[29] *CCC Minstrel Revue*, in addition to the racial implications of its title, reflects the racially homogeneous profile of the camps. In fact, a great deal of the humor in the play stems from the manner in which ethnic minorities and women are objects of ridicule. To cite just a few examples: The local doctor supposedly had been treating "a man for three years for yellow jaundice before he found out his patient was a CHINAMAN!"[30]; there is discussion about a girl whom GREEN says has hands like petals, "Yeah . . . BICYCLE PEDALS!"[31]; and finally, BLACK says about a woman GREEN used to date: "That was the one who was always blushing! At least, you *thought* she was blushing . . . He went with her for three months before he found out SHE WAS AN INDIAN!"[32] By making the boys the focus and participants in a play like *CCC Minstrel Revue*, the show is an occasion for defining and celebrating the exclusive nature of the community.

These characteristics are also evident in the most famous production to derive from the marriage of the CCC and the Federal Theatre Project, *The CCC Murder Mystery*. The play was written by Grace Hayward a playwright and novelist, and who was also the wife of George M. Gatts, the New York State director of the Federal Theatre Project. *The CCC Murder Mystery*, which is referred to as a "Comedy Drama in Two Acts, with a Five Minute Intermission," is a simulated courtroom trial taking place in the camp in which it is performed. In it, a CCC boy is tried for murder, and the crime is revealed and solved by the testimonies (and outbursts) of a number of witnesses. The play's melodramatic plot-line also pits the boys of the camp against the malicious D.A., who badgers the defendant and strives to discredit all of the CCC boys. In the end, however, the defendant is declared not guilty, the D.A. is shamed, and the honor of the CCC is restored. Professional actors played the roles of the court personnel, the boy's mother, his sister, his girlfriend, and "Mugs," a witness who is described in the script as a "*Gracie Allen* type," and "One not afraid to mix with the boys and make herself generally liked." With some coaching beforehand, enrollees took the parts of the defendant, witnesses, and the jury. In all, the script calls for twelve professional, traveling actors (which includes two understudies and a stage manager), twenty-six CCC youths, one noncommissioned officer and educational adviser, and five boys in the audience whose names are mentioned during the performance.[33]

The CCC Murder Mystery debuted in May 1936 in Peekskill, New York with a production by the Suitcase Theatre of New York City's Federal Theatre Project division. Subsequently, touring productions traveled from Syracuse, New York; Manchester, New Hampshire; Boston, and Philadelphia. Although each touring company traveled with no scenery, no special costumes, and just a few props, the logistics of touring the show were rather complicated. A few days before the performance, a production representative, referred to as an "advance instructor," visited the camp and helped the educational advisor prepare a place for performance, such as a recreation room or mess hall. Converting such a space into a theatre was not difficult as the set required only a few tables, chairs, and makeshift stands for the judge, witnesses, and jury. The advance instructor helped select the boys appearing in the play and rehearsed them. Although they were instructed to adhere to the sides given to them (they were not given the full script so that they too would be surprised by the events of the play), the boys were asked to inject their performances with their "own personalities." Hence, the enrollees were not expected to play "assumed characters," a directorial decision intended to make the play even more realistic. When the company arrived, the stage manager led the boys through a final rehearsal and prepared the professional actors with information about the camp, the enrollees taking part, and the local community.[34]

Great lengths were taken to conceal the details of the plot from the entire camp before the performance. For instance, the educational advisor at the camp was urged to keep the complete manuscript of the play "under lock and key" to maintain the surprises surrounding the events and outcome of the murder mystery. In addition, the boys taking part in the play were coached privately, sworn to secrecy, and asked not to talk about what they knew of the "case." For the performance itself, camp residents were given special "court passes" to attend the performance, which helped insure that enrollees from neighboring camps would not receive advance knowledge of the play.[35]

The script of *The CCC Murder Mystery* is a constant string of Civilian Conservation Corps allusions and in-jokes. While casting the enrollees, for example, the directions state that boys should be chosen for their reputations so that *Bud Granger* (character names are provided in the script for convenience, but the boys' real names are used) is played by "the famous fighter of the camp;" *Tony Farrell* is "Known as a lady's man;" and *Butcher* is "Spoken of as having oiled hair." Allusions to life in the camp including references to fighting forest fires, K.P. duty, and camp dances serve to bolster the communal spirit. Although advertised as an evening of "amusement and entertainment [for] the entire camp,"[36] the play's primary purpose was to validate the organization and produce a sense of commonality among the enrollees. In short, the play was a unique and experimental form of traveling propaganda.

The origin of the production is not clear, but Hallie Flanagan, director of the FTP, assumes credit for it in her autobiography. In a letter sent to Federal Theatre directors around the nation, she wrote:

> Three hundred thousand boys in the C.C.C. camps throughout the United States want dramatic entertainment. [. . .] They do not want from us pallid productions of the classics or lukewarm imitations of Broadway. The camps deserve and should have the best that we can send out. Recognizing the limited stage facilities of the camps, can't some of you evolve a technique whereby a company acts in the center of the mess hall, drawing the audience into the show, catching in dramatic form the spirit which makes *Happy Days*, the camp newspaper, so exciting?[37]

The technique that evolved was an environmental, interactive theatre experience that attempted to erase the boundaries between the spectators and actors.

Not only were they subjected to social and medical tests (in fact, the frequent medical examinations and the constant attention to the enrollees' bodies were key plot points in one of the agency's prizewinning plays called *C.C.C.* by George Gill and Bernard Winstock),[38] but the enrollees were cultural guinea pigs as evident by the well-publicized experimental nature of this production. Yet the tremendous success of the "new and different form of theatre" is well documented in camp and organization reports.[39] Even many local and national newspapers covered the event and reviewed the play, including *Variety*, which wrote:

> There is plenty of adlibbing by conservation youths, imparting to the play a naturalness and pungency lacking in orthodox productions . . . No doubt as to audience reaction. Every youth laughed, due, in part, to the fact that the boys' real names are used and the gags are built on the boys' appearances or characteristics.[40]

The CCC Murder Mystery toured for two years, but in its first year alone, the show had played in more than 189 camps and was performed by a total of nine companies.[41] The show was so popular and had received so much praise from enrollees and camp staff, that the directors of the FTP CCC Division suggested that the participatory theatre techniques be the sole methods of presentation in the camps. In a special release to New York State papers on December 18, 1936, Division director Earl House stated: "All activities having as their objective mass entertainment are being discontinued; in their place is being introduced entertainment in which the boys take an active part, and from which they can benefit both in experience and knowledge."[42] The script for *The CCC Murder Mystery* reflects the specific forms of "experience and knowledge" the Division deemed essential to the boys' education and these were bolstered by the participatory quality of the show.

One of the most obvious goals of the production is to celebrate and inscribe conceptions of all-American manhood, which was one of the underlying objectives of the Civilian Conservation Corps. When Roosevelt created the CCC, for instance, he explained that the organization would rescue the nation's "two most precious resources": its land and its young men. According to the world of the play, exemplary manhood is defined by white middle-class values such as hard work, virility, and chivalry toward women. The patriarchal society mirrored in the play reflects a man's position rather distinctly. The judge, lawyers, and bailiff are all men (as would be rather standard of the time), and the women of the play are characterized as either mothers or girlfriends of the boys. The women assume an Otherness, which is heightened by the fact that their presence in the camp mess hall, after all, would have been an extremely unusual occurrence.

The woman with the greatest amount of stage time and the most significant part in the proceedings is Mugs, who flirts with at least a dozen of the boys by name, sits on the laps of several spectators, and has dialogue comprised mostly of innuendo to affirm the sexual attractiveness of the boys. For example, when she takes the witness stand, she states, "I don't care what the court does, but I really do want to please you gentlemen. Honestly, I'd just do *anything*—."[43] Throughout, her dizzy responses and sexual overtones confound the court and her removal is threatened several times. Mugs provides most of the fun in the play, but she complicates the case by providing misinformation about the moon on the night of the murder. Even the defendant's mother entangles the plot because of her concealment of the switched babies at birth, and Marjorie, the defendant's girlfriend, spends most of her time on the stand sobbing. The women have a limited usefulness in the play and are defined in terms of the men in the play, who manipulate and control them. In fact, Robert Vorlicky explains that the female characters in a great deal of American drama "remain heavily coded, gendered bodies that are subjected to the power of male authority and privilege."[44]

The play not only attempts to bolster the self-esteem of the boys in an era in which maleness, "a precious resource," was seemingly under direct assault because of the paucity of jobs available, but it also provides a model of masculine behavior. One of the tensest moments in the play occurs when the D.A. torments Marjorie, the defendant's girlfriend, on the witness stand. One of the CCC boys heroically interjects to save her honor. A mini ruckus ensues and *Bud Granger* steps forward and challenges the D.A.:

Bud

My name's *Bud Granger*, and I've stood just as much as I can from this guy. He's been pulling a line about us boys, and he better lay off. We ain't a lot of sissies.

Jenkins

The government don't pick that kind.

Toby

(From audience)

You bet they don't, *Buddie.*[45]

Within this scene, the boys have an opportunity to rehearse at being "men," based on familiar cultural constructs. A man's duty is to defend women and protect his own masculinity if it is called into question. If he is accused of being less than a man—that is, a "sissy"—the appropriate response is to fight.

In addition to modeling acceptable masculine behavior, the play also allows the boys a chance to experience American democratic principles firsthand through its manipulation of reality. As Elin Diamond writes, "Realism is more than an interpretation of reality passing as reality; it *produces* 'reality' by positioning its spectator to recognize and verify its truths."[46] *The CCC Murder Mystery* pushes the notion of realism even further. The play's *ultra*-realistic form, i.e., the incorporation of the camp's here and now, references to the enrollees by name and characteristics, and bits such as swearing in each witness and juror, offered the boys a chance to encounter the American judicial system, and the experience reinforced the notion that justice in a democratic society will always be served. "Reality" in *The CCC Murder Mystery* is based on hoary stage conventions from melodrama, vaudeville, and burlesque, but it provides the boys with an unequivocal encounter with romanticized American truth and justice. The play creates a fun house mirror effect in which the untrue (the fictional murder case) merge with the *apparently* real (the recognizable courtroom procedures), and the real (the boys' own situation). For this reason, a central function of *The CCC Murder Mystery* appears to be to prepare the boys for a patriarchal society in which American ideals such as truth and justice always prevail. Just when things look particularly bleak for the defendant and the enrollees, for example, the benevolent and fatherly Judge proclaims: "You boys, out there, just be patient, and I'll promise you I'll do my best to keep things right and see that justice is done for everyone."[47] In Grace Hayward's simulation of the "real" world as experienced by the enrollees, good and evil are easily distinguished, and even in Depression-stricken America, life is ordered and fair. The participatory nature of the play offered tangible proof of this American ideal.

Participatory theatre was not unique to the CCC in the 1930s. In fact, Hayward seems to have drawn on a number of devices that to some degree had been used in other courtroom melodramas of the period. In 1927, for instance, Bayard Veiller's *The Trial of Mary Dugan* had experimented with audience participation. In that play, the audience served as the jury, and a plant at the end delivered the final verdict. The play was a hit in New York and successfully played London, Paris, Berlin, and Budapest. The novelty of involving the audience was praised, but the play had additional merits to earn a following.[48] Ayn Rand's *Night of January 16*, although not as critically praised as *Mary Dugan*, employed a similar device in the way it implicated the audience. When Brooks Atkinson reviewed the production, he described the play's invention: "As a sagacious manager's compensation Mr. Woods therefore offers the fillip of drawing the jury from the audience, seating them on stage, asking them to give the verdict and paying them, it is said, three dollars for that whimsical service."[49] Yet while *The CCC Murder Mystery* took the participatory effect further than these other productions, the desire to completely eliminate the separation between the actors and the spectators for social, educational, and political purposes had a rather chilling theatrical corollary.

In her study of theatre in Nazi Berlin, Yvonne Shafer documents the efforts of the infamous Nazi propagandist Joseph Goebbels to conceive a mass audience united in allegiance to the Party through dramatic presentations. Shafer contends that Goebbels' ideas developed out of director Max Reinhardt's idea of a theatre, which he articulated in 1919:

> We must move out of the proscenium and eliminate the division between the actor and the public! But it is not enough to bring the stage into the auditorium; no, the whole tired tradition that the stage and the auditorium are two realms separate from one another must be destroyed. The viewer must feel that he is a participant in the development of the proceedings. But the curtain must disappear, the actor should, whenever it is possible, move through the auditorium, and it should be decorated in harmony with the scenery.[50]

For Goebbels, the theatre represented an ideal space to gather the masses and as an arena to espouse Nazi principles. It was also, as Shafer points out, an excellent way to bring the workers together in order for the Party to "control their leisure time."[51]

Goebbels particularly recognized the propagandistic power of interactive theatre after attending a performance of a political revue in the mid-1930s called *Trotz alledem!* The experience strengthened his resolve that theatre offered a tool in reinforcing the Party's notion of a homogeneous—politically, ethnically, and spiritually—people united by a single cause. After attending the performance of *Trotz alledem!* Goebbels wrote:

> The masses began to participate. The theatre was reality for them, and soon it no longer was stage against auditorium, rather a *single* great auditorium, a *single* battleground, a *single* great demonstration. This unification on this definitive evening was the evidence of the power of agitation of political theatre.[52]

Similarly, *The CCC Murder Mystery* concludes with a rousing, comical song intended to heighten the communal spirit of the camp. Pamphlets were distributed, and at the end of the performance, one of the actors led the crowd in a song, written by Hayward, which extols the virtues of being a part of the CCC. The song begins, for instance, with an affirmation of the boys' patriotic commitment:

> We're just a lot of guys—who work for Uncle Sam
> We help him out without a doubt
> When he gets in a jam.

And the morale-boosting chorus, reiterates this commitment by exclaiming, "We're

Figure 2. A CCC Classroom. "Work, Play, Study, and Health" were the watch words of the CCC. Educational programs, under which drama activities flourished, occurred in makeshift classrooms. Reproduced from the Collections of the Library of Congress.

wards of Uncle Sam." The lyric also emphasizes the masculinity of the enrollees (referred to here as "rollies") who are presumably adored by women because of their association with the stalwart governmental organization:

> We're CCC rollies now, and we all have "tuck" our vow
> We never bow, or cow-tow-tow
> The dames avow, we're a wow-wow-wow!

Hayward's song epitomizes the efforts of the CCC to minimize notions of individuality and diversity among the boys. The song in effect affirms the boys' allegiance to the State and to the masculinizing principles it represents.

The comparison between theatre in the CCC camps and Nazi propagandistic theatre is not at all meant to imply that the Federal Theatre Project and the Nazi Party used theatre to advocate similar political viewpoints or that Hallie Flanagan and Joseph Goebbels had formed a coalition. But the intriguing connection between the two dramatic forms and the philosophies informing them point to the power theatre wielded in the 1930s. The similarities also highlight the potentially transformative potential that interactive performance offers. These historical instances indicate a belief that identities and allegiances could be formed and rehearsed through an integration of actors and spectators, fiction and "real life," and the stage and the auditorium.

The CCC prided itself in its ability to physically mold the boys into men during their time spent in the camps. In a frequently quoted 1940 report, the director of the Civilian Conservation Corps wrote: "The tanned, healthy, well-muscled men who are discharged from the Corps at the end of their enrollment are in marked contrast to the pale, oft-times stoop-shouldered, undernourished youths who replace them in the camps."[53] While the rigorous lifestyle, disciplined living arrangements, and hard work affected the youths physically, the educational and experiential nature of many of the theatre productions culturally shaped the boys into what were deemed model democratic male citizens (See Figure 2). Plays like *CCC Minstrel Revue* and *The CCC Murder Mystery*, although entertaining and certainly a welcome break from the enrollees' rough and tumble lives, reflect the process of normalization in which traditional images of gender were modeled and rehearsed.

NOTES

[1] "Greetings to the Civilian Conservation Corps," reprinted in *The Public Papers and Addresses of Franklin D. Roosevelt*, Vol. 2, 1933 (New York City: Random House, 1938), 271.

[2] Production is described by a former CCC enrollee, Robert Casemore, in "Thespians in the Forest," *Michigan History* (January/February 2001), 12-17.

[3] "Footlights," *Happy Days* (December 14, 1935). Library of Congress Federal Theatre Project Collection, George Mason University, Fairfax, Virginia.

[4] Ibid.

[5] Ibid.

[6] "Special Release to Boston Papers" (August 1, 1936), issued by the Works Progress Administration, Federal Theatre CCC Project states: "In a survey covering CCC camps

in 26 states undertaken at the suggestion of Hallie Flanagan, national director of the WPA Federal Theatre Project, Major House found that an average of less than 60 per cent [sic] of the enrollees had ever seen a professional stage play. These findings were, in large part, responsible for the development of the new CCC project" (Document in the Library of Congress Federal Theatre Project Collection, George Mason University, Fairfax, Virginia), 2.

[7] Eleanor Scherr Shibley. Interview by Lorraine Brown (August 5, 1976). Tape recording of interview in Library of Congress Federal Theatre Project Collection, George Mason University, Fairfax, Virginia.

[8] Charles Monroe. Interview by Lorraine Brown (November 9, 1978). Transcript of interview in Library of Congress Federal Theatre Project Collection, George Mason University, Fairfax, Virginia.

[9] Included in the packet "From Notes Taken at a Conference on CCC Camp Play Needs," dated August 1936 and signed S.B. Dona. Library of Congress Federal Theatre Project Collection, George Mason University, Fairfax, Virginia.

[10] Ibid.

[11] Ibid.

[12] Qtd. in Roger L. Rosentreter, "Roosevelt's Tree Army," *Michigan History* (January/February 2001), 18.

[13] Gorham cites two "book-length academic studies" that concentrate on the organization and implications of the CCC including John A. Salmond, *The Civilian Conservation Corps, 1933-1942: A New Deal Case Study* (Durham, North Carolina: Duke University Press, 1967), and Michael Sherraden, "The Civilian Conservation Corps: Effectiveness of the Camps" (Ph.D., University of Michigan, 1979), but see also Kenneth Holland and Frank Ernest Hill's *Children and Youth: Youth in the CCC* (Reprint edition, New York: Arno Press, 1974).

[14] Gorham, 232.

[15] Ibid., 235.

[16] Compare to Michel Foucault and his discussion of the "time-table" and its relation to the "control of activity": "But an attempt is also made to assure the quality of the time used: constant supervision, the pressure of supervisors, the elimination of anything that might disturb or distract; it is a question of constituting a totally useful time" (150). Michel Foucault, *Discipline and Punish: The Birth of the Prison System*, trans. by Alan Sheridan (New York: Vinatge Books, 1979).

[17] Holland and Hill, 38-42.

[18] The most controversial aspect of the organization remained the army's involvement throughout its nine year history. The maintenance of the program was divided among four governmental agencies, and the War Department was specifically responsible for the enrollment and transportation of the men to the work sites, as well as provision of their food, clothing, housing, and training in the camps. Because each camp was staffed with army personnel, many were wary of the role the camps were serving. In particular, they perceived the education of the youths as being military-centered and geared toward combat preparation. As the country's entrance into World War II seemed more and more likely, the debate ensued as to whether or not the camps should indeed focus on military training, but a congressional decision was ultimately made to keep them strictly *civilian*-oriented (see Salmond, 194-196). This issue was the subject of a workers theatre production about the CCC called *The Young Go First*, by Peter Martin,

Charles Friedman, and George Scudder, and was staged by Alfred Saxe and Elia Kazan for the Theatre of Action at New York's Park Theatre in May 1935. Broadway program and review clippings in Billy Rose Theatre Collection, New York Public Library, New York City.

[19] Holland and Hill report: "As to data, we have figures for 101,856 white junior enrollees in the eleventh to fourteenth enrollment periods, inclusive, showing their height and weight on entrance to the camps and on discharge. The different age groups made varying gains in both height and weight, the average being .38 of an inch in height and 10.16 pounds in weight for those 25 years of age, and .60 inch in height and 12.97 pounds in weight for those 17 years of age. The 18-year-old group gained 13.07 pounds, and the average for the entire number of men examined was about 12 pounds. Even when it is granted that many of the youth are still growing, the gains are impressive" (191).

[20] Luther C. Wandall, "A Negro in the CCC," *Crisis* 42 (August 1935): 244, 253-254.

[21] Foucault, 138.

[22] Holland and Hill provide the following example: "In one camp it was discovered that many of the boys did not know how to dance. Several of them who had got drunk and made themselves generally objectionable at a camp dance confessed that they had behaved as they did because they felt out of place and resentful. The camp adviser promptly started a class in social dancing. In the group the men were taught how to introduce each other to girls, how to dance, and — in so far as possible — how to carry on a conversation. A number of the men who had misbehaved attended this course, and at a later dance conducted themselves well and agreed that they had had a much better time" (213).

[23] Ibid., 217.

[24] Unpublished script in the Library of Congress Federal Theatre Project Collection, George Mason University, Fairfax, Virginia.

[25] Earl L. House, *CCC Division: As of June 30, 1937,* a comprehensive report contains titles requested from the Federal Theatre Project as well as letters and comments from CCC personnel regarding the dramatic activities sponsored by the Federal Theatre Project. Document labeled "Mrs. Flanagan" is located in the Library of Congress Federal Theatre Project Collection, George Mason University, Fairfax, Virginia.

[26] The playwriting contest was announced in August 1936, which further encouraged the enrollees to take an active role in drama in the camps. The winning script was to receive a production by the Federal Theatre Project. Actually two scripts were chosen, *C.C.C.* by George Gill and Bernard Winstock, and *Return to Death* by P. Washington Porter. Over a year later with some negative publicity for the delay, only *Return to Death* was actually mounted. Unpublished scripts, readers' reports, and correspondences are located in the Library of Congress Federal Theatre Project Collection, George Mason University, Fairfax, Virginia.

[27] *CCC Minstrel Revue*, II-26.

[28] Wandall, 254.

[29] "CCC Youth Refuses To Fan Flies Off Officer; Is Fired," *Norfolk Journal and Guide* (January 13, 1934): 7.

[30] *CCC Minstrel Revue*, II-18.
[31] Ibid., II-14.
[32] Ibid., II-14.
[33] See also Alan Kreizenbeck, "The C.C.C. Murder Mystery," *The Drama Review* (December 1979).
[34] Procedures for presenting the play described in the "Form Letter" to the camp educational advisor accompanying the script of *The CCC Murder Mystery.*
[35] Ibid.
[36] "Federal Theatre Troupe Goes to CCC Camps," From *Progress*, a Delaware WPA magazine circa 1936.
[37] Reprinted in Hallie Flanagan, *Arena: The History of the Federal Theatre* (New York: Benjamin Blom, Inc., 1940).
[38] *C.C.C.* unpublished script in Library of Congress Federal Theatre Project Collection, George Mason University, Fairfax, Virginia. See also Gorham's discussion of the frequent medical experiments on the boys of the CCC: "A number of camps became laboratories for federal and army scientists who wanted human guinea pigs on which to try out vaccinations and medications. Medical experiments were conducted on the enrollees, including malaria and typhoid prevention, and experimental vaccines were tried for pneumonia and meningitis. Agency regulations prevented the enrollee from refusing treatment, testing or experimentation" (241-2).
[39] House's *CCC Division* contains a comprehensive report containing letters and comments from CCC personnel regarding success of the *CCC Murder Mystery. Excerpts From Company Commander Reports* also includes comments from the various regional units where the production played. Undated document in the Library of Congress Federal Theatre Project Collection, George Mason University, Fairfax, Virginia.
[40] Bahn, *Variety* (September 23, 1936). Review in *CCC Murder Mystery* Clipping File, Billy Rose Theatre Collection, New York Public Library, New York City.
[41] "'CCC Murder Mystery' in 189 Camps" Undated document in the Library of Congress Federal Theatre Project Collection, George Mason University, Fairfax, Virginia.
[42] "Special Release to New York State Papers" (December 18, 1936), 1. Library of Congress Federal Theatre Project Collection, George Mason University, Fairfax, Virginia.
[43] *CCC Murder Mystery*, II-22.
[44] Robert Vorlicky, *Act Like a Man: Challenging Masculinities in American Drama* (Ann Arbor: The University of Michigan Press, 1995), 18.
[45] *CCC Murder Mystery*, II-12.
[46] Elin Diamond, *Unmaking Mimesis* (New York: Routledge, 1997), 4.
[47] *CCC Murder Mystery*, II-13.
[48] Some critics remarked that the participatory nature of the play was not wholly new for that time either. Phillip Carr of the *New York Times* (February 24, 1929), when writing about the French production said: "The device of enlisting the public as the jury in the trial, and making them, in some degree, into actors as well as spectators, is not, however, in itself considered to be inconsistent with dramatic art. It is, indeed, admitted to have high classical authority behind it, for is it not to be found in the *Clouds* of Aristophanes? It might have been added that the art form of the masque, so popular in Shakespearean times, depended essentially upon the audience, at certain moments,

taking part in the action and especially in the final dance."
[49] Brooks Atkinson, *New York Times* (September 17, 1935).
[50] Qtd. in Yvonne Shafer, "Nazi Berlin and the Grosses Schauspielhaus," *Theatre in the Third Reich, the Prewar Years: Essays on Theatre in Nazi Germany* (Westport, Connecticut: Greenwood Press, 1995; 103-119), 104.
[51] Shafer., 106.
[52] Qtd. in Shafer, 105.
[53] Qtd. in Holland and Hill, 191.

James Wilson is Assistant Professor of English at LaGuardia Community College. He is currently working on a book about gay and lesbian theatre and performance in the Harlem Renaissance entitled *"Bulldykes, Pansies, and Chocolate Babies": Performance, Race, and Sexuality in the Harlem Renaissance.*

Theatre History Studies 23 (June 2003)

The Gestus of Scene Design: Mordecai Gorelik and the Theatre Union's Production of Brecht's *The Mother*

ANNE FLETCHER

Known for his work with the Group Theatre, his metaphorical approach to scene design, and his seminal history of the theatre, *New Theatres for Old*, Mordecai ("Max") Gorelik was also the first American theatre practitioner to unconditionally embrace the emerging theories of Bertolt Brecht![1] The Theatre Union, with Gorelik as designer, produced the first Broadway production of a Brecht play, *The Mother*, in 1935.[2] This production tested several Brechtian conventions that have since become commonplace, even clichéd — among them projections and visible lighting apparatus. One elusive Brechtian idea, "*gestus*," can be reexamined in the light of this production and thus reveal Brecht and Gorelik as proponents of a new design process—one based on function rather than beauty. Neither Brecht not Gorelik identified the design approach to *The Mother* (or any other production) as specifically "*gestic*," (*Gestus* is most often considered a performative device.) but Gorelik eagerly seized Brecht's concept and applied it to the design process.

Brecht appears to have first used the term "*gestus*" in "Notes on the Opera," an essay that followed the published text of his opera with Weill, *Aufstieg und Fall der Stadt Mahoganny*.[3] John Willett's interpretation of the term as meaning "both gist and gesture, an attitude or a single aspect of an attitude"[4] is particularly useful in applying the concept to scene design. Brecht refers to the "scenic *gestus*" as the essence of a written scene. He discusses "*gestus*" at great length with regard to acting, and he broadens the scope of the concept to include costuming in his writings; however, he never expressly uses "*gestus*" when speaking of scene design. Why he ignores scene design in his gestic compendium is not known. This omission may be due to the fact that Brecht's principal designer, Casper Neher, inherently grasped the concept and employed it in his work. To Brecht, mentioning the term in this light, then, would seem redundant. Nonetheless, Brecht's thoughts on scene design in general are expressed often, and with great respect to the designer's part in decision-making.

Brecht's placement of the designer at the hub of theatrical activity would have appealed to Mordecai Gorelik who felt strongly about the designer's role in creating a production. By 1935, Max Gorelik had already designed five productions for the Group Theatre[5] where he played a significant role in establishing concepts. Gorelik describes his Group Theatre experiences in an article for *Theatre Arts* entitled "I Design for the Group Theatre" (1939). Group participants often acknowledge his pivotal place in the Group's conscience, especially anecdotally in Wendy Smith's *Real Life Drama: the Group Theatre and America 1931-1940* (1990). Even Harold Clurman gave Gorelik "credit where credit was due" retrospectively in *The Fervent Years*. He had also closely collaborated with John Howard Lawson, John Dos Passos and others in the New Playwrights Theatre. He designed this company's logo and brought constructivism to the New York stage in his design for Lawson's political satire *Loud Speaker*. In fact, Mordecai Gorelik might well be considered the first American scene designer (concurrent with Boris Aronson who substituted for him at the Group Theatre when he was away) who followed a truly collaborative process.[6] Undoubtedly, Max Gorelik felt he had something to gain, artistically and intellectually, by allying himself with the man most of the Theatre Union members came to despise. It is fair to say that Brecht's rationality would appeal to Gorelik, as he approached theatre (and life) through a similarly objective yet opinionated lens.

Gorelik continued to champion Brechtian principles for the rest of his life[7], utilizing them in his design process, incorporating Brechtian theory into his playwriting and directing in academic theatre.[8] The choice Gorelik made in 1935 to follow the path of Brecht (and not that of Stanislavsky) frequently brought him derision rather than acclaim.

Characteristically, Gorelik refused to veer from his aesthetic and persevered. As a result of this tenacious designer's attempts to marry his dramatic theory with practice in the 1930s, we cannot only chronicle the career of a single theatre artist, but we can examine Gorelik's career as an emblem for the changing American theatre. The much ignored Theatre Union production of Brecht's *The Mother* offers an early example of the contentiousness that often arises between proponents of Brecht's theories and those who prefer a more realistic route. In the case of *The Mother*, the only theatre personnel representing Brecht's side were Brecht himself, sometimes composer Hans Eisler, and Max Gorelik.

Manuel Gomez served as Brecht's official translator, but it was the other German-speaking member of the Theatre Union, designer Mordecai Gorelik, became intrigued by Brecht's theories, if not by his demeanor. While Brecht criticized Gorelik's work as overly "picturesque" at first, Gorelik quickly figured out how to wed his style of production to Brecht's dramatic form.[9] Although he knew nothing of *Verfremdung*, Gorelik knew a great deal about the German theatre.[10] He was even better acquainted with the workers' theatre in America. Breaking the "fourth wall" was an impassioned goal Gorelik shared with John Howard Lawson and others from the New Playwrights Theatre. Gorelik "had what it took" to design the American premier of Brecht's *The Mother*. Despite some criticism of the Theatre Union designer, Brecht thought so, too, and, in retrospect, he wished the designer had been given more leeway in the production process.[11]

Four published photographs of the play in production have emerged for this study. (See Berlau, Brecht, Hubalek, Palitzsch, Rulicke, nd, 334). They and photographs of Mordecai Gorelik's model reveal him to have been extraordinarily farsighted in his application of a screen and projections.[12] The promptbook reveals that more than thirty-five slides were used in the production! Stage Manager Peter Xantho kept copious notes, among them a list of the slides, in order, by title.[13] The technical complexity of the production is alluded to in Xantho's daily log on numerous occasions; often there are references to glitches regarding the slide projector. In addition, there are much more detailed sketches in this particular promptbook than in others assembled for Theatre

Union productions by the same stage manager. This one includes a rudimentary light plot and very specific lighting areas. A large "Thank God!" is scrawled at the end of the scene change list![14]

The difficulties involved in executing the design concept with 1935 technology and its overall effects were not the most pressing problems the Theatre Union faced with regard to Bertolt Brecht. The most striking conflicts arose between Brecht and the director (Victor Wolfson) or the adapter/translator (Paul Peters). The overall atmosphere, throughout the rehearsal process and the run of the show, was unpleasant. The stage manager's daily log is filled with actor and musician infringements from tardiness to drunken behavior.[15]

From its outset, Brecht's association with the Theatre Union was an unlikely and unpleasant one, plagued by miss-communication after miss-communication. He apparently pinned his hopes for widespread acclaim in the United States on this production while the company was not even aware of the theoretical underpinnings of his work. The Theatre Union found *The Mother* compatible with its ideals,[16] but its members scarcely knew who Bertolt Brecht was, let alone suspected whom he might become. Theatre Union board member and playwright Albert Maltz recalled: "To my best recollection none of us had any knowledge of Brecht's concept of the epic theatre. . . ."[17] The Theatre Union entered its alliance with Brecht with the characteristic naiveté of "bleeding heart" liberals of depression era America. Nonetheless, and despite themselves, the German playwright and the company (much credit owing to its set designer, Mordecai Gorelik) produced what can be viewed as ***the first "Epic Theatre" production in America!***

Problems with the Theatre Union's production of *The Mother* began early with the selection of a script translation. The company thought it had obtained permission from Brecht to utilize Paul Peters' translation. They believed that Brecht's initial dislike for the version had been alleviated when they dispatched board member Manuel Gomez to Denmark to negotiate with Brecht. Therefore, when Brecht arrived in New York, his passage paid for by the Theatre Union, company members were taken aback by his rage at the script they were only days away from performing. With no knowledge of Brecht's Epic theories, Theatre Union members could not understand why he would be outraged at the addition of [melodramatic] scenes and the omission of others. Ironically, Peters had struggled to overcome what he and the company believed to be weaknesses in Brecht's text: "its fragmentary quality, its abrupt changes of mood and style and its insufficient dramatizations of personal scenes. . . ."[18] Theatre Union members, although champions of the working class, had no idea of how Brecht's political views and dramatic theories informed his productions.[19] By employing a "fourth wall" approach, the very first stage moments of the Theatre Union's production, then, violated the major Brechtian principle — "alienation."

Brecht vehemently criticized the Theatre Union director's treatment of the scene in which the Mother rises from her sickbed to her revolutionary calling. Brecht's intention was the juxtaposition of discrete scenes and music, not the blending of book and music here:

> The chorus 'Die Partei ist in Gefahr' upset the whole production. Instead of placing the singer (or singers) near the musical apparatus or else offstage the

> director had the singers burst into the room where the mother lay ill, inviting her with emphatic gestures to come to the Party's aid.[20]

"Educated workers," according to Brecht would have realized that the expunged scenes were crucial to the political impact he desired; they would have understood that the efficacy of the production was paramount. The Theatre Union, although obviously sympathetic to the workers' cause, wanted its audience to follow the play's action, to be swayed toward political action by *empathizing* with the workers' plights, and to remain for the duration of the show.[21]

Brecht had added scenes in his adaptation of Gorki's novel through Stark-Weisenborn; Peters removed some of them, including the Mother's tearing of a page from the Bible.[22] Peters also rearranged the order of the scenes. Brecht's placement of scenes was crucial and in keeping with his Epic structure and efforts to minimize pathos. In Brecht's version, the Mother is informed of her son's death early enough in the course of the action to continue her revolutionary work with a clear head; in the Peters' translation, news of the son's death arrives too close to the sickbed scene to avoid a tendency toward melodrama. The final assault on Brecht's Epic sensibilities came when director Victor Wolfson refused to allow the use of slogans shouted by the Bolsheviks to the masses in the final scene. Peters was building dramatically, from an emotional and psychological approach, to the climax of what he saw as a workable dramatic structure — the antithesis of what Bertolt Brecht extolled. "The result was a hybrid production which satisfied no one."[23] It lacked the Epic structure and hardline political punch Brecht sought; at the same time, it failed to satisfy the traditional well-made-play-goer.

Rehearsals with Brecht in the room were chaos. Brecht did not speak English, but no translator was needed for the resounding expletives, "Das ist Scheisse! Das ist Dreck!" that shook the Civic Repertory Theatre. Brecht continually bullied twenty-three-year-old director Victor Wolfson[24] to whom he had apparently taken an immediate dislike.[25] Gomez, Maltz and Sklar offered similar recollections of the rehearsal process. Maltz described Brecht's behavior:

> He tried to take over the direction by badgering Wolfson with constant comments, by running up on stage and trying through an interpreter to tell the actors how to play their parts . . . he had a voice that would have humiliated the fight announcer at Madison Square Garden; it blasted out of him.[26]

Sklar recalled:

> Brecht would sit in the audience, mutter to himself, then take off like a beechcraft plane, hop up on stage and start screaming. . . . Day after day he'd come in with 'rewrites'— one scene at a time. It was soon clear that the 'rewrites' were simply reversions to the original script.[27]

Finally, when Wolfson could see no other alternative, he seized Brecht by the collar, literally dragged him up an aisle, and threw him out the theatre door, locking it behind him.[28] Mordecai Gorelik found Brecht and Eisler on the street, near the stage door.

Apparently afraid to attempt to go back inside, they asked Gorelik to fetch them their caps![29]

In retrospect, it is easy to see what frustrated Brecht. From his perspective, the company's production was an inept and bourgeois interpretation of his theories. At the time, he even took his complaints to V. J. Jerome, chief cultural officer of the Communist Party in the United States. "Comrade" Jerome listened to the arguments on both sides and mediated, assigning responsibilities to the Theatre Union and to Brecht. Brecht broke with the established agreement almost immediately, stating that he was not a Party member and therefore was not bound by the agreement. The Theatre Union members were not members, either, so the arbitration failed miserably and the rehearsal process returned to mayhem.[30]

Almost twenty years later, in an article entitled "Brecht: I am the Einstein of the New Stage Form," Gorelik acknowledged that the set for *The Mother* was primarily Brecht's creation. With insight and humor, he recalled his naiveté, his fascination with Brecht's mercurial personality— and the speed with which he had comprehended Brecht's scenic intentions. Apparently when the designer challenged Brecht with the question, "Why don't you simply say you don't want settings — only properties?" the playwright answered in the affirmative, and the two of them took it from there.[31] Gorelik's description of the set corroborates Brecht's:

> A small revolving stage partitioned through the center stood just under a projection screen. At stage right were two grand pianos. The stage was illuminated by rows of visible spotlights. . . . The projection screen was in constant use as an editorial commentary. . . . For many people the screen was especially disturbing; it was resented as making obvious statements and detracting from the action.[32]

In a letter written more than thirty years after the fact, Gorelik recalled how he used the screen:

> One example bore the caption 'Class Struggle.' Another showed a grocery list written down by Mother, imitating her untutored writing — written for projection with my left hand. On occasion the screen complemented the setting below it. For instance, the factory scene was represented only by an acetylene tank with workers grouped around it. Projected on the screen was a photo of the outside of the factory, combined with a photo of Mr. Suekhlinov [sic], the owner.[33]

The production promptbook's list of the slides utilized augments Gorelik's description, the production photographs, and the extant photographs of Gorelik's model. This list corroborates the idea of ***gestus* of scene design** by the way it indicates the reduction of each scene to its most essential element. The approach differs from the concept of metaphor that would pervade Gorelik's later designs and is most publicly apparent in such pieces as *The Golden Boy.*

In the list of representative slides that follows, my commentary on the slides is in bold type. The total number of slides utilized appears to total thirty-seven—in 1935!

Slide 1 (See Figure 1)- "The life of the revolutionist Pelagea Vlasova of Tversk" (In this visual equation or metaphor, the revolutionist is Pelagea; Pelagea = revolutionist, the essence of, and revolutionist= Pelagea.)

Slide 3- shopping list in kopeks (written with Mordecai Gorelik's left hand, this list shows the cost of groceries, item by item, in kopeks; in this manner, the list offers up the essence of poverty in an objective, "factual" way that can be, at best, more effective than a photograph of the impoverished, and at least, an earlier example of Brecht's theory in practice. This exemplifies the *gestus* of scene design at its most successful.)

Slide 4- "Women like Pelagea Vlasova. In every country of the world there are... (Four faces of working women in photograph)- (Now, the issue is extended to one of gender; Pelagea= woman= worker, etc.)

Slide 8- "Factory" (This is the slide to which Max Gorelik alludes—and which Brecht explains in *Brecht on Theatre*, stating that the importance lay in the fact that the factory was owned by Mr. S., not the workers.)

Remember, the stage was relatively bare. In keeping with Brechtian principles, the lighting apparatus was exposed and the pianos were visible (but, as Brecht complained, they were not lit well enough to make a statement). As script and ground plans indicate, there was some furniture and there were realistic props, but the thrust of the visual impact was relegated to the projections—a technique with which the 1935 audience was unaccustomed.

Slide 14- "Membership card of Pelagea Vlasova in the Russian Social Democratic Labor Party" (The membership card is the physical object that connotes the revolutionary spirit in all its manifestations; this slide is the essence of the scene and the play.)

Slide 15- "The mother learns to read and write." (This is probably one of the slides found problematic by auditors of the production. Those projecting words also uttered in the text were most likely considered redundant by audience members and critics.)

Slide 16- "Worker"

Slide 17- "Class Struggle"

Slide 19- "In Praise of Learning"

Slide 23- "Prisoners—in circle." (photograph) - (The prisoner's circle, connotes unity among the prisoners.)

Slide 28- "Picture of Pavel" (standing)

Slide 29- "Picture of Pavel" (rogues' gallery)

Slide 31- " Soldiers running to battle" (photograph)

Slide 32- " Statistics of Russian soldiers killed and wounded in battles in World War" (Of course, this selective use of statistics would become more familiar to the American public with the Federal Theatre Project's Living Newspapers.)

Slide 33- "Dead Soldiers" (photograph)[34]

Although the slides from this production of *The Mother* do not survive and only a few production photographs exist, the list alone is a telling artifact for an examination of the scenography of early Epic theatre in America.

While Epic design involves the placement of objects on the stage according to their respective functions and without a deliberate attempt at achieving either artifice

Figure 1. The set showing the first slide: "The life of the revolutionist Pelagea Vlasova of Tversk." Courtesy of Special Collections, Morris Library, Southern Illinois University.

or beauty, like any design, its creation involves a process of selectivity. Points of emphasis, in keeping with a Marxist prospective, are established. For example, in *The Mother*, with reference to SLIDE 8:

> the factory was represented not so much by a photograph of the building as by the picture of the owner; the point of the scene was not that workers were in a factory, but that the factory belonged to Mr. Sukhlinov and not to them...[35]

This exhibition of the kind of slide usage, descended from Piscator's "Schweik" and adapted to suit Brecht's needs, is undoubtedly **the first in America!** Yet, it comes as no surprise that at the time it was not recognized as groundbreaking. The technique (and its companion theories) was not understood.

At the time, predating even the Federal Theatre Projects' *Triple- A Plowed Under*, the screen effect was considered unusual: " the screen . . . on which titles and photographs are flashed while the action transpires below, is not a success."[36]

Reviews of *The Mother* indicate that critics found the style of production baffling. Opinions of its effectiveness varied greatly and many reflected the same irony that has come to characterize Brecht's subsequent work and that of those who emulate him: The harder he tried to "distance" his audience, the more his audience seemed to want to empathize with his protagonists: "Miss Henry has a quiet dignity about her that gives the piece a quality of genuineness despite its tendency to spell everything out on a black-board or throw it on a screen."[37] Arthur Pollock of the *Brooklyn Daily Eagle*, Richard Lockridge of the *New York Sun* and an anonymous reviewer for *Women's Wear Daily* all weighed in on the negative side regarding the set as well: "The proscenium arch bears quotations from Thomas Jefferson and Karl Marx."[38] "The scenery is only intimated, and after a thing has been said four or five times, and sung twice, it is spelled out on a motion picture screen. There is certainly no excuse for anyone's missing the point."[39] ". . . one wondered why the audience should learn from screen titles what the dialogue can and does describe."[40]

Brooks Atkinson stood alone in his defense of the production. While he found the dramaturgy lacking, he was intrigued by the style of production:

> The style of production is considerably more interesting than the drama. . . . The scenery is hardly more than a skeletonized background lighted by batteries of lamps that are quite visible. Above the background is a screen where movie titles are shown to clarify the story, to announce the title of the chant or to show photographs that symbolize the significance of the scene. In the shadows of the wings are two pianos. . . . Although the style of production may sound eccentric in this description, it seems thoroughly logical in the theatre, and in its free confession of stage mechanics it has a refreshing frankness. All the bars are down between the actors and the audience.[41]

In his review, Atkinson even acknowledged Brecht's indebtedness to Piscator. It is also interesting to note how Atkinson chose the phrase "stage mechanics."

Independently of each other, Bertolt Brecht and Mordecai Gorelik had selected similar phrases to articulate their respective aesthetics.

By the time Gorelik met Brecht, the designer had already codified much of his own theory of the theatre; for example, he had already published "Theatre is a Weapon"(1934).[42] His conversations with Brecht undoubtedly confirmed his beliefs about the purpose and process of the theatre. Gorelik did not simply adopt Brecht's theories and methods wholesale; he sought to expand his own thinking, to develop it, to study and interpret Brecht. He would follow Brecht back to Europe and question the playwright/theorist incessantly. Some of this study would express itself later in the section entitled "INDUCTIVE SETTING" in *New Theatres for Old* (1940). Here, in retrospect, Gorelik explains Epic design. In this chapter, Gorelik emphasizes that the fundamental scenic principles of Epic scene design require the creation of settings that are non-illusory, utilitarian, and *functional.* The purpose of the Epic setting is not to imitate, but, rather, to elucidate. Gorelik carefully contrasts Epic design with other styles of production. He is precise in his explication of the Epic design process.

> It is the *function* which is essential. Hence, Epic design, instead of reproducing the object . . . or symbolizing it by means of a significant part . . . represents the object by means of its *function.* [emphasis mine][43]

By 1940, Gorelik had internalized the Epic design process. Five years earlier, under Brecht's supervision, Gorelik had followed this process in the creation of his design for *The Mother.* His depiction of the factory scene clarifies the Epic design process as parallel to the Epic idea of *gestus* in acting. According to Brecht,

> the factory was represented not so much by a photograph of the building as by the picture of the owner; the point of the scene was not that the workers were in a factory, but that the factory belonged to Mr. Sukhlinov and not to them. . . .[44]

The selection of the precise object or property to epitomize an idea is at the root of Epic design. Gorelik was quite proud when Brecht complimented him on his knack for identifying the "right" objects.[45]

Even at the outset of his relationship with Brecht, Gorelik sensed that he was "in on the ground floor" of something big. Even he, though, was taken aback by Brecht's bold introduction:

> 'I am the Einstein of the new stage form,' he announced calmly.
> 'What stage form is that?' I asked.
> 'Epic theatre.'
> 'Never heard of it.'
> 'You will.'[46]

In 1935, Gorelik's newly formed alliance with Bertolt Brecht may have given him the courage to follow his instincts — even if it meant going against the tide of the American theatre. While his place as Brecht's interpreter would be usurped by Eric

Bentley, Gorelik would go on writing about Brecht well into the 1950s, as Brecht's popularity in America burgeoned, and beyond. Brecht's impact on Gorelik's career cannot be overemphasized. *The Mother* was a watershed for Mordecai Gorelik; it seems he chose his path as a non-realistic designer based on this experience. Gorelik's concept of the scenic metaphor stems, in part, from his idea of Epic design.

The Theatre Union's production of *The Mother* introduced Bertolt Brecht as a player on the New York stage, and, while the production was a nightmare for many of its participants and did not win critical acclaim, it further established the Theatre Union as America's only professional leftist theatre. It also established the career path of designer, Mordecai Gorelik. *The Mother* epitomized the *gestus* of Max Gorelik's approach to scenography.

WORKS CITED

Atkinson, B. 1935. *New York Times*. 20 November: n.p.
Barnes, H. 1935. *New York Herald Tribune*. 20 November: n.p.
Baxandall, L. 1967. "Brecht in America, 1935" *TDR Drama Review* vol. 12: 69-7.
Berlau, Brecht, Hubalek, Palitzsch, Rulicke, ed. *Theaterarbeit*. Progress-Verlag Johann Fladung Düsseldorf n.d.
Brecht, B. 1965. *The Mother*, Lee Baxandall trans. New York: Grove Press.
Fuegi, J. 1972. *The Essential Brecht*. Los Angeles, CA: Hennesser & Ingalls
Gomez, M. 1965. Letter to Lee Braxanall as quoted in Braxanall, 71. 12 July.
Gorelik, M. 1957. "Brecht: I Am the Einstein of the New Stage Form," Theatre Arts March
__________ 1967. Letter to Lee Baxandall. 17 January.
__________ 1940. *New Theatres for Old*. New York: Samuel French.
__________ 1935. Photographs of *The Mother* model. Gorelik Collection, Special Collections, Morris Library, Southern Illinois University-Carbondale.
Larkin, M. n.d. *The History of the Theatre Union*. New York: Billy Rose Theatre Collection, New York Public Library.
Lockridge, R. 1935. *New York Sun*. 20 November: n.p.
Lyon, J. 1980. *Bertolt Brecht in America*. Princeton, NJ: Princeton University Press.
Maltz, Albert as quoted on Braxanall, 71.
The Mother 1935. Program. New York: Billy Rose Theatre Collection, New York Public Library.
The Mother 1935. Promptbook. New York: Billy Rose Theatre Collection, New York Public Library.
Pollock, A. 1935. *Brooklyn Daily Eagle*. 20 November: n.p.
Sklar, George. 1966. Letter to Lee Braxanall as quoted in Brazanall, 71
Waldorf, W. 1935. *New York Evening Post*. 20 November: n.p.
Willett, J., ed. 1964. *Brecht on Theatre*. New York: Hill and Wang.
Wolfson, V. 1990. "Brecht Harangued in German, But the Elegant Man Said Nothing," *The Dramatist Guild Quarterly*. Winter: 30.
Women's Wear Daily. 1935. n.a., n.p., n.d.

NOTES

1. Gorelik's work with Brecht predates that of Eric Bentley, although Bentley went on, of course, to translate and represent the German's theories in America.
2. In 1935, apart from a couple school productions of *He Who Says Yes* and the Philadelphia Symphony's performance of the music from *The Flight of the Lindberghs*, Bertolt Brecht was known in the United States only by a short-lived English version of *Three Penny Opera* staged in New York in 1933. (Lyon 1980, 6) He received scant mention in even the most leftist American publications; in fact, Brecht took a backseat to the now forgotten Friedrich Wolf (*The Sailors of Cattaro*) and Hans Eisler (composer for *The Mother*).
3. Willett 42
4. Willett 42
5. *1931-, Success Story, Big Night, Men in White,* and *Gentlewoman*
6. Gorelik studied with Robert Edmond Jones, assisted Cleon Throckmorton, and competed with Lee Simonson among others. These designers are known for establishing production concepts rather than eliciting them from a production team as Gorelik did.
7. Gorelik died in March, 1990.
8. Gorelik retired from his position as Research Professor of Theater at Southern Illinois University-Carbondale in 1972. During the later part of his time in academia, Gorelik traveled extensively across the United States, conducting seminars in his "scenic imagination" process and promoting his plays. He remained active for most of his remaining years.
9. Mordecai Gorelik, "Brecht: I am the Einstein of the New Stage Form," *Theatre Arts* March 1957: 72
10. Gorelik traveled to Europe in 1922 and again in 1932, witnessing many productions, including *Massemensch* at the Volksbühne (Gorelik, Copy of Letter to Gregory Stragnell, p. 23 Gorelik Diary, Special Collections, Morris Library, uncatalogued.) On the 1922 European tour, Gorelik met up with Robert Edmund Jones and Kenneth McGowan

as they prepared to write *Continental Stgaecraft.*

11. We were extremely surprised to see the excellent designer given so little chance to carry out his aims. He had no say in the grouping and positioning of the actors, nor was he consulted about the costumes...

> Even the lighting was planned without him. His construction allowed the lighting mechanism and the music mechanism to be plainly seen. But as the pianos were not illuminated during the musical numbers it looked as if there had merely been no room for them anywhere else... Eisler experienced the same treatment with his music. (Willett, 82)

12. Gorelik Collection, File 9/22, Special Collectons, Morris Library, Southern Illinois University, Carbondale.
13. Promptbook, *The Mother*, Billy Rose Collection, NCOF+ Acc. No. 92795ZA, .New York Public Library, Lincoln Center, New York, New York.
14. Promptbook, *The Mother*
15. Promptbook, *The Mother*, Billy Rose Theatre Collections, New York Public Library (Examples include entries from 26 March, 1935; 27 March 1935; 4 April 1935; 20 November 1935; 24 November 1935; 3 December 1935)
16. The Theatre Union's Mission Statement (as it appears on each of the company's programs):

WHAT IS THE THEATRE UNION?

The Theatre Union is the first professional social theatre in America. It was founded on three main ideas, which, interlocking as they do, differentiate it from all other theatres.

First— we present plays that deal boldly with the deep-going social conflicts, the economic, emotional, and cultural problems that confront the majority of the people. Our plays speak directly to this majority, whose lives usually are caricatured or ignored on the stage...

Second — we have established the lowest price scale in New York... People who have been barred from the theatre by high prices can attend our plays.

Third— we organize our own audience, through subscriptions and through theatre party benefits...

17. Lee Baxandall, "Brecht in America," *Tulane Drama Review*, vol. 12 (1967): 71
18. Ibid.
19. In retrospect, Brecht said:

> Politically-educated workers...would never have accepted the theatre's view that the big (though only seven-minute-long) anti-war propaganda scene in the third act must at all costs be cut, on the grounds that limiting the play to two hours was all-important to the public. (Willett 82)

20. Willett 82-83
21. The reworking of two particular scenes and Brecht's comments on Peters' alterations to *The Mother*'s text explain the source of Brecht's rage. Gorki's novel opens with a panoramic view of the city, gradually focusing in on the Vlassov family as exemplars of the broader situation. (Fuegi 1972, 55; 53) The Stark-Weisenborn version provides exposition at its opening through a traditional "fourth wall" scene in which Pelagea Vlassova discusses her son Pavel's (and her own) economic situation with a neighbor. (Willett 84) Brecht keeps the character of the son onstage, but he remains silent throughout the protagonist's direct expression of her circumstance to the audience. Pavel exits and a chorus follows. Paul Peters conflates the two openings,

reverting to an intimate dialogue between mother and son.(Fuegi, 53)

22. Lyon 9

23. Lyon 9

24. Wolfson 1990 30

25. Baxandall 73

26. Baxandall 74

27. Baxandall 75

28. Wolfson 30

29. Gorelik, Letter to Lee Baxandall, 17 January 1967

30. Baxandall 76

31. Gorelik, "Brecht..." 72-73

32. Gorelik, *New Theatres For Old* 396

33. Gorelik, Letter to Baxandall

34. Promptbook *The Mother*

35. Willett 83

36. Howard Barnes, 20 November 1935, np. Of note as well, the screen effect in *The Glass Menagerie* was cut for the original production in 1945, a decade later.

37. Wilella Waldorf, *New York Evening Post*, 20 November 1935, np

38. Arthur Pollock, *Brooklyn Daily Eagle*, 20 November 1935, np

39. Richard Lockridge, *New York Sun*, 20 November 1935, np

40. *Women's Wear Daily*, nd, np

41. Brooks Atkinson, *New York Times*, 20 November 1935, np

42. By this time, Gorelik had already written "Theatre is a Weapon" and "The Conquest of Stage Space."

Brecht's use of such words as "apparatus" and "mechanism" (Willett's trans.) are similar to Gorelik's vocabulary in discussing, for example, *Sailors of Cattaro*. "Workmanlike" is a term often applied, in a positive sense, to Gorelik's designs, and by Gorelik in speaking of design.

43. Gorelik, *New Theatres for Old*, 423

44. Willett 83

45. Gorelik, "Brecht: I Am the Einstein of the New Stage Form," 87: "As a designer, the highest praise I ever received from Brecht came during a visit to the staging of his *Round Heads and Peaked Heads* in Copenhagen...Brecht was especially troubled by the major setting—that of a town square. For this the designer had furnished a view of houses in an open area, center stage. I suggested that the property man bring in all the shopkeepers' signs he could round up: a sugar cone from a confectioner's; a wooden

umbrella; a big, gloved hand from the mercer's; an enormous pretzel from the baker's, and so on. Hung in one assortment in the middle of the stage, these conveyed some of the activity of small business in the center of a modern town. 'The Gorelik effect,' according to Brecht."

46. Gorelik, "Brecht" 73

Anne Fletcher is an Assistant Professor in the Theater Department at Southern Illinois University-Carbondale. Her work has appeared in Theatre History Studies, Theatre Journal, and Theatre Symposium. She has presented at ATHE, ASTR, IFTR, MATC, and the SETC Theatre History Symposium. Her book on Group Theatre designer Mordecai Gorelik's experiences and insights into the 1920s and 1930s is forthcoming from SIU Press.

Book Reviews

Staging Desire: Queer Readings of American Theater History. Edited by Kim Marra and Robert A. Schanke. Ann Arbor, MI: The University of Michigan Press, 2002. pp. x + 404. $60 cloth, $22.95 paper.

During my early years in graduate school, I immersed myself in pre-twentieth century dramas written by United States authors: Tyler, Dunlap, Mowitt, Stone, Bird, Howard, Aiken, Boucicault, Daly, Herne, and Harrington, to name a few — even the works of more obscure authors immortalized in the multivolume *America's Lost Plays* series (Indiana UP, 1975). Imagine my pleasure when I would bypass familiar monologues from Williams, Miller, Mamet, or even Shepard for audition material in favor of a juicy speech of Clyde Fitch's, especially from *The City*. Regardless of the quality of my actorly efforts (and my appropriateness, or not, for the role), directors always were hooked on the material: "Tell me more about the play?" "Funny name, Clyde Fitch. Never heard of the guy." "American? When did he write?"

George Rand, the conflicted protagonist in Fitch's *The City*, provided the male actor with pools of emotion to dive into. It was outright fun to flirt with the edges of melodrama within the realist acting traditions encouraged by directors, both inside and outside the academy. And while I knew about the popularity of Fitch's plays in turn-of-the-century New York, and I enjoyed thinking — at the time — about Fitch's texts in relationship to other literary genres in late nineteenth-century America (prose fiction and essays, in particular), it would not be until the application of new historicism, stage semiotics, auto/biography studies, and gay/lesbian/queer theory that the breadth of perspectives from which to explore Clyde Fitch's life, times, and creative output was fully acknowledged. I certainly did not know as much about Clyde Fitch as I do now, and for that, I am grateful to the rise in diversified fields of critical inquiry — especially those that respect the advances made in queer theory — and to the scholarly team behind *Staging Desire*.

The University of Michigan Press is once again at the forefront in publishing noteworthy contemporary theater scholarship with its recent title, *Staging Desire: Queer Readings of American Theater History* (2002), a volume in its impressive series, "Triangulations: Lesbian/Gay/Queer Theater/Drama/Performance" (general editors, Jill Dolan and David Roman). Under the astute editorship of Kim Marra and Robert Schanke (who also are contributors to the volume), twelve additional essayists in *Staging Desire* bring further into the light of theater history studies the unheralded along side the more well-known writers, lyricists, critics, dancers, and designers whose careers peaked toward the end of the nineteenth-century to the mid-twentieth century. *Staging Desire* is a "sequel" to Marra and Schanke's well-received *Passing Performances: Queer Readings of Leading Players in American Theater History* (U of Michigan P, 1998). Together, these two volumes stand as significant contributions to the field of theater history studies — to a broadening of the ways in which drama, theater, and performance histories and historical *information* are read, interpreted, and disseminated by and throughout culture. It is also critical to note the useful coordination of the contents in Marra and Schanke's two books — that is, the ways in which the collections "speak to one another." For example, it is very good planning on the part of the editors to have had an article on Elizabeth "Bessie" Marbury in *Passing Performances*, since her personal and professional lives crossed so many of the artists who are highlighted in *Staging Desire*. These useful connections between theater personnel occur frequently throughout the two books.

The collection is divided into three sections: "Playwrights and Lyricists," "Critics and Audiences," and "Designers and Dancers." The opening division focuses on eight playwrights and lyricists in U.S. theater: Clyde Fitch (in an essay by Kim Marra, who, I'm pleased to note, quotes George Rand's famous monologue from *The City* in its entirety), Rachel Crothers (by J. K. Curry), Mercedes de Acosta (by Robert Schanke), Djuna Barnes (by Susan Clark), George Kelly (by Billy Harbin), Cole Porter (by Mark Fearnow), Lorenz Hart (by Jeffrey Smart), and William Inge (by Albert Wertheim). Characteristic of the entire collection, each of the essays in the opening section of the collection are well-researched, written in lively, engaging prose, and filled with intelligent, insightful commentary about their subject matters. Rarely, however, do anecdote, gossip, and innuendo — references difficult to substantiate — filter into the critics' arguments. These few instances undercut the historians' otherwise scrupulous attention to defensible arguments and detail that mark the collection. Documented evidence is a lasting commodity in a collection that links the personal to the professional — and all the more so in queer readings of specific subjects because so many continue to resist the applicability of this evidence to strategies of (historical) interpretation and analysis.

An invaluable service to the reader is the care which the editors have taken to ensure that the goals of individual essays are clearly articulated at the beginning of each piece (this feature is often sorely missing in most collections, an absence that only emphasizes the arbitariness of a collection's selections, which in turn calls attention to a collection's lack of focus). By providing this clarity, each essay is linked to the strategies, definitions, and intentions established by the editors in their "Introduction." Furthermore, the collection is graced with extremely useful intertextual references. For example, the significance of a particular kind of lifestyle in Greenwich Village as lived by Djuana Barnes (as explored by Susan Clark) is linked to a comparable life experienced by Robert Edmond Jones (the Barnes connection is made in Jane Peterson's piece on Jones), which serves to enhance the sexually-inflected contours of both artists' lives. Likewise, it is extremely helpful to read about the diverse images of masculinity in the Harlem Renaissance (in James Wilson's article), and then to be referred to Lisa Merrill's essay (in Wilson's text itself and not in an endnote) on the nineteenth-century constructions of masculinity embodied in actors Edwin Forrest and Edwin Booth. This attention to intertextual detail — a conscious choice by the editors to help the reader make connections throughout a sizable chunk of American theater history — stitches the essays together as a coherent collection, and it is an editorial strategy that reinforces the value of the queer readings it offers.

Focusing on the individual essays, I recommend Billy J. Harbin's "George Kelly,

American Playwright: Characters in the Hands of an Angry God" as an exemplary piece that juggles appealingly the critic's various roles of historian, social commentator, theater scholar (and advocate), and "queer" reader. Throughout his essay, Harbin strikes an agreeable, effective balance among biographical information (much culled from personal interviews with Kelly's family members), literary analyses, and theoretical application when focusing on George Kelly's life and contributions to the theater. Harbin sets out to deepen one's insight into Kelly's craft and art by focusing on "two complex influences at work in Kelly's plays" that have hitherto been overlooked in Kelly scholarship: "Kelly's rigid Irish Catholic upbringing, overseen by . . . the domineering presence of his mother, Mary Kelly, and, secondly, his homosexuality" (126). In the hands of Harbin, what might have become a jargon-ridden psychoanalytic detour (which is not to imply that a psychoanalytic reading would be inappropriate) is, in fact, a skillful, layered reading of biography (without overstatement) — it progresses from a discussion of Kelly as one of the youngest children in a family of ten (and the imbalanced relationship between his mother and father) to a measured account of Kelly's class-conscious relationship to his lifetime partner, William Weagly. These discussions invite the reader to think about George Kelly as he experiences life inside and outside the queer spaces of his particular time and place. These events, the critic demonstrates — and not simply intimates — directly impact the art that Kelly produces, much of which is "managed as a legitimate outlet for his homoerotic persona . . . [his] secret self" (141). Harbin invites us to consider, amid his own opinions on the matters, why Kelly seems to write with a gender bias against women, why Kelly incorporates such "stringent moral judgments" (138) in his plays, and how the productions of Kelly's work are situated among those of his contemporaries. Harbin's assessments are logical, insightful, and clearly argued.

This correlation between one's personal, queer history and the evolving nature of one's "queer" creative expression is demonstrated with much aplomb in the essays throughout the collection. Among the pieces that reflect the range of scholarly approaches that create the foundations for the "queer readings" that typify the collection are: biographical study and correspondences that ground Kim Marra's compellingly documented essay that convincingly argues for the lasting influence of Oscar Wilde's brief, but highly influential relationship with Clyde Fitch on the latter's American's theatrical contributions; Robert Schanke also substantiates for the theater historian the value of "queering" letter exchanges as he constructs an 'epistolary' foundation for his study of Mercedes de Acosta in "Say What You Will about Mercedes de Acosta"; J. K. Curry and Albert Wertheim rely upon sharp, nuanced analyses of texts (i.e., character development, dialogue, and thematics) to "queer" their readings of the writings of Rachel Crothers and William Inge, respectively; and in "Djuana Barnes: The Most Famous Unknown," Susan Clark astutely refers to a variety of prose sources, written by Barnes, to contextualize her critique of the layered, poetic language in Barnes's dramas that invite a "queering" of the playwright's dense, literary theatricals.

In the second section of the collection, "Critics and Audiences" and the final section, "Designers and Dancers," the essayists continue to vary their critical approaches to provide "queer readings" of people, places, and products residing within American theater history. James Wilson's lively piece of cultural and performance history — the reception of audiences to the Lulu Belles in the Harlem Renaissance — highlights the intersections of racial politics, theatrical representation, and economic currencies across cultural /sexual boundaries in the 1920s. His piece, as well as so many throughout the collection, point to the need for more scholarship in the area of audience receptions to queer materials, throughout history, on the local and national levels. Focusing on the critic in a straightforward, clearly documented essay, Daniel-Raymond Nadon, in "The Gay Man as Thinker: Eric Bentley's Many Closets," maps out a trajectory of Bentley's coming out process by examining the critic's reviews, essays, and finally, the chronology of his own dramas. One's writings in a variety of genre (here embodied by Bentley's oeuvre) are observed as historical documents that continue to reveal to oneself, and to the researcher, an identity that is in constant formation and revelation.

At the other extreme from language-driven theater critics are the collection's designers and dancers whose artistry is not language bound. In these cases, the evidence upon which the scholars draw for support of their "queer readings" is, according to Jane Peterson who focuses on Robert Edmond Jones, "What is *not* disclosed and *why*" (339). Peterson's task is a slippery one in her approach to Jones. At its best, Peterson's "Not as Other Boys" sheds useful light on the relationship between Jones's "subaltern sexuality" (read queer) as a "lens through which to read both his life and his work" (340), citing Jones's family as a significant power in maintaining secrecy about the designer's private life. Peterson's focus on four pre-Zurich productions as "ways homoerotic desire permeates Jones's work" (348), while providing interesting reading, often leaps in directions that are unconvincing. For example, Eugene O'Neill, not Jones, created the language to describe the world and set design for *The Hairy Ape*; if anyone's homoerotic desires need to be examined vis a vis this illustration, it is O'Neill's. This does not imply that *The Hairy Ape*, or any of the other named productions, did not provide artistic outlets for Jones's imagination, but the originating source for *guiding* or *directing* the imagination, at least in the design of his plays, resides with language-obsessed and detail-oriented O'Neill. Similarly, the dance historian faces comparable challenges to those who document the other ephemeral aspects of theater production. Bud Coleman's queer reading of Loie Fuller, choreographer extraordinaire and the highest paid performer in vaudeville at the turn of the twentieth century avoids some of the pitfalls that can plaque dance criticism. Queering the performances of Fuller's choreography and career as a dancer, Coleman wisely relies upon local reviews of the artist's performances, a challenge made all the more difficult when the historian deals with the transitory artistry, the undocumented (i.e., non-textual) origins that reside at the heart of early dance scholarship.

Residing at the center of the collection is a masterful essay written by Lisa Merrill, "'Appealing to the Passions': Homoerotic Desire and Nineteenth-Century Theater Criticism." Merrill skillfully approaches her fascinating subject through a rich, multidimensional argument — one that embraces both theater and cultural histories as her context in order to demonstrate how "homoerotic passion informed the aesthetic and critical responses" of arts' commentators James Oakes, James Rees, and Adam Badeau to the leading male stage stars of the nineteenth century, Edwin Forrest and Edwin Booth. From an array of research sources, Merrill constructs a tightly defended position that highlights the "depiction of Forrest and Booth by male critics, reviewers, and biographers" in order to reveal "the role played by an economy of homoerotic desire in the anonymous and pseudonymous theatrical notices and reviews published in the nineteenth-century American periodical press" (222). Transgenerational in its implications for future research that investigates critic-artist "relationships" (both in- and outside printed material), the specificity of Merrill's argument resonates in numerous dynamic directions, including how nineteenth-century actor training is affected by a homoerotics of critically well-received public performances by notable male actors, how men's bodies created a "potential male homoerotic public space" on stage (229), and how the power of homosocial (let alone homoerotic) desire experienced by the critic can inform his critical writing. Merrill connects the dots among performance, homoeroticism, and criticism in ways that stay with the reader long after the essay is completed. Her essay certainly positions the critic — the evaluator of artists' work — as an equally viable focus of scrutiny when it comes to deconstructing *all* the components that contribute to the cultural dialogue surrounding an artist and a work of art.

One comes away from reading *Staging Desire* with the knowledge that none of its subjects lived unproblematic, unexamined lives. While these artists chose careers that kept them in the public eye, their personal lives were under constant scrutiny (albeit to different degrees of accountability and society's interest). Regardless if one was an "out" or closeted gay, lesbian, or bisexual in the United States during the time span covered in this collection, the queer artist — one who experimented with or embraced non-normative sexualities — did not live free from a stifling social bias and oppression that either kept her/his private life completely secret or comfortably sheltered. In some cases, as with Cole Porter (as vividly discussed by Mark Fearnow) and Clyde Fitch, for instance, personal wealth and fame granted them a kind of open passage through New York's social circles, protecting them from the harsher anti-homosexual sentiment that threatened others' ability to be open. Women artists, from Rachel Crothers, Mercedes de Acosta, and Jean Rosenthal (discussed in a beautifully written, well-argued essay by Jay Scott Chipman) to Djuana Barnes were often polarized between the reemerging feminist politic of independence, outspokenness, and self-reliance on one hand, and a compulsion for complete secrecy and painful self-examination on the other. Their lives were constantly framed by a patriarchal construct that confronted them with hyper-restrictive gender and sexual politics espoused by the dominant culture at every turn.

Still other queer artists, specifically Lorenz Hart (as argued effectively by Jeffrey Smart), for instance, lived in between the cracks of social conformities of gender standards (that is, the conventional gender standards to be a "man's man") and his compulsive drive for sex. Unlike the majority of theater practitioners highlighted in this collection, Hart — and arguably Mercedes de Acosta — may well be the one who will feel most contemporary to the reader because of his clearly delineated *outsider status.* For today's reader, who is living in a sexually liberated country yet witnessing an urgent conservative attempt by Washington to strip human rights from sexually diverse communities, the queer outlaw remains the radical citizen. Hart's coded lyrics, his efforts to enjoy an erotics that were often denied him because of his physical appearance, and his frequently marginalized complement to Richard Rodgers's heteronormative life add up to a kind of post-modern journeyman's existence in a landscape that does not welcome him on his own terms. Hart's life on the edge is not dissimilar in the (manic) energy directed toward pursuit of the love object derived from Schanke's portrait of the captivating Mercedes de Acosta. The queer artists in *Staging Desire* who *lived* most explicitly sexual existences are the ground, in fact, upon which this collection's varied approaches to its usages of "queer" is established. Just as "queer" itself continues to evolve and accommodate a range of non-heteronormative diversities (as evidenced by the artists in this collection and the essayists' varied approaches to their biographies and artistic creations), so, too, may theater historians appreciate the necessity to queer their subject matter, when warranted, because to do anything less is to deny a more complete, truthful recreation of personal and theatrical histories. The time in which we live demands that we continue to open up ourselves as theater historians to diversified kinds of critical inquiry. In terms of its specific goal to investigate the significance of queer readings of American theater history, *Staging Desire* has opened up one of the most compelling doors for us to walk through and to take notice.

Bob Vorlicky
New York University

On the Edge of Your Seat: Popular Theater and Film in Early Twentieth-Century American Art. Edited by Patricia McDonnell. New Haven, CT: Yale University Press in association with Frederick R. Weisman Art Museum, University of Minnesota, 2002; pp. xii + 220. $45.00 cloth.

A wealth of images — color reproductions of paintings, posters, sheet music, song slides, and postcards; beautiful silver gelatin photographs of theatre façades and interiors; film stills; drawings — complement ten chapters by ten scholars of art, theatre, film, and cultural history. Published in conjunction with the exhibition of the same title, this attractively designed book offers a loving and vivid evocation of American popular entertainment as a component of the urban visual landscape between 1890 and 1930.

Patricia McDonnell's introductory overview, the book's longest chapter, lays the foundation for the more focused essays that follow. She relates modernism's "heightened stress on visual sensation" (6) to aspects of urbanization: electric lighting, department-store shopping, plate-glass display windows, the mingling of economic classes in public transportation, the street as spectacle. The public's craving for novelty found gratification in disjunctive forms of mass entertainment, notably vaudeville and early motion pictures. The painters who chose popular entertainment as their subject matter also adopted its aesthetics: fragmentation, speed, strong contrast between bright colors and dark masses. Paintings that show nickelodeon or vaudeville audiences often include someone gazing directly out toward the viewer of the painting, perhaps echoing the famous closeup of the bandit who shoots out at the audience in Edwin S. Porter's 1903 film *The Great Train Robbery*, and certainly analogous to the mutual visual connection between vaudeville performers and their audiences.

Awareness of the multiplicity of sights to be visually consumed characterizes the period and the popular arts it produced. The dilemma of the serious painter was to capture that variety and disjointedness within a work having some kind of coherence. According to Laurel Weintraub (Chapter 6), Charles Demuth's vaudeville watercolors of the 1910s use jazz rhythms. Edward Hopper's approach, as Robert Silberman shows in Chapter 7, was to use framing devices and to keep the focus on the audience, a "separation between the seer and the seen" (151). Everett Shinn emphasized "the sense of community" (158) by "introducing the viewer as a participant in the scene" (161), according to Sylvia Yount. Rebecca Zurier notes that although John Sloan was an avid theatergoer, he painted the streets as spectacle with the implicit acknowledgment that "comprehension is only partial" (178).

For theatre scholars, Chapter 3 by Robert C. Allen, on cinema, vaudeville, and burlesque, is the core of the book. While acknowledging influences like dime novels, amusement parks, dime museums, puppetry, tableaux vivants, minstrels, and burlesque, he elucidates the close interconnection between moving pictures and vaudeville in such areas as programming, demographics, audience behavior, "continuous performance" policy, and architecture. Just as cinema progressed from kinetoscope to "attractions" to nickelodeon to picture palace, so vaudeville might be said to have grown from displays of inanimate objects through the carefully calculated arrangement of acts on a bill to the musical revues of the 1920s.

David Nasaw's chapter on electric lighting's impact on urban nightlife offers a pithy context for many of the social changes of the era. C. Lance Brockman focuses on technological milestones — the chariot race in *Ben Hur*, panoramas, dioramas, moving panoramas, a vertical panorama, Steele MacKaye's vision of a Spectatorium, the Maréorama, the Balloon Cineorama — that paved the way toward motion pictures. Leo Charney presents another take on fragmentation and order, claiming that both "vaudeville and cinema offered coherence with a veneer of incoherence" (120). In the final chapter, "A Company of Ghosts, Playing to Spectral Music; Gesamtkunstkino and the Future of Digital Cinema," Walter Murch takes us on whimsical time travels bringing the past, present, and future into a coherent whole. The charming playfulness that infuses his expertise and vision strikes just the right note to round off the book.

Although the selection of illustrations is truly dazzling, it is in the visual aspect of this book about visual spectacle that I must register my only (mild) disappointment. While the wide page and glossy stock allows most of the paintings to be reproduced quite beautifully (usually about five inches wide), some illustrations are relegated to the margins with widths of little over two inches. The tiny reproductions of Everett Shinn's "Concert Stage, 1905" and "The Vaudeville Act, 1902-3"on page 35 made me yearn to see them in larger format. With a small sigh, the reader understands that choices must be made and moves on. But then it is shocking to discover that some large reproductions from Chapter 1 get reproduced on even larger scale in Chapters 6 and 8. Could not some of the space devoted to twice reproducing Shinn's wonderful "The Orchestra Pit, Old Proctor's Fifth Avenue Theatre, c.1906-7" (5 on 34, 7 on 168) or Demuth's "Acrobats" (38 and 133) have been allotted to show the Shinn pieces to better advantage? And why is the still from "The Kiss" (1896) reproduced on page 179 where it is barely mentioned and not on page 65, where it is actually discussed? In truth, these complaints are trivial when one considers that throughout the book the careful placement of so many pictures on the very page on which they are discussed make it all marvelously convenient for the reader.

A twelve-page Selected Bibliography and an Index augment the scholarly side of a book that will simultaneously enhance any coffee table.

Felicia Hardison Londré
University of Missouri-Kansas City

The Roots of Theatre: Rethinking Ritual & Other Theories of Origin. By Eli Rozik. Iowa City: University of Iowa Press, 2002; pp. xix + 362. $49.95 cloth.

A professor of theatre studies at Tel Aviv University, Eli Rozik has set himself the task of disproving most of the accepted ways of talking about the origins of theatre. He especially is critical of the School of Cambridge and the anthropological work of James G. Frazer in the attempt to link ritual and theatre. Rozik believes that ritual and theatre are ontologically different and mutually independent, although ritual can use theatre and theatre might describe ritual. But more important, he sees the quest for origins as essentially misleading: "Rather than searching for previous forms that could have engendered theatre, we should seek its roots in the psychological constitution of human beings and sociocultural structures of human societies"(xiv). Eli Rozik has written a thoughtful book that is certain to provoke discussion and debate.

Rozik has organized his book in three parts. In "Theories of Origins" he reviews the evidence for and provides criticism of the origins of theatre in ritual. He includes chapters on tragedy and comedy, Shamanistic sources, Christian recreation of theatre, Mummers' Plays, and adoptation of theatre by Judaism. Rozik concludes the first part by reexamining Aristotle's comments on the origins of theatre, noting that Aristotle did not connect Attic tragedy to ritual. This part is aimed at refuting the prevailing arguments that place the origins of drama in ritual.

In the second part "Criticism of Theories" he examines Richard Schechner's notion of Performance which includes activities with a performance-audience relationship such as ritual, theatre, play, sports, dance, and games. "Reintroducing" ritual participation into the theatre interests Schechner but Rozik does not accept the theory that theatre evolved out of ritual and consequently finds little to learn here about the roots of theatre. Other chapters reference the theories of Erving Goffman, Mikhail Bakhtin, and Johan Huizinga, among others, as Rozik attempts to connect theatre with a wide variety of human activity. In the end, however, he finds their theories reductive and not helpful in determining the roots of theatre.

In the third part, Rozik proposes his "Theory of Roots." He explains that dreams and the theatre share the same principles of representation through symbolic and metaphorical images. And he makes a connection between theatre and imaginative play, daydreams, and dreams in their methods of representation. In a chapter on "Mythical Representation," he makes the point that myth like theatre communicates through an "imagistic method of signification." Rozik finds the roots of theatre in dreams, play, and myths.

Finally, the author suggests a theory of roots that reveals the "necessary psycho-cultural conditions for the medium of theatre to come into existence"(342). He suggests a progression from daydreaming through children's imaginative play to a "eventual crystallization in theatre"(345). He concludes that imagistic activities such as daydreaming and imaginative play get suppressed in the normal course of human development, and theatre provides a "socially permitted" way of experiencing them in our adult life.

An interdisciplinary study, *The Roots of Theatre* provides not only a good review of current literature on the subject but seminal thinking about the nature of creativity. Rozik's research methods include structuralism and semiotics, and at times his language gets in the way of his meaning. Also, redundancies throughout bog down his arguments. But the book is provocative and, for the most part, compelling reading, and will stimulate thinking about these issues.

Tice L. Miller
University of Nebraska-Lincoln

The Undiscovered Country: The Later Plays of Tennessee Williams. Edited by Philip C. Kolin. New York: Peter Lang Publishing, Inc., 2002; pp. 240. $32.95 paperback.

The post-*Night of the Iguana* plays of Tennessee Williams have more often than not been judged harshly by critics and audiences, the majority of whom considered them to be merely boozy autobiographies of a waning playwright that pale in comparison to his earlier masterpieces. However, *The Undiscovered Country: The Later Plays of Tennessee Williams*, a collection of fifteen essays assembled by editor Philip C. Kolin, squarely challenges the notion that these works are "problem plays." The essays of *The Undiscovered Country* instead reveal these later works to be the products of a playwright who consciously and vigorously experimented with diverse theatrical styles, in a sense learning and employing other languages in a quest to better and more fully express himself. Sadly, while Williams the artist was still evolving, his critics and audiences for the most part were not.

The number of plays that Williams wrote in the period after *Night of the Iguana* to his death is incalculable; not all have been published, produced, or accounted for, but the number certainly far exceeds that of those created in the seventeen years between the premieres of *The Glass Menagerie* and *Iguana* (1). Kolin's collection examines only a fragment of these later works, including: *The Milk Train Doesn't Stop Here Anymore; The Gnädiges Fräulein* (which Kolin suggests is Williams's "least understood and most denigrated" play); *In the Bar of a Tokyo Hotel; Small Craft Warnings; A Lovely Sunday for Creve Coeur; Clothes for a Summer Hotel; Out Cry; Two Character Play; Vieux Carré; Red Devil Battery Sign; Something Cloudy, Something Clear;* and *A House Not Meant to Stand* (3). The essays' contributors, including such esteemed Williams scholars as Felicia Hardison Londré, Michael Paller, Annette J. Saddik, Una Chaudhuri, Robert Bray, and Kolin himself, examine the later plays through an astounding array of lenses, including Postmodernism, Artaudian and Brechtian theories of performance, cinema, philosophy, theology, painting, and the Nô theatre of Japan.

Perhaps the most remarkable essays are those that deal with the most maligned plays of the later canon. Una Chaudhuri's essay on *The Gnädiges Fräulein*, a strange, haunting play about a seal-trainer's assistant who assumes the seal's role in the act and can then only provide for herself by abandoning her humanity, is particularly powerful. Chaudhuri explores the awkwardness of the encounter between art and animality in this play, considered to be Williams's most avant-garde, which she posits calls for a rethinking of the animal made possible by postmodernism (54-55). Kolin's essay on *Small Craft Warnings* is also engaging; *Small Craft Warnings* has perhaps been considered the most autobiographical play of Williams's later offerings, possibly because it deals in a naturalistic way with individuals wrestling with demons that Williams himself battled — most prominently alcoholism, as the piece is set in a bar — and, most importantly, because Williams himself chose to act in the production. But Kolin reveals *Small Craft Warnings* to be a Christian play by a self-identified Christian playwright. The play is not the seedy, *Lower Depths*-esque ramblings of the morally bankrupt, but rather a hymn to the presence of God, forgiveness, and love in the darkest of places. Too, Michael Paller's thesis that *The Milk Train Doesn't Stop Here Anymore* is William's richest synthesis of "Nô philosophy and dramaturgy with his own unmistakable brand of Western theatre" (27) is also compelling and soundly argued.

Only one essay left me wanting more: Terri Smith Rukel's "*Ut Pictura Poesis, Ut Poesis Pictura:* The Painterly Texture of Tennessee Williams's *In the Bar of a Tokyo Hotel.*" While I found her thesis to be interesting —Williams the hobbyist painter employed "painterly techniques" in his later writings, most notably in *Tokyo Hotel* — I believe that her assertions could have been augmented by more visual support (i.e., more reproductions of Williams's paintings) to demonstrate effectively her argument. Her writing, though, is thoughtful and intelligently crafted (as are all of the essays in this volume.)

The Undiscovered Country is a potent little book, providing much needed scholarship on Williams's later canon. Kolin and his contributors also valiantly rehabilitate the playwright. While certainly troubled in his private life, Williams did not spend his later years fruitlessly attempting to rehash his major successes, only to fail because of drugs, alcohol, or conflict with his sexual identity; instead, he was a vibrant, experimental, and maturing artist. But most importantly, perhaps, *The Undiscovered Country* spurs the reader to reread, or perhaps discover for the first time, these enigmatic buried treasures.

W. Douglas Powers
Susquehanna University

Performing History: Theatrical Representations of the Past in Contemporary Theatre. By Freddie Rokem. Iowa City, IA: University of Iowa Press, 2000; pp. ix +241. $42.95 cloth.

The nature of the relationship between History and Theatre has been an issue of concern in dramatic theory and criticism since (at least) the time of Aristotle. Though this interest in the intersections of History and Theatre continued through the 20th century, few book-length studies have addressed this intersection in historical drama written after the cataclysmic events of World War II. While Herbert Lindenberger's 1975 *Historical Drama* and Matthew Wikander's 1986 *The Play of Truth & State* are both useful, comprehensive studies of historical drama, for instance, neither devotes significant, sustained attention to the tremendous impact World War II (and, in particular, the Shoah) has had on plays and productions depicting historical events. Other more recent works — notably *Stages of Annihilation* by Edward Isser and *Staging the Holocaust* edited by Claude Schumacher — have specifically addressed theatrical representations of the Shoah, but devote limited space to considerations of how this monumentally important event has influenced the contemporary theatre's presentation of *other* historical events. Freddie Rokem's *Performing History: Theatrical Representations of the Past in Contemporary Theatre* makes an important contribution to the study of historical drama by acknowledging that "the Shoah has challenged and even radically changed some of our notions of history and historiography" (14) and examining how those challenges and changes are reflected in nearly a dozen post-World War II productions

Rokem's Introduction carefully delimits the scope of his inquiry to productions about the Shoah and the French Revolution — two major turning points in history that Rokem asserts "have formed our modern consciousness, in particular our sense of the historical past as a series of tragic failures of basic human values" (1). Working from this underlying assumption, Rokem endeavors to explore "the restorative potentials of the theatre in trying to counteract the destructive forces of history" (3), to examine how these two "failures of history" have been represented on stage, and to address "the ways in which these performances have communicated in different national and ideological contexts" (5).

Rokem's exploration of these issues proceeds primarily through his detailed, insightful analyses of live or recorded performances, but also makes productive use of published production reviews, programs, interviews, artists' memoirs, and production-related archival documents. Rokem brings a variety of theoretical perspectives to bear in his interpretation of these works, ranging from analyses of narrative and performative strategies to considerations of the historiographic insights of Walter Benjamin and Michel de Certeau, the New Historicist perspectives of Stephen Greenblatt, and the Semiotic analyses of Erika Fischer-Lichte. No single theoretical approach dominates Rokem's investigation of the individual plays and productions under consideration; rather than attempting to prescribe a unified interpretive apparatus for the examination of all post-World War II drama, Rokem uses his broad theoretical arsenal to elucidate ways in which the selected works move beyond merely theatricalizing the past to "Performing History," a concept developed progressively through the book.

The Introduction establishes the centrality of the actor in works that perform history, arguing that an actor performing a historical figure on stage "in a sense becomes a witness of the historical event" (9). The actor is, in Rokem's conception, a "hyper-historian" who serves "as a connecting link between the historical past and the 'fictional' performed *here* and *now* of the theatrical event" (13). Rather than attempting to elide the differences in time between the historical event and its theatrical performance—as happens in many traditional historical and documentary dramas — Rokem's "notion of performing history is based on strengthening or reinforcing the dialectics between" those times (19).

The first three chapters of *Performing History* provide theatrical case studies allowing Rokem to articulate the concepts of performing history and the actor/witness as "hyper-historian" in greater, more concrete detail. Chapter One, the longest in the book, examines Yehoshu Sobol's "Ghetto Triptych" (comprised of the plays *Ghetto, Adam* and *In the Underground*), Dudu Ma'ayan's production of *Arbeit macht frei vom Toitland Europa*, and Hanoch Levin's production of his play *The Boy Dreams*. Rokem's detailed discussions of these productions consider a variety of narrative and performative strategies employed to confront the difficulties inherent in aesthetic representations of the Shoah. Broadening his consideration of the plays themselves to issues of audience reception, Rokem argues that Israeli plays about the Shoah must "be seen as an integral aspect of the more comprehensive 'work of mourning' and 'working through' which is an important element in the Israeli ideological texture, occupying Israeli society and culture in innumerable ways" (27).

Chapter Two devotes less attention to the national or ideological context of performances as it considers three European productions about the French Revolution: Peter Brook's production of Peter Weiss' *Marat/Sade*, Ariane Mnouchkine's production of *1789*, and Ingmar Bergman's production of Yukio Mishima's *Madame de Sade*. Though all three productions examined in this chapter relate to the French Revolution, the plays form a less unified grouping than found in Chapters One or Three. Two of the plays deal with the Marquis de Sade, the other does not; two are considered experimental works of collaborative creation, the other is not; two feature metatheatrical elements, the other does not; two depict "public events from the French Revolution which had very clearly defined effects on the public sphere" (117-8), the other does not. As a result, it is difficult to draw broader typological conclusions regarding these works; one of the plays generally stands as an exception to the principle under investigation. The consistency found in this short chapter resides less in the plays themselves than in Rokem's more focused attention on performative strategies that foreground the act of witnessing historical events from the stage.

Chapter Three has a much more pronounced inherent unity as it focuses on three different American productions of Georg Büchner's 1835 classic *Danton's Death*: Orson Welles' 1938 production at the Mercury Theatre in New York, Herbert Blau's1965 production in the Beaumont at Lincoln Center, and Robert Wilson's 1992 production at Houston's Alley Theatre. In this chapter, Rokem uses a great deal of documentary source materials to construct his interpretation of these plays, relying heavily on newspaper reviews, production-related publications, artists' memoirs, and interviews. While arguably digressions from his primary focus, Rokem's extended discussion of the behind-the-scenes drama and politics swirling around these productions makes for fascinating reading.

All three of these American productions were based on adaptations of Büchner's script, and more importantly to Rokem's analysis, all three productions were considered commercial and critical failures. In his attempt to discover the reasons these productions failed, Rokem returns to the considerations of national ideology introduced earlier, suggesting these American productions "were unable to domesticate this play, to make it fully or even satisfactorily meaningful in its new social and ideological context, nor to create an aesthetically viable bridge between the historical past and the present" (136-7). Reiterating the centrality of the actor as "hyper-historian" in his conception of performing history, Rokem compellingly suggests that "the directorial concepts apparently took over" (178), diminishing the actors' effectiveness in communicating directly with the audience. In order to perform history successfully, Rokem implies, what is needed is "a performance context that allow[s] the individual actors to communicate the historical past to the spectators in the present" (187). The fourth and final chapter considers the means of establishing that context and facilitating that communication.

Chapter Four's exploration of "Theatrical Energies" raises the question of "how the complex semiotic economy of emotions . . . is transposed, perceived, and experienced in specific performances about history" (188). This return to more abstract theoretical and philosophical questions in the book's final chapter is a bit jarring after three engaging chapters of production case studies. Rather than merely summarizing issues previously explored, Rokem's final chapter "opens up some new issues that are not strictly within the boundaries of performing history" (188). These issues — including the roles of the "eavesdropper" and "deus ex machina" in drama and the differing directorial notions of "energy" as employed by Schechner, Barba, and Brook — are interesting in themselves, yet somewhat dissatisfying as a means of concluding such a well-organized and thought-provoking study.

That said, however, Rokem's refusal to wrap his diverse theoretical speculations and analytical strategies into a concise, universalizing pronouncement hints at the overriding value of the work. The variety of analytical approaches and theoretical perspectives employed throughout *Performing History* provides scholars with a number of intriguing questions that may be productively asked of other post-World War II historical dramas.

Review by Don LaPlant
California State University, Bakersfield

The Staging of Drama in the Medieval Church. By Dunbar Ogden. Newark, NJ: University of Delaware Press, 2002; pp. 251. $39.50 cloth.

Dunbar Ogden's *The Staging of Drama in the Medieval Church* is, first and foremost, an exploration of medieval dramaturgy. Ogden's evocative descriptions of medieval liturgical dramatizations are solidly grounded in the vocabulary of modern theatrical realism. *Visitatio Sepulchri* ceremonies, for example, are "performances" with "all of the elements of theatrical production," the *Quem quaeritis* in the Winchester Troper is a "play." Ogden seeks those qualities in medieval texts, music, rubrics, and architecture that resonate with traditional Western stage representation: individualized characterization, gestures drawn from everyday life, realistic props and costumes, vocal qualities expressive of human emotion. "Throughout this study of staging," the author writes, "we are searching through original records of liturgical observance to discover rare bits of evidence of the drama: the glimmering of what we might call *play* instead of *rite*, *ludus* instead of *ordo* or *officium*, *Spiel* instead of *Feier*, *jeu* instead of *rituel*" (p. 179).

Numerous recent scholarly efforts have shown the problems inherent in applying post-Renaissance concepts of drama and theatricality to medieval texts and music. Though some critical readers might find Ogden's approach to be nostalgic, even Romantic, in its quest for glimmers of the modern in the medieval, *The Staging of Drama in the Medieval Church* provides an essential resource for directors and performers attempting to create emotionally effective reconstructions of medieval religious dramas and ceremonies. Ogden's study does not set out to analyze his sources (drawn largely from Karl Young and Walter Lippardt as well as manuscripts), reassess the historiography that informs his interpretations, or engage critical material on gender, violence, memory, ritual, or medieval representational practices. His purpose is to explore medieval texts and music traditionally known as "liturgical drama" for their aesthetic value as stage pieces. This study offers meticulous comparisons of familiar texts such as the *Peregrinus, Officium Stellae, Ordo Prophetarum,* and *Visitatio Sepulchri,* revealing a wide range of interpretive possibilities.

The Staging of Drama in the Medieval Church covers six centuries of English and Continental church dramas. Prof. Ogden does not tie liturgical dramatization to liturgical practice or theology, or delve into historical conditions that might have informed variations in representational practice. He is deeply invested in the relationship between performance rubrics and space, based on finely honed interpretations of the internal evidence for performance in liturgical texts, music, and architecture. The texts chosen for detailed description in Chapter Three are those which can be assigned to specific churches and cathedrals. Ogden renders his texts in three dimensions by matching references to altars, tombs, chapels, movement, and other features to their original physical spaces (p. 41).

The dramaturgical strategy does often lead to observations of historical change. Ogden suggests, for example, that performances of the *Visitatio* ceremony as documented in the English *Regularis Concordia* took place in The Old Minster of Winchester and in Christ Church, Canterbury; the difference in architecture reflects "a transition at the birth of ecclesiastical drama from a processional liturgy . . . to a liturgy celebrated within a single church building" (p. 26, 27). Likewise, Ogden's presentation of internal evidence indicates how dramatic action could take place anywhere in a given church: choir, organ loft, crypt, nave, in front of the façade. He concludes that "the [historical] process from this kind of theatre to that of the Renaissance is largely a process of confinement, of separation between actor and audience, of formal physical restrictions on distinct playing space versus distinct viewing space" (p. 40). Ogden's focus on theatrical performance does not require elaboration on conclusions such as these, or speculation on issues of the alterity of medieval drama raised by Hans Robert Jauss and Rainer Warning in the late 1970's. These historical conclusions do, however, very effectively support Ogden's underlying claim (most evident in Chapter Six, *The Music*) that despite radical differences in representational practices between modernity and the Middle Ages, hints of emotional realism bind medieval religious presentations to modern theatre.

Throughout *The Staging of Drama in the Medieval Church,* floor plan diagrams, sketches and photographs of church interiors, photographs of iconography, drawings of liturgical garments, transcripts of musical passages, as well as lengthy reproductions of the texts themselves provide a reader with abundant visual resources with which to mentally reconstruct a church drama as a medieval *Gesamtkunstwerk* (p. 175). Pictorial evidence such as Hartker's *Liber responsalis*, the *Benedictional* of Bishop Ethelwold, and twelfth-century replicas of the Holy Sepulchre help the author explore dramaturgical questions, such as "what did the Sepulchre look like," "where was it positioned in the church," and "where were the actors positioned" (pp. 30-31, 33). Likewise, glossaries of medieval terms for "set pieces" (pp. 120-121) and vocal qualities (pp. 156-58), provide useful references for interpreting texts as effective productions.

Ogden's focus on physical movement and gesture as bodily expressions of emotion in Chapter Three and on costume as "a formal mode of character portrayal" in Chapter Four is clearly written with an eye to modern reproductions. Along the way, Ogden also lays foundations for historical work that extends beyond production dramaturgy. Chapter Five, *Acting*, for example, lays out differences between texts written to be performed by women and those written for men. The differences Ogden notes invite intriguing questions outside the scope of this study: Why were women's texts written in the vernacular and with indications of prompting? How and why did the texts for women's performances allow for a greater expression of emotion in language and gesture? What do thirteenth-century purification rituals for women suggest about the relationship between Christian worship and dramatic representation in convents? How did the invention of "fresh musical composition, a new ceremonial moment, a unique gestural pattern" around the figure of Mary Magdalen in the twelfth century challenge conventional images of sacred women?

The search for theatrical verisimilitude in *The Staging of Drama in the Medieval Church* remains carefully, if not critically, balanced between religious ceremony on one side and theatre as a secular art form on the other. In his chapter on music, Ogden is very aware (citing Susan Rankin and John Stevens in particular) that plainsong was not constructed as a mirror to dramatic characterization. Still, he seeks those conjunctions between words, melodies, instrumentations, and modes in which "a spark of a *ludus* contrasts with the generally cool temper of an *ordo* or *officium*" (p. 179). As in his analysis of the multiple uses of architectural space, Ogden's search through chant notation reveals wide variation in relationships between language, movement, and musical settings. The dramatic effects, following Ogden, are conditioned by the degree of ceremony or theatricality indicated in the text (p. 200). Chapter Six also opens up possibilities for much needed work on the interaction between physicality and music in liturgical practice in light of studies by Christopher Page, Margot Fassler, Nancy Van Deusen, Timothy McGee, Ruth Steiner, Ulrike Weithaus, and Constant Mews, as well as examination of musical treatises in relation to dramatic performance.

As a dramaturgical manual informed by the author's many stagings of medieval liturgical plays, *The Staging of Drama in the Medieval Church* does not problematize traditional arrangements of information or ideas about medieval theatricality. In the tradition of Clifford Davidson, David Bevington, Audrey Ekdahl Davidson, and Peter Meredith, Ogden's study sets out a clear, stunningly detailed, and immensely practical guide for understanding medieval drama as theatrical performance in modern church settings. While the application of modern terminology to medieval practices might trouble some historians, Ogden's clear prose identifies fine gradations between modern theatre and medieval representation, and between Christian ritual and theatrical performance that serve recreations of the texts and their music. His sensitivity to performance is everywhere evident, as is his admirably thorough knowledge of his sources. *The Staging of Drama in the Medieval Church* is an elegant and readable book, supplemented beautifully with well-chosen visual images, which offers a complete comparative study of new and familiar medieval liturgical dramas. As such, Dunbar Ogden's study has numerous immediate applications in contemporary dramaturgy and pedagogy, and will be a valuable resource for historians as well as practitioners for decades to come.

Donnalee Dox
Texas A&M University

Bernard Shaw and the French. By Michel W. Pharand. Gainesville, Florida: University Press of Florida, 2000; pp. xviii + 413. $55.00 cloth.

In 1884, while studying French, George Bernard Shaw wrote his first complete work for the stage, a playlet entitled *Un Petit Drame.* This early piece, a parody of French melodrama, manifested a tension that existed within Shaw throughout his career: the simultaneous and conflicting desire to both absorb and critique French culture. Shaw was both a"Francophobe"and a"Francophile"; and his reception in France later proved equally ambivalent. Although translation of his plays into French began in 1904, Shaw did not achieve a major success on the French stage until 1925.

In *Bernard Shaw and the French,* Michel W. Pharand explores this complex relationship between Shaw and the French theatrical and literary worlds. In doing so, Pharand follows a tradition of scholarship that includes Geert Lernout, Yves Hernouet, Edwin Sill Fussell, and others who have examined the relationships between Anglophone writers and French culture and literature. Apart from Mina Moore's untranslated work, *Bernard Shaw et la France,* published in 1933 (xv), no study has focused specifically on Shaw, making Pharand's work particularly needed.

Pharand chronicles Shaw's reception in France and explores the reasons for what appeared at times to be a mutual dislike. According to Pharand, Shaw and the French were victims of a culture gap: whereas "French audiences and readers were disconcerted at unorthodox ideas cloaked in levity, paradoxical or ironic situations, cerebral discussion, assertive women, and an eclectic philosophy and similarly dismayed by "Shaw's aggressive, deliberately clownish self-promotion"(279), Shaw scorned French aesthetics. Pharand uses Shaw's response to Sarah Bernhardt's acting as an illustration of the differences between him and the French: the histrionic acting style of the Comédie-Française, although lauded by French critics, was not complementary to Shavian ideology or dramaturgy.

Shaw and the French is divided into six parts according to topic — for example, Shaw and French Theatre, Shaw Translated, and Shaw and Joan of Arc. The arrangement of these parts is loosely chronological. Each part is subdivided, creating a total of sixteen chapters. Pharand begins by examining Shaw's responses to the French artistic world of the late 1800s; this is followed by two chapters exploring issues surrounding translation. After this, there are four chapters on Shaw's appropriation of French historical figures, followed by an investigation of the effects Shaw had on contemporary French thinkers. As Pharand notes, however, "the primary focus" of his text "is on people (xv). While Pharand looks at larger issues, such as differences in the French and Shavian theatrical aesthetics, he does so within the context of Shaw's attitudes toward specific playwrights or artists. For example, Pharand points to ways that specific French playwrights may have influenced Shaw. Eugene Scribe's well-made play structure, in particular, can be seen in a subverted form in a number of Shaw's plays.

Pharand pays special attention to those artists for whom Shaw felt an affinity, astutely pointing out that this was a kinship based more on shared political ideology than on artistic merit. One such artist was the playwright Eugène Brieux, whom Shaw helped bring to English audiences because he shared Brieux's interest in drama that broke taboos in its discussion of social issues. Similarly, shared ideology caused Shaw to choose Augustin and Henriette Hamon as translators of his plays. The chapter treating Shaw's translators is among Pharand's greatest contributions. He argues that the choice of the Hamon's greatly impeded Shaw's success in France. Augustin Hamon had no theatre background, a limited knowledge of the English language, and an inability to see the humor in Shaw's comedies. Because of their shared interest in anarchism, Communism, and Socialism, Shaw chose the couple who, for his lifetime, were his sole translators into French. Although the Hamon's translations were condemned by critics, Shaw defended them — perhaps out of a desire to maintain control. Shaw's choice of translators, Pharand suggests, helps a great deal to explain his ambivalent reception in France.

In addition to examinations of Shaw's relationship with his contemporaries, *Bernard Shaw and the French* also looks at the playwright's attitudes toward historical figures such as Napoleon and Joan of Arc. In three interesting chapters, Pharand traces how Shaw went about writing *Saint* Joan — particularly how he was affected by the portrayals that came before. With *Sainte Jeanne* in 1925, Shaw finally had his first major French success. Pharand suggests that Shaw's depiction may have been successful with French audiences because of Shaw's ability to present an unromantic portrayal of a figure who had been overly romanticized in the preceding French depictions. Nevertheless, the work's favorable reception apparently required French mediation. Shaw objected to Ludmilla Pitoëff's performance of a"frail, vulnerable Joan"(I 5 8); however, it was the combination of Pitoëff's popular, emotional portrayal with Shaw's writing that allowed for the play's success.

In later chapters, Pharand departs from his discussion of Shaw's attitudes toward the French to suggest ways in which Shaw may have influenced French thinkers. Pharand points out similarities between Shaw's Life Force and the theology of Teilhard de Chardin; he suggests ways that Jean Anouilh's *L'Alouette* may have been a response to *Saint Joan;* and he identifies Shaw as a"protoexistentialist," drawing parallels between Jean-Paul Sartre's *Huis clos* and the "Don Juan in Hell" section of *Man and Superman.* Although the comparisons Pharand suggests are provocative, the points he makes would seem to merit further investigation.

At times, the focus on relationships between individuals obscures Pharand's critical argument. Although some chapters may have been strengthened by a more narrow focus, Pharand provides a wealth of information on a relatively neglected subject. *Bernard Shaw and the French* is highly readable and devoid of jargon. Whenever Pharand quotes a passage in French, he includes his own original translation. Readers may find especially useful the many appendices, including a chronological bibliography of sources on"Shaw in French" and on"Shaw and French Culture and Literature" (289). By including such an in-depth bibliography, *Bernard Shaw and the French* will prove useful to those conducting further research on this quite specific subject. By illuminating the cultural dissonance that exists between an Anglo-Irish author and French audiences, Pharand suggests ways in which cultural differences cause aesthetic differences. By examining this cultural gap and its many facets, Pharand has created a book that will be useful to Literature, Theatre, and Cultural Studies.

David J. Eshelman
University of Missouri-Columbia

The New York Concert Saloon: The Devil's Own Nights. By Brooks McNamara. Cambridge and New York: Cambridge University Press, 2002; pp. xxi+148. $55 cloth.

The concert saloon and related forms of popular entertainment, features of nineteenth-century American culture, are frequently noted in performance histories, but rarelv elaborated upon. The concert saloon, a site familiar to fans of Hollywood Westerns, emerged in the frontier setting and became popular in urban areas, and by the Civil War period was a fixture of Manhattan nightlife. Historical novels, such as Michael McDowell's 1980 *Gilded Needles*, feature Harry Hill's and other New York establishments, replete with gambling, waiter-girls and female pugilism.

Brooks McNamara's *The New York Concert Saloon* is the first full-length study of this popular entertainment venue. He discusses the concert saloon's cultural context and significance, reputed links to prostitution, known facts about arrangement of physical space, the acts that were performed there, and the people who were present. He calls his work a "detective story" that endeavors to solve the mystery of what actually constituted the nineteenth century American concert saloon. Although citing the importance of the guidebooks to the city of James McCabe, as well as the *Police Gazette*, McNamara relies primarily on two sources: the *New York Clipper's* coverage of popular entertainment forms, particularly around 1864; and the reports of the Society for the Reformation of Juvenile Delinquents, which investigated the activities of concert saloons from 1874 to 1884, and determined whether or not the establishments were in conformance with the Concert Bill. This legislation, passed in 1862, and revised in 1872 (to cover virtually all forms of popular entertainment) was a licensing act that banned performances that were not strictly musical in nature. It also prohibited the sale of alcohol in the presence of "waiter-girls." The Society went so far as to investigate the activities of any suspect performance venue, from the lecture rooms of dime museums, to amateur medicine and magic shows in multipurpose meeting halls, to determine if they violated the Concert Bill. Some venues rather blatantly advertised their violations of the Concert Bill in announcements of their nonmusical acts (47)

McNamara discusses the concert saloon's relation to other kinds of performance, such as the British music hall, as well as its influence on the entertainment forms to follow. He suggests that it was "a kind of early musical theatre" that also anticipated the night club and early burlesque, though distinguished from the variety theatre (5). At times, it certainly did include some sort of "leg show" amongst the requisite musical entertainment, which frequently included minstrel performances. In the latter regard, McNamara notes the "frankly racist" nature of some of these comic numbers, but also contends that "there was little understanding at the time of the implications of racism"(57). McNamara also notes that he is looking beyond the obvious musical influences, with the added purpose "to suggest that there is a link between entertainment and the growth of advertising in America after the Civil War" (xiii). Specifically, he considers advertising's use of popular entertainment as a tool, as he did in his valuable study of the medicine show, *Step Right Up.*

Particularly engaging is the chapter on the arrangement of the physical spaces - the signs on the exteriors, lighting set pieces, stages, balconies, racial and sexual mix of clientele, employees and performers; as well as the ways in which concert saloons managed to get around laws by offering "entertainment" that was not "performance," from billiards to stereopticons.

McNamara notes the concert-saloon as a unique place where all sorts of people gathered. It "existed, not for regulars, but for every sort of "fast" men, "respectable" men, boys and girls, for soldiers and sailors, for working men out for a night on the town, and for visitors from the country and from other towns and cities, who had heard how things were carried out in New York. And it genuinely transcended the usual class, gender — and perhaps to some extent — racial lines" (94). The concert saloon offered entertainment initially to attract a male clientele; its height of popularity was from the 1860s to 80s. The entertainers themselves were itinerant — and also performed in the circus, pleasure gardens and other venues. But it was the combination of liquor, women and performance was regarded by some as the inducement to immoral behavior; not those three things individually, but together they were considered a virtually lethal mixture. McNamara addresses the conflation of the waiter-girl and female concert saloon performer with prostitutes — although it seems that certainly some of them were prostitutes - and sexual commerce certainly occurred in private rooms on the premises of many venues. The women seemed to have worked under strict rules, and were often performers as well. McNamara's discussion of who some of the owners of the concert saloons were is also of note, as they were frequently colorful characters who frequently emceed the entertainment, and included several strong female proprietors as well.

Related forms, the dance house and the German beer garden -one focused on a male clientele and the other more respectable and family-oriented - are discussed in the concluding section. The appendices provide the text of the 1872 licensing act, as well as the list of popular songs and singers in concert saloons collected by the Society for the Reformation of Juvenile Delinquents.

My complaints are not concerned with the substance of the study — and certainly it is one that needed to be done — but more with the need for some exertion of editorial control, in areas ranging from the author's fondness for filler phrases such as "at any rate"and "all in all" to the larger problem of the circular, repetitious writing in the book's initial sections. The reader is also reminded numerous times of the demise of the waiter-girl after the Civil War, when several mentions would have been sufficient. Finally, given the specific topic of *The New York Concert Saloon*, it's odd that the cover illustration is of a Cheyenne venue, not one in New York. However, McNamara does accomplish his stated intention, to illuminate what the concert saloon was, what happened there, who worked in and patronized it, and how it influenced the popular entertainment forms that followed.

Noreen Barnes-McLain
Virginia Commonwealth University

***The Theatre of Sabina Berman.* The Agony of Ecstasy *and Other Plays*.** By Sabina Berman. Translation and introduction by Adam Versényi. Essay by Jacqueline E. Bixler. Carbondale/Edwardsville: Southern Illinois University Press, 2003. xxvi + 169 pp. $21.00 paper.

Actor, director, novelist, poet and journalist Sabina Berman is Mexico's leading contemporary woman playwright and one of the country's most successful dramatists. Born in 1955, Berman is Mexican by historical chance: while fleeing Nazi Europe, Berman's Polish Jewish parents were forced to land in Mazatlán when the attack on Pearl Harbor diverted their Japanese ship from San Francisco. Such accidents of nationality aside, Berman stands out among her peers for her fascinatingly critical dramatic revisions of Mexican history. Outside Mexico Berman is better known for her wickedly humorous deconstruction of gender roles. Adam Versényi's translations into English of four early Berman plays provide excellent examples of the Mexican dramatist's engagement with her country's political and cultural history as well as its sociosexual obsessions. As Versényi aptly notes in his "Translator's Introduction" opening the collection

> A feminist perspective on sexuality and gender, a constant questioning of the meaning of identity, a frequently searing and satirical treatment of official discourse, and a resuscitation of historical presences willfully ignored are all characteristics of Berman's dramaturgy. . . . (xviii-xix)

The edition also includes an extensive primary and secondary bibliography, compiled by Jacqueline E. Bixler, who also contributed the study, "From Ecstasy to Heresy: The Theatre of Sabina Berman." Bixler provides a succinct overview of Berman's life and work as well as capsule analyses of her early plays, all four of which are included in this collection: *El suplicio del placer [The Agony of Ecstasy]* (1978); *Yankee* (1979); *Rompecabezas [Puzzle]* (1981); and *Herejía [Heresy]* (1983). The latter three received Mexico's prestigious National Theatre Award and clearly established Berman's prominence on the national stage.

The Agony of Ecstasy's one-act playlets stage three encounters between a man and a woman. In *The Mustache*, an androgynous upper-class couple shares a fake mustache. While the man uses the mustache to seduce younger women, his wife employs the prop to keep other men at bay as she vicariously enjoys her husband's latest conquest. Over morning tea the couple argues about the mustache, the previous evening's events, and their own neurotic co-dependence. *The Love Nest* presents a man berating his "kept" lover as she gets ready for their evening out. The man interrupts his rant to call home with an excuse about working late; he is completely undone when his beloved teenaged daughter informs him that "there aren't any virgins" anymore. The play completes its brutal portrayal of *machista* splitting of Woman into Virgin/Whore as the man falls between his lover's legs, crosses himself and declares, "My wife's a wonderful woman!" *The Pistol* explores a younger married couple's already bored relationship. The action revolves around a gun the husband has surreptitiously brought into the home. Through a series of cat-and-mouse intrigues (augmented by absurd exchanges about dinner), the couple makes us aware that they are engaged in a game. The man shoots the gun at the woman, but it's unloaded; he reloads the gun only to be shot when his wife takes him for an intruder, but he apparently remains unwounded. The play ends with the man regaining the pistol, reloading and hiding it somewhere else, just before he takes his wife into the bedroom and locking the door behind them.

Yankee, a psychological thriller told with a sparse realism punctuated by nightmarish flashbacks (or flashforwards), takes place in the port-city of Puerto Vallarta. The gringo Bill has insinuated his way into Rosa and Alberto's lives, and the play focuses on this emotional triangle. We never learn for certain who Bill is (CIA agent, English teacher, Vietnam vet, tourist, U.S. Embassy guard?), but his internal demons propel the play toward its violent yet ambiguous end. *Yankee* is as much a metaphor for turbulent U.S.-Mexico relations as an exploration of tangled sexual and ethnic/racial dynamics.

Leon Trotsky's 1940 assassination during exile in Mexico is the subject of the complex *Puzzle* (whose English title loses the pun contained in the Spanish *rompecabezas*, a puzzle whose literal translation as "head-splitter" describes the way in which Trotsky was killed). Berman's play presents multiple versions of Trotsky's death and ends without our learning his murderer's true identity or motives. Through switches in points of view (conveyed through powerful visual tableaux and lyrically rich monologues), Berman clearly wishes us to see the ideological forces at work behind Mexican historiography.

Heresy recounts a rarely noted episode in early Mexican history: the persecution of Mexico's colonial Jews. The particular case is that of a converted Jew, Luis de Carbajal the Younger, his secret return to his Jewish faith, his struggles with his Dominican priest brother, and the family's subsequent martyrdom in 1649. The play transcends mere retelling through a fragmented, episodic structure allowing for multiple viewpoints, extremely powerful corporeal imagery, anachronistic effects such as machine-gun fire, and the inclusion of the southern Spanish *cante hondo*, whose percussive clapping heightens dramatic tension as it underscores ongoing Old World cultural persecution. Both *Heresy* and *Puzzle* anticipate Berman's later plays in dramatizing how traditional Mexican history has not only erased but also distorted events in a quest for a "homogenized" Mexican history.

All four plays have been skillfully translated by Adam Versényi. Inevitable quibbles with the translation are few and minimal. (In *The Love Nest* why are the Woman's head, bust, waist and hip measurements given in centimeters? In *Heresy* why are certain Judaic ritual elements described in English [e.g., *challah* as "braided bread"] while others simply given in Hebrew and left undescribed [e.g., *chupa*]?) I would have appreciated additional informative annotations, which I believe would not necessarily detract from any stageworthiness but on the contrary provide information useful to any potential production, especially of the more "historical" plays.

This important collection begins to address a long overdue need for stageable English-language translations of Sabina Berman's plays. I hope that it proves to be the first volume of her complete dramatic works in English translation.

Jean Graham-Jones
Florida State University

A Beautiful Pageant: African American Theatre, Drama, and Performance in the Harlem Renaissance, 1910 – 1927. By David Krasner. New York: Palgrave Macmillan, 2002; pp. xii+370. $35 cloth.

In *A Beautiful Pageant*, David Krasner examines the ways in which dramatists and performers of the early Harlem Renaissance negotiated the pressures of appealing to diverse audiences within a shifting social and political environment. That is, in order to thrive professionally, individuals needed to accommodate the demands of black, white, middle-class, and working-class audiences while simultaneously balancing the expectations for presentation of hoary stereotypes carried over from blackface performance and the desire to create new positive images of African Americans. This paradox, as Krasner forcefully demonstrates, was the guiding force behind the cultural and aesthetic milieu of the era.

A Beautiful Pageant is a follow-up to Krasner's own *Resistance, Parody, and Double Consciousness in African American Theatre, 1895 – 1910* (St. Martin's, 1997), which explores early black drama and popular performance. In this recent work, Krasner focuses his attention on the Harlem Renaissance, also referred to as the New Negro Movement, which was a period of tremendous artistic output. Acknowledging the tricky proposition of trying to pinpoint the exact dates of the Harlem Renaissance, Krasner wisely settles on the Great Migration of African Americans as the initiator and the end of World War II as its culmination. The focus in this book, though, is on 1910–1927, an era that represents a transition in African American life from a primarily rural to urban existence and one marked by a burgeoning political and social spirit. As a result, there was a conscious development of a "black modernity," which reflected "a desire to *transform the image of black culture from minstrelsy to sophisticated urbanity*" (10; emphasis in original). But, as this study shows, cultural perceptions are not easily changed, and the nurturing "Mammy" figure, slow-moving "Uncle Tom," and irrepressible "Pickaninny" figures continued to hold the stage and cultural imagination throughout the era. *A Beautiful Pageant* presents numerous instances in which African Americans resisted these representations, while paradoxically often embracing elements of the depictions.

Extending his definition of performance beyond popular theatre and traditional drama, Krasner covers a great deal of ground in this book. His highly varied sites of exploration include prizefights, dance performances, historical pageants, civic parades, community theatre productions, and black Broadway musicals. Highlighting such issues as primitivism, gender constructions, class-consciousness, and political autonomy, these instances offer a complex view of the ways in which the seeds of a rising black nationalism and a unique cultural expression were sown in the inexorable terrain mined with racism and violence.

Boxer Jack Johnson (1878-1946) and dancer Aida Overton Walker (1880-1914), for example, provide insight into the ways in which black bodies carried the weight of cultural attitudes and supposed evidence of "white superiority." Johnson's highly publicized heavyweight title fight in 1910 with white boxer Jim Jeffries (1875-1953) revealed the national anxieties around racial integration and the search for a fixed definition of (white) manhood in an age of uncertainty and change brought on by industrialization. Johnson's victory provoked violence across the country, but it also served as an inspiration for African Americans to confront racism and degrading stereotypes. Similarly, Walker's polished performance in *Salome*, a faddish ballet usually danced by white women in the 1910s, offered a stark contrast with the typically frenetic choreography associated with black women of the era. Walker's choice to perform the role was most likely a rejoinder to the widely held perception of black women as "primitive" and "sexually voracious." As Krasner explains, "By incorporating the popular dance of *Salome* into her repertoire, Walker may have been seeking an artistic response to the demeaning impressions held by many" (69). The bodies of Johnson and Walker may be regarded as sites of resistance, which contested — through performance — ingrained assumptions around race, class, gender, and sexuality.

Likewise, *The Star of Ethiopia*, a historical pageant written by W.E.B. Du Bois (1868-1963), reflected an attempt to overturn racist presumptions on a grand scale. Performed with a cast of hundreds in various cities throughout the 1910's, the pageant attempted to "celebrate black uniqueness" by depicting "African history, the Middle Passage, slavery, emancipation, and Reconstruction" through "music, dance, and historical reenactment" (83). In addition to challenging black stereotypes, the spectacle also endeavored to promote black solidarity and stimulate interest in an indigenous African American folk drama. According to Krasner, "In reaction to racist misrepresentations, Du Bois wrote the pageant in order, he said, to achieve three goals: to 'get people interested in the development of Negro drama'; to teach 'the colored people themselves the meaning of their history and their rich emotional life through a new theatre'; and 'to reveal the Negro to the white world as a human, feeling thing'" (82). Although the pageant was not financially profitable, it certainly contributed to the increased interest in folk drama among black audiences, especially in the work of Georgia Douglas Johnson (1877-1966) and Willis Richardson (1889-1977).

Performance of a black nationalism was perhaps most powerfully embodied by black activist and leader, Marcus Garvey (1887-1940), whom Krasner describes as a consummate "performance artist." Krasner explains, "Through pomp and ceremony, a resonant voice, superlative stage presence, and a physical self-confidence, Garvey displayed a sense of pride and fashion to black people who had felt removed from the growing economic and cultural advances of Americans in general" (170). In addition, the parades that Garvey organized aroused a sense of solidarity among the black working class, who seemed to have been captivated by the theatricality of Garvey's comportment.

The final third of the book focuses on the popular theatre of the 1920s, primarily looking at the complex artistic and social compromises black performers made while performing for primarily white audiences or in productions created by whites. For instance, Krasner devotes a chapter to actor Charles Gilpin (1878-1930), who is best remembered for originating the role of Brutus Jones in Eugene O'Neill's *The Emperor Jones* (1920). Gilpin is generally regarded historically as a recalcitrant drunk, who often changed O'Neill's dialogue during the more than two hundred times he played the role on Broadway and on tour. Krasner shows how these accounts are greatly exaggerated, and he makes a strong case for the motivations behind Gilpin's substitutions in O'Neill's language (particularly in the use of the word "nigger"). Proclaiming Gilpin a complex and accomplished artist, Krasner presents a sound argument for stating that the actor's impetus for modifying the role "had less to do with egocentrism and more to do with solidarity with the spirit of the Harlem Renaissance" (192).

The book concludes with an examination of the black musicals of the 1920s, which began with *Shuffle Along* in 1921. The musicals have by and large been dismissed by theatre scholars because of the shows' perpetuation of black stereotypes, which were rooted in minstrelsy and blackface performance. Yet rather than condemning white audiences and producers for preserving the degrading images and giving black performers little choice but to embody them, Krasner also makes a compelling argument concerning the complex attitudes held by African Americans, who, in their own way, were complicit in the continuance of these representations. Minstrelsy, Krasner argues, was something of a "guilty pleasure" for black audiences who had grown up with it as one of the few forms of entertainment available to them. Also, lacking their own dramatic traditions due to slavery, African Americans considered minstrelsy one of the few artistic legacies they had. Krasner writes, "Perhaps the most important ingredient to the success of blackface shows to black audiences was the belief that blackface comedy, however self-mocking, was part of a cultural heritage" (277). This contention helps explain why blackface and minstrelsy had such a stranglehold on black performance of the era even as black cultural leaders railed against its debilitating effects.

A Beautiful Pageant is impeccably researched, and it captures the richness and importance of the multiple forms of black performance and drama from 1910-1927. And while many theatre historians have designated the Harlem Renaissance a failure because of its inability to produce an enduring African American theatre tradition, Krasner shows how the period laid the aesthetic and nationalist foundation for black artists who followed. The book's main appeal, however, lies in its ability to capture a historical era in which racial and cultural identities were forged through public and artistic representations. As this study indicates, this was a time in which theatre and performance truly mattered.

James Wilson
LaGuardia Community College
City University of New York

Theatre, Society and the Nation: Staging American Identities. By S.E. Wilmer. Cambridge: Cambridge University Press, 2002; pp. 202. $60.00 cloth.

Theatre, Society and the Nation surveys seven sites of performance activity over three centuries, which the author, S.E. Wilmer, thinks have defined or challenged "national values and the notion of the nation" (p. 3). This `argument without an opposite' offers an organization of existing scholarship about these seven sites with an eye to presenting "various notions of national identity" (p. 4). As Wilmer puts it, "Divided into chapters relating to specific political and social movements, the book discusses representative plays and performances that emerged out of these movements" (p. 3). The sites are: the shift from colony to nation in the eighteenth century (Ch. 1); the rivalry between Federalist and Democratic Republican playwrights/ theatres, 1797-1803 (Ch. 2); American Indians and the Ghost Dance, 1889f (Ch. 3); the Paterson Strike Pageant of 1913 (Ch. 4); staging 1960s rebellions (Ch. 5); suffragist and feminist plays of the twentieth century (Ch. 6); and deconstructions of the multicultural nation in the 1990s (Ch. 7). Chapters 3, 5, and 6 are quite short — 17 to 23 pages of text — the remaining chapters somewhat fuller (ranging from 26 to 36 pages).

Chapter 1 makes use of pamphlet plays, which "helped formulate a new national identity and promoted a nationalist struggle for independence" (p.52). It is the longest chapter in the book. Chapter 2 focuses upon four plays of either a Federalist or Democratic Republican stripe — John Burke's *Bunker-Hill* (1797) and *Female Patriotism* (1798) and William Dunlap's *André* (1798) and *The Glory of Columbia* (1803). According to Wilmer, "Both writers used the theatre to encourage particular social attitudes, to clarify the relationship of the United States with foreign countries, and generally to help construct a self image of the new nation," "not just to foster a spirit of nationalism, but also to represent what the writers hoped would become the core values of the contry" (p. 79). Chapter 3, the shortest in the book, argues "the Lakota Ghost Dance reconfigured the nation, but from a Lakota perspective and in a Lakota idiom" (p. 81). Wilmer likens the Ghost Dance to Mercy Otis Warren's eighteenth century pamphlet plays urging rebellion against Great Britain, in that "the Ghost Dance encouraged Indian patriots to resist assimilation and assert their right to their own independence" (p. 97).

The 1913 Paterson Strike Pageant (Chapter 4) was presented in New York as a fund and support raiser for the New Jersey silk-workers strike, then in progress. The workers performed the pageant as well as the strike, and Wilmer sees its spectators as participants in a public ritual (p. 117) which "displayed an alternative vision of America as a multi-ethnic and multilingual mass of men, women, and children cooperating to overcome oppressive conditions of employment" (p. 111). Supported by a rich body of existing Paterson Strike Pageant scholarship (reflected in twice as many notes to this as any other chapter in the book), Wilmer claims that "By analyzing and rehearsing their roles in a major industrial strike and re/presenting themselves on stage for thousands of others, the Paterson workers acknowledged their position as makers of history and their potential strength as part of a class that could transform the structures of society" (p. 126). Chapter 5 surveys social rebellions staged in the 1960s, particularly those reflected in the work of Amiri Baraka, El Teatro Compesino, and Vietnam Veterans Against the War.

Split approximately in half between plays and productions (chiefly pageants) of the suffragist movement in the early twentieth century and post-1960 feminist plays and companies, Chapter 6's sources confine the data about women in theatre to Chinoy's and Jenkins's 1981/7 survey of plays by women produced on Broadway and in regional theatres (p. 161) and feminist theory ("liberal," "radical," or "materialist") to Dolan's 1988 introductory text (pp. 161-162), while the histories of feminist companies reflect somewhat more recently published sources. Chapter 7 concludes the book with a survey of "multicultural" theatre in the U.S. in the 1990s, chiefly the work of Anna Deavere Smith, Tony Kushner, Velina Hasu Houston and Brenda Wong Aoki, the Coatlicue Theatre of Elvira and Hortensia Colorado, and the theatre of Guillermo Gómez-Peña. Wilmer ends the volume quoting Cherríe Moraga's 1994 call for "an identity that dissolves borders" (p. 202).

Theatre, Society and the Nation was clearly designed to touch the sites currently associated with national identity issues in America (U.S.): the role of theatre in early nation building and early national (political) definition; a performative context for America's non-white races (Amerindian, Hispanic American, African American, Asian American) and for combinations of racial and ethnic identities; and a performative history for workers (especially European immigrants), women (especially white), and for political movements (civil rights, gay and lesbian, cultural diversity, anti-war, and women's liberation). The intellectual benefits of such a survey are less clear, since it can hardly be assumed that the historical circumstances affecting "nation" and "national identity" in America in the late eighteenth century are the same as those pertaining to "nation" and "national identity" at scattered points in the nineteenth and twentieth centuries, nor, indeed, that race, class, or gender float free of the historical circumstances that construct them in a given time and space.

In addition to generalized historical information where those constructing contexts need to be, and the distortions of large claims where the careful construction of argument needs to be, particularly claims concerning difference (Chapter 3) or historical impact (Chapter 4), *Theatre, Society and the Nation* touches theories of the "nation" and "national identity" (Anderson, Said, Bhabha, Greenblatt, Carlson, Higson, Dolan, Mulvey, Chinoy and Jenkins, Canning, Case, Shohat and Stam, Bharucha, hooks, and others cited) that vary widely and often disagree. To be sure, historical practice offers examples of how different ages, places, and persons have performed "nation" and "national identity." These enactments require an historiographical reading which Wilmer does not provide. Without that analysis and absent new historical information, connections among diverse practices and between those practices and national identity theory are at once elementary, overstated, and vague.

One place to begin this analysis is to overturn the notion of the hegemonic "nation" which informs this book and to replace that idea with careful study of the constructed nature of the "nation" throughout U.S. history, a construction which was and is the product of all the races and groups surveyed here (and of others as well). The rigor and benefit of this approach is on view in Philip J. Deloria's *Playing Indian*, one of many works of cultural deconstruction (including my own) absent from Wilmer's select bibliogrphy. What "theatre," "society," and "nation" would emerge from American history if we constructed these "notions" from Henry Louis Gates's idea of culture as "mutually constitutive and socially produced," rather than, as here, from a view of culture as definitive or exclusive?

Rosemarie K. Bank
Kent State University

Teaching Performance Studies. Edited by Nathan Stucky and Cynthia Wimmer. Carbondale and Edwardsville: Southern Illinois University Press, 2002; pp. xiii + 290. $25 paper.

"None of us follows a single vision; instead, our very visions are products of growth and adaptation, not fixed but emergent."— Mary Catherine Bateson, *Composing a Life*

The editors of *Teaching Performance Studies* launch their introduction with a provocative statement: "Beginning a book with the words *performance studies* announces at the outset 'turbulence ahead.' The methods and purposes of its practitioners vary, and the extent of its domain engenders disagreement" (1). These statements aptly establish a framework for their book: 1) that the essays contained within will contest the boundaries of performance studies, particularly in the realm of pedagogy, and 2) that the collection will be far-reaching. As I read *Teaching Performance Studies*, I re-discovered the richness of my field and found myself rejoicing at the centrality of performance in contemporary discourse. Performance is essential, indeed it occupies the core of what it means to be human as Stucky and Wimmer point out: "Performance studies concerns itself broadly with culture and identity; it involves a study of the human as a performing being" (11).

Frequently in the volume, authors ruminate on the slipperiness of the content of performance studies itself, beginning with the foreward by Richard Schechner: "A happy Sisyphus, that's who an accomplished teacher of performance studies is, one whose task is never ending because the field is always changing" (ix). In the first essay of the book's first section, Joseph Roach explores the interlocking, contested nature of the vocabularies that define performance studies in "Theatre Studies/Cultural Studies/Performance Studies: The Three Unities." Roach sets the tone for the contextual wrestling of interdisciplinarity in the volume when he states: "If *performance* is a fundamentally contested term, then it is also an extraordinarily opportunistic one, skating rings around other, more rigid concepts as they take their spills on the slippery surfaces of postmodern culture" (33).

The constant shifting of figure and ground points to the elasticity of performance studies pedagogy and the necessity of practitioners and theorists to continually re-assess and reinvent conceptions, strategies, and the scope of the very terrain they occupy. While the very instability of the field, like the act of performance itself, preserves invention and prevents stagnation, it also ensures that any study of its pedagogy will not fit neatly into the pages of any one book. Extending Schechner's analogy, as a reader I happily chased boulders as they alternately inched up and cascaded down the hill, occasionally dodging dislodged pebbles or avoiding rocks too slippery to stand upon, but I sometimes longed for a guide to steady my progress. Given that the book is divided into three sections, Positioning Performance Studies,

Embodiment and Epistemology, and Negotiating Borders, response essays or editors' commentary at the end of each section would have helped tremendously in guiding the reader to make optimum use of the material, particularly in illustrating pedagogical applications in performance studies research, whether in the classroom, in the field, or on the page.

That observation aside, *Teaching Performance Studies* is a much-needed and incredibly rich resource for critics, teachers, and practitioners of performance studies. Elyse Lamm Pineau, in "Critical Performative Pedagogy," establishes one of the key concerns at issue in the book when she addresses issues of actual and ideological bodies: "I think we can agree that bodies in the classroom are overwhelmingly inscribed as *absence*. Steeped in the tradition of Cartesian dualism, students and teachers effectively have been schooled to 'forget' their bodies when they enter the classroom in order that they might give themselves more fully to the life of the mind" (45). Pineau's call for a "body-centered, performance ethnography" is echoed and augmented in varied ways in later essays by Joni L. Jones in "Teaching on the Borderlands", Michelle Kisliuk, in "The Poetics and Politics of Practice: Experience, Embodiment, and the Engagement of Scholarship," Judith Hamera, in "Performance Studies, Pedagogy, and Bodies in/as the Classroom," and Nathan Stucky, in "Deep Embodiment: The Epistemology of Natural Performance." And, implicitly, Linda Park-Fuller embeds the body through the metaphor of improvisation into her essay "Improvising Disciplines": "I explore performance studies as a postmodern, improvisational discipline, as an institutional course of study, and as a teaching philosophy, subject, and tool. I will attempt to stress performance studies as an improvisational *method* of pedagogy..." (208).

Given that embodiment has always been a cornerstone of what makes performance unique as a way of knowing, it is not surprising that in a book on pedagogy the theorization and integration of the body would occupy center stage. I was arrested by a fascinating observation by Hamara, I suspect shared by many teachers of performance studies, "It has taken me a long time to realize that, to borrow a formulation of Clifford Geertz, we don't just perform as bodies, we perform in bodies" (121). She relates that in spite of physical training (in dance, sports, etc.) she and her students are often reluctant to acknowledge or foreground this experience in performance autobiographies. She discusses in fascinating ways how the physical self is held apart from the conceptual self and raises consequent issues about spectatorship: "Most students write their accounts of disciplined bodies rather than perform them, and this has given rise to discussions about whether or not the choice to write is a further flight from the corporeal" (123). Hamara suggests that performance doesn't heal the mind-body split but rather acknowledges it and frames "how we, as embodied educational subjects, survive and what we survive" (130).

Other authors in the collection make use of writing as performance and as another dimension of embodiment, as Craig Gingrich-Philbrook details in "The Queer Performance That Will Have Been: Student-Teachers in the Archive," and Michael S. Bowman and Ruth Laurion Bowman describe in "Performing the Mystory: A Textshop in Autoperformance." Gingrich-Philbrook asks his students to write, to produce a series of documents or archives: "I do this to contest their perception of the performance as an isolated set of moments on stage, to help them recognize those moments as the surfacing, perhaps, of a larger project" (74). The texts the students write demonstrate queer performance "as an ongoing, embodied process" (73). In another extensive use of writing as performance, Bowman and Bowman experiment with autoperformance and also seek to extend Linda Park-Fuller's and Ronald Pelias' questions (in a 1995 essay in *Communication Education*) about the "evaluation and appropriateness" of this genre of performance. Their use of Gregory Ullmer's "textshop," a laboratory incorporating autobiographical writing and culture, borrows experimental methods from the social sciences for use in exploring performance knowledge. A central question they consider is "How might performance studies classes also take into account the inventive strategies of texts and performances they encounter and learn invention from the performing arts, without forsaking interpretation and criticism?" (163). The intricate relationship between written and performed texts is enhanced further by Nathan Stucky's essay "Deep Embodiment: The Epistemology of Natural Performance" as he details how everyday speech is first recorded, then transcribed, studied, and almost dissected as students re-inscribe the words, inflections, and behavior of another in their own performance: "Conversational performance (as well as some other modes of performance) allows the performer to *act as*, not *act as if*" (136). Stucky discusses the work of Anna Deavere Smith which re-enacts conflict in multi-ethnic communities using a similar method; both Stucky and Smith employ versions of ethnographic practice. As Joni L. Jones says in "Teaching in the Borderlands," a discussion of her classroom as "a laboratory for the exploration of race and ethnicity" (175), "The body as a set of learned and repeated behaviors that constitute the performance of the self, what Pierre Bourdieu calls *habitus*" (177). The use of performance ethnography to incorporate students' participation in other cultures as a way of expanding their own cultural knowledge is evident also in Michelle Kisliuk's essay, "The Poetics and Politics of Practice: Experience, Embodiment, and the Engagement of Scholarship:" "When we commit our bodies to practice and presence on various levels, and in so doing examine the qualities and complexities of that participation within our thinking and writing, we cannot presume to stand either outside or above the subject of our research—but instead become embedded in it and implicated by it, just as we do in live performance" (106).

Teaching Performance Studies, as I stated earlier, is wide-ranging and its eighteen essays address many other aspects of performance pedagogy from theories and practices of acting (Phillip B. Zarilli, "Action, Structure, Task, and Emotion") to employing performance studies outside the academy (Cynthia Wimmer, "'I Dwell in Possibility — 'Teaching Consulting Application for Performance Studies") as well as intriguing forays into neuroscience (John Emigh, "Performance Studies, Neuroscience, and the Limits of Culture") and technological interventions (Eric Dishman,"Performative In(ter)ventions: Designing Future Technologies Through Synergetic Performance"). Perhaps a kind of capstone essay to the volume can be found in Arthur J. Sabatini's essay "The Dialogics of Performance and Pedagogy" which brings together performance and pedagogy in its very textualization. Employing the theories of Bakhtin, Sabatini describes a theory of teaching that creates a dialogic context from its presuppositions to its practice. He states that "both culture and knowledge exists on the borders *between* human beings" (194) and he promotes discourse in his classes that identify, acknowledge, and bridge those boundaries.

In their Editors' Introduction, "The Power of Transformation in Performance Studies Pedagogy," Nathan Stucky and Cynthia Wimmer do a wonderful job of connecting their volume to many traditions of educational philosophy and pedagogical methods as well as delineate major and emergent research directions in performance studies. They present a complex gallery of pedagogical strategies and meditations of great value to practitioners, teachers, and scholars in many fields beyond the obvious ones of theatre, performance studies, communication studies, and anthropology. It is my hope that this volume, the most comprehensive collection of essays on pedagogy in performance studies to date, will lead to other studies of classroom practice, strategies of learning, and methods of evaluating performance.

Teaching Performance Studies points out to us in myriad ways that what we teach, how we teach, the ways our students teach us, and all the ensuing collaborations that result validate the theoretical structures of a discipline. Our students keep us honest by demanding that we ground our ideas in some reality where they can have use and purpose. Jane P. Tompkins puts it succinctly in "Pedagogy of the Distressed": "First, what we do in the classroom is our politics. No matter what we may say about Third World this or feminist that, our actions and our interactions with our students week in and week out prove what we are for and what we are against in the long run. There is no substitute for practice" (660).

Works Cited:
Bateson, Mary Catherine. *Composing a Life*. New York: Plume, 1990.
Tompkins, Jane. "Pedagogy of the Distressed." *College English* 52 (1990): 653-660.

Lynn C. Miller
University of Texas at Austin

Theatre History Studies 23 (June 2003)

Books Received

The listing of a book in this section does not preclude subsequent review.

Beckman, Karen. *Vanishing Women: Magic, Film, and Feminism.* Durham, NC: Duke University Press, 2003. pp. xiii + 239. $59.95 cloth, $19.95 paper.

Blackmore, E.H. and A.M. and Francine Giguère, trans. *George Sand: Five Comedies.* Albany, NY: State University of NY Press, 2003. pp. 272. $65.50 cloth, $21.95 paper.

Bradby, David and Maria M. Delgado, eds. *The Paris Jigsaw: Internationalism and the City's Stages.* New York, NY: Manchester University Press, 2002. pp. xvi + 302. $74.95 cloth, $27.95 paper.

Brandon, James R. and Samuel L. Leiter, eds. *Kabuki Plays on Stage: Villainy and Vengeance, 1773-1799*, vol. 2. Honolulu, HI: University of Hawaii, 2002. pp. xiii + 413. $50 cloth.

Brandon, James R. and Samuel L. Leiter, eds. *Kabuki Plays on Stage: Darkness and Desire, 1804-1864*, vol. 3. Honolulu, HI: University of Hawaii Press, 2002. pp. xv + 397. $50 cloth.

Brandt, Nat. *Chicago Death Trap: The Iroquois Theatre Fire of 1903.* Carbondale, IL: Southern Illinois University Press, 2003. pp. xxiv + 181. $25 cloth.

Brown, Pamela Allen. *Better a Shrew Than a Sheep.* Ithaca, NY: Cornell University Press, 2003. pp. xi + 263. $49.95 cloth, $19.95 paper.

Chambers, Colin, ed. *The Continuum Companion to Twentieth Century Theatre.* New York, NY: Continuum Publishing, 2002. pp. xxv + 865. $150 cloth.

Conolly, L. W., ed. *Bernard Shaw and Barry Jackson.* Toronto, Canada: University of Toronto Press, 2002. pp. xliv + 218. $60 cloth.

Cushman, Robert. *Fifty Seasons at Stratford.* Toronto, Ontario: Madison Press Books, 2002. pp. 224. $45 cloth.

Dessen, Alan C. *Rescripting Shakespeare: The Text, The Director, and Modern Productions.* New York, NY: Cambridge University Press, 2002. pp. xi + 268. $65 cloth, $23 paper.

Egan, Gabriel, ed. *Thomas Heywood & Richard Brome, "The Witches of Lancashire."* New York: Routledge, 2002. pp. xii + 167. $17.95 paper.

Egginton, William. *How the World Became a Stage: Presence, Theatricality, and The Question of Modernity.* Albany, NY: State University of New York Press, 2002. pp. viii + 208. $65.50 cloth, $21.95 paper.

Enders, Jody. *Death by Drama and Other Medieval Urban Legends.* Chicago, IL: University of Chicago Press, 2002. pp. xxx + 324. $35 cloth.

Everett, William A. and Paul R. Laird, eds. *The Cambridge Companion to the Musical.* New York, NY: Cambridge University Press, 2003. pp. xvii + 310. $65 cloth, $23 paper.

Foakes, R.A. *Henslow'e Diary,* 2nd edition. New York, NY: Cambridge University Press, 2002. pp. lxiii + 368. $75 cloth, $27 paper.

Friedland, Paul. *Political Actors: Representative Bodies & Theatricality in the Age of the French Revolution.* Ithaca, NY: Cornell University Press, 2002. pp. ix + 351. $21 paper.

Greenberg, Richard. *"The Dazzle" and "Everett Beekin."* New York: Faber and Faber, 2003. pp.198. $16 paper.

Grote, David. *The Best Actors in the World: Shakespeare and His Acting Company.* Westport, CT: Greenwood, 2002. pp. xv + 298. $39.95 cloth.

Harris, Susan Cannon. *Gender and Modern Irish Drama.* Bloomington, IN: Indiana University Press, 2002. pp. x + 307. $41.95 cloth.

Henke, Robert. *Performance and Literature in the Commedia dell'Arte.* New York, NY: Cambridge University Press, 2003. pp. xiv + 263. $60 cloth.

Hischak, Thomas S. *Boy Loses Girl: Broadway's Librettists.* Lanham, MD: Scarecrow Press, 2002. pp. x + 277. $39.95 cloth.

Honigmann, E.A.J. *Shakespeare: Seven Tragedies Revisited: The Dramatist's Manipulation of Response,* 2nd edition. New York, NY: Palgrave, 2002. pp. ix + 275. $21.95 paper.

Hüsken, Wim and Konrad Schoell, eds. *Farce and Farcical Elements.* New York, NY: Rodopi, 2002. pp. 223. $51.50 cloth, $23 paper.

Jenkins, Annibel. *I'll Tell You What: The Life of Elizabeth Inchbald.* Lexington, KY: University of Kentucky Press, 2003. pp. 596. $39.95 cloth.

Knapp, Jeffrey. *Shakespeare's Tribe: Church, Nation, and Theater in Renaissance England.* Chicago, IL: University of Chicago Press, 2002. pp. xvi + 277. $36 paper.

Kolin, Philip C., ed. *The Undiscovered Country: The Later Plays of Tennessee Williams*. New York, NY: Peter Lang, 2002. pp. viii + 223. $32.95 paper.

Kramer, Larry. *Women in Love and Other Dramatic Writings*. New York, NY: Grove Press, 2003. pp. xiii + 482. $16 paper.

Krasner, David. *A Beautiful Pageant: African American Theatre, Drama, and Performance in the Harlem Renaissance, 1910-1927*. New York, NY: Palgrave Macmillan, 2002. pp. xii + 370. $35 cloth.

Lee, Carol. *Ballet in Western Culture: A History of Its Origins and Evolution*. New York, NY: Routledge, 2002. pp. xiv + 368. $33 cloth.

Lennard, John and Mary Luckhurst. *The Drama Handbook: A Guide to Reading Plays*. Oxford, England: University of Oxford Press, 2002. pp. xii + 416. $14.95 paper.

Levy, Shimon. *Samuel Beckett's Self-Referential Drama: The Sensitive Chaos*. Portland, OR: Sussex Academic Press, 2002. pp. viii + 187. $65 cloth, $27.95 paper.

Loehlin, James N., ed. *Shakespeare in Production: Romeo and Juliet*. New York, NY: Cambridge University Press, 2002. pp. xv + 270. $65 cloth, $23 paper.

Loewenstein, Joseph. *Ben Jonson and Possessive Authorship*. New York, NY: Cambridge University Press, 2002. pp. xii + 221. $60 cloth.

Lowenthal, Cynthia. *Performing Identities on the Restoration Stage*. Carbondale, IL: Southern Illinois University Press, 2003. pp. x + 270. $40 cloth.

MacDonald, Joyce Green. *Women and Race in Early Modern Texts*. New York, NY: Cambridge University Press, 2002. pp. ix + 188. $55 cloth.

Mangan, Michael. *Staging Masculinities: History, Gender, Performance*. New York: Palgrave, 2003. pp. x+ 276. $75 cloth.

Marra, Kim and Robert A. Schanke, eds. *Staging Desire: Queer Readings of American Theater History*. Ann Arbor, MI: University of Michigan Press, 2002. pp. x + 404. $60 cloth, $22.95 paper.

McAllister, Marvin. *White People Do Not Know How to Behave at Entertainments Designed for Ladies and Gentlemen of Colour*. Chapel Hill, NC: University of North Carolina Press, 2003. pp. x + 239. $45 cloth, $18.95 paper.

McNamara, Brooks. *The New York Concert Saloon: The Devil's Own Nights*. New York, NY: Cambridge University Press, 2002. pp. xxi + 148. $55 cloth.

Marker Frederick J. and Lise-Lone Marker. *Strindberg and Modernist Theatre: Post-*

Inferno Drama on Stage. New York, NY: Cambridge University Press, 2002. pp. xi + 176. $55 cloth.

Mertz, Annelise, ed. *The Body Can Speak: Essays on Creative Movement Education with Emphasis on Dance and Drama*. Carbondale, IL: Southern Illinois University Press, 2002. pp. xiv + 148. $25 paper.

Michalos, Alex C. and Deborah C. Poff, eds. *Bernard Shaw and the Webbs*. Toronto, Canada: University of Toronto Press, 2002. pp. xxxi + 311. $65 cloth.

Miles, Julia, ed. *A Theatre for Women's Voices: Plays and History from The Women's Project at 25*. Portsmouth, NH: Heinemann, 2003. pp. x + 309. $25.95 paper.

Mitchell, Rick. *The Composition of Herman Melville*. Portland, OR: Intellect Press, 2002. pp. vii + 96. $29.95 paper.

Munday, Anthony and others. *Sir Thomas More*. Manchester, England: Manchester University Press, 2002. pp. xvii + 258. $21.95 paper.

Nyusztay, Iván. *Myth, Telos, Identity: The Tragic Schema in Greek and Shakespearean Drama*. New York, NY: Rodopi, 2002. pp. 202. $30 paper.

Ogden, Dunbar H. *The Staging of Drama in the Medieval Church*. Newark, NJ: University of Delaware Press, 2002. pp. 251. $39.50 cloth.

Otten, Terry. *The Temptations of Innocence in the Dramas of Arthur Miller*. Columbia, MO: University of Missouri Press, 2002. pp. xvi + 280. $37.50 cloth.

Owen, Susan J. *Perspectives on Restoration Drama*. Manchester, England: Manchester University Press, 2002. pp. vii + 198. $74.95 cloth, $27.95 paper.

Park, Chan E. *Voices From the Straw Mat: Toward an Ethnography of Korean Story Singing*. Honolulu, HI: University of Hawaii Press, 2003. pp. xii + 338. $44 cloth.

Reynolds, Bryan. *Becoming Criminal: Transversal Performance and Cultural Dissidence in Early Modern England*. Baltimore, MD: Johns Hopkins University Press, 2002. pp. xi + 217. $41.95 cloth.

Roudanè, Matthew, ed. *The Cambridge Companion to Sam Shepard*. New York, NY: Cambridge University Press, 2002. pp. xix + 329. $60 cloth, $22 paper.

Rozik, Eli. *The Roots of Theatre: Rethinking Ritual and Other Theories of Origin*. Iowa City, IA: University of Iowa Press, 2002. pp. xix + 362. $49.95 cloth.

Segal, Erich, ed. *Oxford Readings in Menander, Plautus, and Terence*. Oxford, England: University of Oxford Press, 2001. pp. xxvii + 280. $74 cloth, $29.95 paper.

Shimakawa, Karen. *National Abjection: The Asian American Body Onstage.* Durham, NC: Duke University Press, 2003. pp. xi + 192. $54.95 cloth, $18.95 paper.

Silk, M.S. *Aristophanes and the Definition of Comedy.* Oxford, England: University of Oxford Press, 2002. pp. 456. $26.95 paper.

Silverbush, Rhona and Sami Plotkin, eds., *Speak the Speech: Shakespeare's Monologues Illuminated.* New York, NY: Faber and Faber, 2002. pp. lviii + 1028. $35 paper.

Smith, Emma, ed. *King Henry V.* New York, NY: Cambridge University Press, 2002. pp. xvi + 244. $65 cloth, $23 paper.

Sternlicht, Sanford. *A Reader's Guide to Modern American Drama.* Syracuse, NY: Syracuse University Press, 2002. pp. xi + 260. $19.95 cloth.

Stucky, Nathan and Cynthia Wimmer, eds. *Teaching Performance Studies.* Carbondale, IL: Southern Illinois University Press, 2002. pp. xiii + 290. $25 paper.

Thacker, Jonathan. *Role-Play and the World as Stage in Comedia.* Liverpool, England: Liverpool University Press, 2002. pp. xv + 202. $52.95 cloth.

Traub, Valerie. *The Renaissance of Lesbianism in Early Modern England.* New York, NY: Cambridge University Press, 2002. pp. xvi + 492. $80 cloth, $29 paper.

Ulea, V. *A Concept of Dramatic Genre and the Comedy of a New Tyype: Chess, Literature, and Film.* Carbondale, IL: Southern Illinois University Press, 2002. pp. xvii + 196. $45 cloth.

Versenyi, Adam, trans. *The Theatre of Sabina Berman: "The Agony and the Ecstasy" and Other Plays.* Carbondale, IL: Southern Illinois University Press, 2002. pp. xxvii + 169. $21 paper.

Vickers, Brian. *Counterfeiting Shakespeare: Evidence, Authorship and John Ford's Funerall Elegye.* New York, NY: Cambridge University Press, 2002. pp. xxvii + 568. $75 cloth.

Voss, Ralph F., ed. *Magical Muse: Millennial Essays on Tennessee Williams.* Tuscaloosa, AL: University of Alabama Press, 2002. xii + 251. $39.95 cloth.

Wells, Stanley. *Shakespeare For All Time.* Oxford, England: University of Oxford Press, 2003. pp. xxi + 442. $40 cloth.

Wells, Stanley and Sarah Stanton, eds. *Shakespeare on Stage.* New York, NY: Cambridge University Press, 2002. pp. xvi + 322. $ 60 cloth, $22 paper.

Wertenbaker, Timberlake. *Timberlake Wertenbaker: Plays Two.* New York, NY: Faber and Faber, 2002. pp. ix + 374. $15 paper.

Whitfield White, Paul and Suzanne R. Westfall, eds. *Shakespeare and Theatrical Patronage in Early Modern England.* New York, NY: Cambridge University Press, 2002. pp. viii + 326, $60 cloth.

Wikander, Matthew H. *Fangs of Malice: Hypocrisy, Sincerity, and Acting.* Iowa City, IA: University of Iowa Press, 2002. pp. xxii + 238. $32.95 cloth

Williams, Gary. *Our Moonlight Revels: A Midsummer Night's Dream in the Theatre.* Iowa City, IA: University of Iowa Press, 2002. pp. xiii + 344. $24.95 paper.

Wilmer, S. E. *Theatre, Society and the Nation: Staging American Identities.* New York, NY: Cambridge University Press, 2002. pp. vii + 281. $60 cloth.

Wolf, Stacy. *A Problem Like Maria: Gender and Sexuality in the American Musical.* Ann Arbor, MI: University of Michigan Press, 2002. pp. xx + 289. $49.50 cloth, $20.95 paper.